SENT
FOR YOU
YESTERDAY

JOHN
EDGAR
WIDEMAN

VINTAGE BOOKS

A DIVISION OF RANDOM HOUSE ■ NEW YORK

First Vintage Books Edition, September 1988

Copyright © 1983 by John Edgar Wideman

Library of Congress Cataloging-in-Publication Data
Wideman, John Edgar.
Sent for you yesterday.
Reprint. Originally published: New York, N.Y.:
Avon Books, c1983.
I. Title.
PS3573.I26S4 1988   813'.54   88-14305
ISBN 0-679-72029-4 (pbk.)

Manufactured in the United States of America

10 9 8 7 6 5 4 3 2 1

To Danny, Jake, Jamila

Past lives live in us, through us. Each of us harbors the spirits of people who walked the earth before we did, and those spirits depend on us for continuing existence, just as we depend on their presence to live our lives to the fullest.

SENT
FOR YOU
YESTERDAY

IN HEAVEN WITH BROTHER TATE

Hey Bruh.

Hey man.

What you thinking, man?

I had this dream. This real bad dream.

Nightmare?

Shit man. Worse than that. Night mare. Day mare. Afternoon mare. Every damn time-of-day mare. Whatever you want to call it. That dream had me by the nuts.

Well, what was it?

Wasn't nothing to it really.

What you talking about then?

Wasn't nothing I could put my finger on. No monsters or funny green mens or nothing like that in the dream. Just a dumb jive ass dream. But it scared the shit out me.

You gon tell it or not?

If you get your lips off that bottle *we* spozed to be drinking maybe some wine help me get started.

Hey man. The *you* part of the *we* done already killed half the Johnson.

Why you got to lie like that? Pass the apple.

Better be a good goddamn story.

Nothing good about it. Ain't hardly no story at all. Just a cripple-ass no-kind-of-sense dream I ain't told nobody never.

Go on and tell it if you gon tell it, man.

See, I was on a train. Don't know where I was going.

9

Where I been. Just knows I'm on a train, and it's pitch black night, inside and outside. Couldn't see the hand in front of my face. It was blacker than the rent man's heart when you ain't got a dime. Blacker than tarbaby's mama. And this train just rattlin on, shakin like it's bout to come apart. Sho nuff shake, rattle and rolling train full all these people. Scared people. And I mean scared, Jack. Stomped down, righteous scared. Too scared to say boo to one another. We's all in there rattling round and nary a word. Nary a peep out nobody. People banging up against you. Knocking your shins and shoulders and what not. Arms and legs and pieces of people slamming all up against you and nobody saying s'cuse me or sorry. People just rolling around like marbles on the floor of that boxcar. Quiet as lambs cept every once in a while all the sudden you hear somebody scream. Ain't no doors nor windows but you know they gone. Nothing left after a scream like that.

Yeah. Funny thing was I knew just why they had to scream. Couldn't put it in words then and can't now. Ain't no words for it, but I knew why. See, cause I wanted to scream. I wanted to cut loose and tell somebody how scared I was. What a evil place I was in. Needed to scream worser than I never needed to pee or needed a woman or needed anything I can think of. But I knew if I'da screamed I'd be gone. If I screamed I'd be like them other poor suckers screaming and flying away. That scream would take me with it. My insides. And all my outsides too. So I didn't scream. Couldn't scream. Just lay there holding it in and shaking with all them wet bodies and pieces of body crashing upside me. Laying there shaking and waiting for one of them lost souls to holler.

Train moving on down the track and I got to sit there and listen and hope it ain't me next time I hear one cut loose.

What happened?

Nothing happened. Told you it was a shitty-tailed nothing kind of dream.

Yeah. But you also said it scared the daylights out you.

Till this day. And still does. Will tomorrow if the truth be told. Tomorrow and the next day and the next.

You leaving something out. Something else musta happened.

Didn't nothing else need to happen.

Aw, man. Gwan. Gimme back the jug. I done had plenty worse dreams than that. Shit man. Freaks be chasing me. And little bitty hairy spiders trying to eat me up. There was one time a whole army of cops be after me and I'm running for days all over Homewood and finally I got away, got home and my heart's pounding so I takes a deep breath and I'm thinking they ain't never gon catch me I'm the gingerbread man and this my briarpatch and shoot I'm opening the back gate of the house on Finance Street and don't you know there was a elephant in there. A big greasy-assed elephant chewing his cud in the backyard. Now that was a dream. That big burly motherfucker in your own backyard after you done outrun the police and marines and FBI. That was a scary motherfucker.

Yeah. That's what I'm talking about. The elephant.

What goddamn elephant?

The one made you stop. Made you hold your breath cause you know if you make a sound you're gone.

That's my dream, fool. I just told it to you. You spozed to be talking bout your own dream.

Couldn't scream. Had to hold it in for sixteen years. Fraid to open my mouth for sixteen years cause I knowed I'd hear that scream.

I

THE RETURN OF
ALBERT WILKES

Brother Tate stopped talking five years after I was born. When he died I was twenty-one and thought myself too grown for the name he had given me in my grandmother's kitchen. Nearly sixteen years altogether of silence, of not saying one word to any human being. By the time I was old enough to notice and care everybody else had gotten used to Brother's silence and paid it no mind. His strange color and silence were part of Homewood, like the names of the streets and the night trains and hills. But it wasn't exactly color and wasn't exactly silence. If you looked closely Brother had no color. He was lighter than anybody else, so white was a word some people used to picture him, but he wasn't white, not white like snow or paper, not even white like the people who called us black. Depending on the time of day, on how much light was in a room, on how you were feeling when you ran into Brother Tate, his color changed. I was always a little afraid of him, afraid I'd see through him, under his skin, because there was no color to stop my eyes, no color which said there's a black man or white man in front of you. I was afraid I'd see through that transparent envelope of skin to the bones and blood and guts of whatever he was. To see Brother I'd have to look away from where he was standing, focus on something safe and solid near him so that Brother would hover like the height of a mountain at the skittish edges of my vision.

And his silence wasn't really silence. Brother made

15

noise all the time. Drumming his fingertips on the edge of the kitchen table till my grandmother yelled at him to stop, cracking his knuckles, patting his feet, boog-eying so outrageously in the middle of the floor you'd hear the silent music making him wiggle his narrow hips and pop his fingers and wag his head like the sanctified sisters moaning their way to heaven. If my grandmother wasn't in the kitchen, he'd sit there at the gimpy table with the checkered cloth and flip his lower lip like it was the string of a bass fiddle. He'd hum and grunt and groan, and Brother could scat sing and im-itate all the instruments in a band. When Brother was around you didn't need a radio. As long as my grand-mother didn't shush him or chase him out her house he would play all the good songs you'd ever heard and make up plenty nobody ever heard before. Brother would make all that music, all that noise, but he never said a word. Not one word in all the years I knew him.

The first time I remember seeing Brother Tate he was scratching the back of his cue-ball head, and the creases at the base of his skull puckered into a kind of mouth that scared me half to death because what I saw was a face without features, a round, empty, flesh lol-lipop licked clean of eyes and nose, a blank skull grow-ing a blubbery octopus mouth. And the first time I remember hearing him he was singing scat. Scat sing-ing *Bodey opp opp boddlely doop*...sitting with my Uncle Carl at the table with the red and white check-ered oilcloth, spooning Kellogg's cornflakes straight from the box between takes. *Opp Dudedly Poop.* And the first time I smelled him was again in the kitchen of my grandmother's house when I got too close trying to fig-ure out the strange noises sputtering from his lips and he reached around and grabbed me and tucked me into his shoulder grinning and looking half at me and half at my Uncle Carl, *Doot. Doot* was what he christened me, tickling a riff with his hard blunt fingers on my ribs. His smell was the wine, tobacco, limburger cheese of my grandfather's flannel shirts.

It seems from the stories I've heard that Brother Tate had a son, a son born about the same time I was, just before or just after World War II began. Brother's son would be my age now. If things had worked out differently we might have grown up playing together, being good buddies, getting into trouble and chasing girls and drinking wine and knowing everything worth knowing about each other. But it didn't happen that way. One of the stories I've heard about Brother Tate tells how his son, Junebug, died in a fire on the Fourth of July. Junebug was albino and ugly like his father even though his mother was a coal-black beautiful woman named Samantha everybody called Sam. The fire occurred a year or so after the war ended, so Junebug was only five or six when he died. They say that's about the time Brother Tate stopped talking for good. He'd never said much before. He'd go for weeks according to my Uncle Carl, without saying word the first. Brother's silence made people think he was feebleminded. That and his strange color, or lack of color, that whiteness which made him less nigger and more nigger at the same time.

Brother's silence can be thought of as a kind of mourning for his lost son. Perhaps the lost son also explains the particular affection and attentiveness Brother always lavished on me. Brother treated me special because he could see Junebug in me. In Brother's eyes I grew up living not only my own life, but the one snatched from Junebug. Brother took on the job of watching me closely even though it must have been hard sometimes for him because I would be a reminder of both the life and death of his son. I couldn't help carrying both seeds. And Brother couldn't help remembering as he stood guard over me what he'd lost.

So I'm linked to Brother Tate by stories, by his memories of a dead son, by my own memories of a silent, scat-singing albino man who was my uncle's best friend.

I am not born yet. My Uncle Carl and Brother Tate hurry along the railroad tracks on the graveled crest of the hillside which parallels Finance Street. It is early in the morning, a summery spring day, and Carl is daydreaming of running away. He feels the sun on the back of his neck, hears the crunch of gravel, but his mind is on the ocean, an ocean he has never seen except in pictures and daydreams. If he closes his eyes he can see an ocean, red and wild as his blood, an ocean surging past the shimmering curtain of heat rising from the steel rails, an ocean rushing to the end of the world. He would run away that far if he could. To the place where the waters roar over the edge and the sky is no thicker than a sheet of paper. He would run or fly or swim to that place where the red sky and red sea meet. If he could.

Brother wants him to play a scare game. One game is cutting across an oncoming train at the last possible instant. First one to start is the loser. You hunker down at the edge of the tracks. You watch the train fill the sky and watch the shoulders of the one next to you for a sign. You juke your own shoulders and scream and snap out of your crouch. You cheat and push the one next to you hoping you'll scare him into flying first across the tracks. Scream as if your voice could drown out the monster engine chewing and spitting rails as it bears down on you. Brother always wins that game, always has one life to spare so he ain't afraid to leave it like a stomped down, bloody overcoat on the tracks. There is always that split second when you're crunched down so low and tight you think you're going to pee your pants if you don't let go, if you don't vault that first rail and hit the ties clean and leap again with both fists grabbing for air, grabbing for gravel as you flatten out and sail over the second rail to the safe place be-tween tracks.

Brother always waits a half second longer, that half second when the train sucks all the air out your chest, when it turns your knees to runny butter, that half second when nothing inside you works because the train has rammed its fist up your hynie. The worst way to lose that game is nailed to the hillside, your heart trying to jump out your mouth, standing there like Okey Doke the damn fool till the train finishes swooshing past and you can see Brother again, not dead like he ought to be, but wagging his bald head and signifying with his whole self in the middle of the right of way.

The other scare game is getting as close as you can to the outside rail and not flinching when the train bears down on you. One player sets the challenge, scuffs a mark as close as possible to the tracks then dares the other to stand in the footprints. The challenger is the judge. Nobody won that one much. Carl waited for Brother to plant himself, then he stood right behind Brother's narrow back, as close as Brother to the track. Carl started yelling before the smoke settled. He tasted ashes and burnt oil and choked getting his words out.

You moved, nigger. You moved.

What you talking about, man?

You moved. You was inched halfway down the hillside by the time the engine hit.

Sheet. Your mama the one moved.

I don't play that.

You just ain't got no heart, that's all.

Listen who's talking. What about the time the man blew the whistle?

Aw, man. He ain't supposed to be doing that, that ain't part of the game.

You set the world record. Ain't never seen nobody jump so high. I thought you was climbing a tree, man. Couldn't see no tree, but I knew you had to be climbing something. Must have been something holding up your big feet cause niggers ain't supposed to be walking on no air.

Whistle ain't part the game.

Scared is scared.

Well, we ain't talking about that now. We talking about *now,* now. And I ain't moved one bit.

You moved. You know you moved.

You're lying, man. You lying and Miss French got a bulldog dick.

Told you I don't play that shit...

So nobody won that game much, but they played it when they couldn't think of anything better to do. But this morning as they hustled along the tracks toward Westinghouse Park they weren't playing anything. My Uncle Carl was dreaming of running away and Brother was chucking rocks, but they had a job and were on their way to do it.

Albert Wilkes is back. Albert Wilkes is back and that means trouble. Carl's job was finding his daddy, finding him and bringing him home.

You tell him I said come home. Right away. You understand? Wait for your father, stay with your father till he starts to move and come back here with your father. You hear me? Don't stop to play. Don't stop for nothing. Albert Wilkes is back in town and if you want to have a daddy tomorrow, you better do just what I told you.

I can see my grandmother shooing Carl out the door, the only door in the row house on Cassina Way. I can hear it slam and echo in the emptiness of the cobblestone alley lined with identical wooden row houses from Dunfermline to Richland. The house on Cassina Way was still there when I was a teenager. Two families still occupied each unit so the people in front lived on Tioga Street and the people in back lived on Cassina Way. You could live in the same house with people and not know their names because of the partition dividing the house and the doors at either end opening in different places. You knew the people across the alley but you seldom went around the block to Tioga, to the little green front porches that made living on Tioga a step up from living on Cassina. Even if you lived in the end house, next to the vacant lot, you seldom had business which carried you around to Tioga. The people who lived on Cassina walked down Cassina to get to Homewood Avenue and the stores. What they knew about each other was enough to keep them knee deep in gossip, so keeping up with Cassina left them uncurious about the strangers whose voices leaked through the thin partitions dividing their houses into two slightly unequal chunks.

That's the way it must have been on Cassina Way. Rows of wooden shanties built to hold the flood of black migrants up from the South. Teeming is the word I think of. A narrow, cobbled alley *teeming* with life. Like a wooden-walled ship in the middle of the city, like the ark on which Noah packed two of everything and prayed for land. I think of my grandmother and grandfather and the children they were raising in that house on Cassina and I see islands, arks, life teeming but enclosed or surrounded or exiled to arbitrary boundaries. And the city around them which defined and delimited, which threatened but also buoyed and ferried them to whatever unknown destination, this city which trapped and saved them, for better or worse, never quite breached Cassina's walls.

The life in Cassina Way was a world apart from Homewood and Homewood a world apart from Pittsburgh and Pittsburgh was the North, a world apart from the South, and all those people crowded in Cassina Way carried the seeds of these worlds inside their skins, black, brown and gold and ivory skin which was the first world setting them apart.

I hear the door slam behind Carl and echo up and down Cassina in the morning stillness. My grandmother cringes because she's told him a thousand times not to run outdoors like a wild Indian, not to bust through doors like a hog out its pen, and each time he flies through the frame and the door swings slamming shut behind him one more nail is driven into her heart. Miss Pollard hears it. She is already stationed in the upstairs window, in the single room she rents from Dot Jones. Miss Pollard. Miss although she's buried two husbands, Miss though ten children who call her Mama are scattered in places like Cleveland, Akron, and Scranton, Pennsylvania. Miss Pollard has the job of watching Cassina from her second-story window and she's on duty and registers the French boy, Carl, whose feet hit the cobblestones before the door bangs shut behind him. Then it's two of them, Carl and the albino who was sitting on the steps, the white boy at his post some mornings before she took hers, early, early before anything moving in Cassina. Like a ghost out there before Miss Pollard settles herself for the day in her fanback rocker next to her window. Maybe he stays out there sitting on those steps all night. He's a peculiar one. Looking and acting. The two of them, the French boy never touching the steps where the white one sits, just flying by straight to the cobbles so the other one must have felt the breeze going by his head cause he's up in a second and clomping after the other one, two pairs of feet trying to wear out the stones of Cassina with their rubber-soled shoes.

Miss Pollard wonders what they're all up to so early

Saturday morning. John French first, easing the door
shut behind him, hefting his tool bag cross his shoulder
and creeping up Cassina like he done robbed his own
house and got it all stuffed up in that sack on his back.
Then Freeda French popping out the door like a bird
out a clock. No coffee cup steaming in her hand this
morning, no sweet little wave up at Miss Pollard's window, no pat for the ghost boy's bald head, nothing but
her eyes running both ways up and down that empty
alley after her man. Then them boys flying. Miss Pollard treats herself to a pinch of snuff to pass the time
till the ice wagon rattles down Cassina. After the ice
wagon and the ice man's song and the horses' hooves
clacking against the cobblestones, Cassina will begin
to fill up. Be so many doors slamming and children in
and out and so and so yelling at so and so across the
way, be so much business out there today it keep a body
weary rocking to keep up. She'll call down to one of the
little rascals go get her some chewing tobacco over to
Indovina's. She'll drop a nickel and drop a penny and
he better get on back here with my Five Brothers. Five
Brothers. You hear me now? Don't let him sell you
nothing else. If he ain't got it, tell him to get it. Hear
me now? Tell him I said get it. Much money as I spend
in there. Little crippled up dago ain't got what you need
half the time no way. Too busy cheating these dumb
niggers round here to stock like he should. Five Brothers. And don't be taking all day, child.

A hophead friend of my brother's will kill Indovina.
Shoot the old man three times in the chest with a .357
Magnum because there was only thirteen dollars in the
cash register, thirteen dollars and change old crippled
Indovina dumped on the floor like he was emptying a
slop jar. Miss Pollard will die in a fire in the single
room she rented on Braddock Avenue. Not a bad fire,
everyone else got out of the apartment building. Smoke
mostly. Enough smoke to suffocate her as she slept because nobody remembered she was up there on the third
floor. She had to move to Braddock Avenue when the
city tore down her side of Cassina. I remember driving
past the row houses where John French and Freeda
French raised my mother and kept me a year or so when

I was a baby. You could see that stretch of Cassina from Susquehanna after the city urban renewed Homewood. Our old house still standing then next to the vacant lot. A row of wooden shanties anchored in rubble, so thin and old and exposed they shamed me and I looked away quickly, the way I averted my eyes from the crotches of ancient women in head rags and cotton stockings rolled to their knees who sat gap-legged on their porches.

The train catches Brother and Carl just before Homewood Avenue. My uncle tries to ignore it but shies a few steps down the embankment as the train passes. Hot, monster breath. His body yanked from the ground and shaken like a rag doll in a giant, black fist. When the air stops heaving and shuddering in the train's wake and he can think his own thoughts again he looks back over his shoulder for Brother. But his shadow is not there.

You're crazy, man. You ain't got good sense, man.

Brother is squatting in the middle of the right of way, soot stained, grinning, the red sweat rag around his bald head, his chest heaving like a little bit of the train's still in there trying to get out.

Ain't no time for games, fool. Come on if you're coming.

Brother stands and pulls off his shirt. The sun strips the skin from his thin chest. Naked bones pulse like wings. Brother catches his breath and strolls nonchalantly toward my uncle, rolling his skinny shoulders. Brother's hands tell a story. His fist is a train humping down the track and two fingers on the other hand are naked little white legs sprinting then leaping over the fist as it lunges past. He tells it again, but this time the fist smacks into his palm and the pale legs fly up in the air and flutter back to earth dead as snow.

You play that shit by your ownself this morning.

If Carl's knees pumped a little higher he'd be running. He hears Brother's breathing over his shoulder, huffing to keep up. After the narrow bridge over Homewood Avenue the tracks stretch straight and shining through the length of Westinghouse Park till they disappear in a molten curve too far away, too bright for his eyes to follow. His father could be down in the park beneath that dusty roof of green, under those trees that look like broccoli, tightly packed heads of fresh broccoli in crates outside Indovina's grocery store. He could call down there if he dared, call *John French, John French,* wake up the winos who would be sleeping in the Bums' Forest now that spring was turning warm as summer. He knew his father slept down there on gambling, wine-drinking nights when he didn't make it home to Cassina Way. But his father had slept in his own bed last night. He'd heard John French leave early in the morning with his paper-hanging tools. Heard him cross the landing and tip down the stairs.

You try the beer garden first. Said he had a job this morning so you try there first. Ask for his tools. Ask if they're behind the bar or if he took them on a job. Damn that Albert Wilkes. Damn his soul.

His mother's eyes had frightened him. His mother only damned people when she was scared. And scared was in her eyes this morning. Damning people and talking fast like she couldn't hardly catch her breath. Wagging a finger in his face. Do you understand this? Do you remember that? Are you listening, boy? Go here, go there as if he didn't know, as if this was the first time he had searched the Homewood streets for his father.

Sunshine, you are my sunshine. His father sang that to his mother when she was scared. When her long hair hung down loose, uncombed the way it was this morning and her eyes were red from crying or no sleep, witchy hair, almost, the way it hung so long over her shoulders and hid so much of her face like a veil. He sang *You are my sunshine* when she left one twin dead in the hospital and brought the other home to die on Cassina. Sang it and hummed it that sad week waiting for the babyboy who was also John French to die. Sadness in her hair, her eyes this morning, sadness which was being scared as much as it was anything else, made her damn Albert Wilkes the way she damned God and all his angels the week his father sang *Sunshine. You are my sunshine.* He was humming it to himself now, his father's song, his mother's eyes, the baby brother who lived only a week on Cassina Way, humming it as he stopped along the tracks and Brother drew up panting beside him.

From where they stood you couldn't see the path cutting up from Finance Street through the trees, and if you couldn't see the path no way you'd see anybody sleeping farther back in the woods.

It's that Albert Wilkes. That goddamn no-good Albert Wilkes got my mama scared. You know who I'm talking about. He used to stay over youall's place before he went away. Piano-playing Albert Wilkes, damn his goddamn soul.

Brother nods, runs his fingers up and down a keyboard.

Yeah, they say he could play. They say he was the best but that don't make no nevermind. He's back from wherever he's been and my mama's scared and we got to find my daddy before she starts crying again.

Brother points to the old station at the far end of the park where the trains used to stop. Carl pictures his daddy on the broken-down steps, sitting regal and laid back as if he owned them and owned the whole wooden-stepped passage from the abandoned train station with its busted windows and crooked sign to Mulberry Way's cobblestones, owned the steps and anything else he chose to claim if he decided something was worth tilting the wide-brimmed hat back off his forehead to stake a claim with his green eyes.

And Carl hopes there won't be too many others sitting on the steps. Because the men were always teasing. Always signifying. Junk about pimples and young boys and nasty stuff said in whispers and winks so you never heard it all, just enough to know they were talking at you, not to you. Signifying so you knew part of what was funny was you. He hated that laughter, felt his face getting hot, already saw Brother acting a fool, making faces to get the men laughing louder. Somebody would poke a wine bottle at Brother and he'd swig it, wipe his chin with the heel of his hand the way the winos did and roll his eyes and cut wobbly-legged monkeyshines till John French snapped his fingers, snapped them once, as loud as breaking a stick.

What you want, boy? And no matter what Carl had to say he'd get choked up. All the men would be listening and he'd stutter and sound simpleminded. The message he'd said a thousand times over and over to himself would sneak off and hide and laugh at him too. He'd wish he was Brother so he could act a fool and cut monkeyshines. Anything be better than opening his mouth and stuttering like he was feebleminded.

He damned Albert Wilkes again and daydreamed the other places his father could be. With Brother like a shadow behind him Carl could enter the dream, get from one place to another in Homewood just by thinking where he wanted to go and then the streets would slip past as he thought of them, Dunfermline, Tioga, Albion, Finance, Susquehanna, Alliquippa, Frankstown, Hamilton, and it wouldn't be a matter of a certain number of steps and turning here and crossing there because the streets were inside him. The streets were Homewood but they were not real till he thought them. Till he glided with his shadow, Brother, up and down and over the streets sleeping inside him.

He knew the idea was silly, but he thought it sometimes anyway: if he didn't wake up one morning, would there still be a Homewood? It was a silly idea because he had a father and mother and they had lived in Homewood before he was born. And plenty of Homewood people much older than his father and mother, people in the stories Aunt May told about Grandmother Gert and her Great-grandmother Sybela Owens. So he knew Homewood was as old as Sybela Owens and slavery days, older than his Uncle Bill and Aunt Aida they called Anaydee, as old as the old dead people in May's stories. Homewood was young too, was starting up again in the kids playing on the sidewalks and alleys and vacant lots where he had played. But he thought his silly idea sometimes anyway. If I don't wake up, Homewood will be gone. If I run away, far away, the Homewood streets will disappear. Mornings like this, this hard, bright spring summer morning when he was sent looking for his father, it would be easier to run away. To lose himself and lose his shadow, Brother, in a daydream of some other place. A place where the streets have new names, a place he cannot see plainly like he sees the Homewood streets unfurling when he shuts his eyes. He wouldn't have to search for his father there. The trees wouldn't look like dirty broccoli. No pee smell along the path. His mother wouldn't be standing in the kitchen of the house on Cassina wringing her hands in her apron.

A silly idea. Like most of the ideas he thought up. But it's like a job. Something he must do no matter what. He had been scared by his mother's eyes. She was a pretty lady. She had skin white as a white woman's and long soft hair she wore piled on top of her head. He loved to see her let her hair down and loved to watch her comb it because she hummed as she combed it down past her shoulders. This morning she damned Albert Wilkes, and her eyes were sad. Red like she'd been crying. But it was his job so he had to make Homewood this morning like he made it every morning when he woke up. Make the streets because that's where his father would be and she needed him to find his father. So he listens to his shadow breathing behind him and stares as far as he can down the tracks. The tracks could take him somewhere else, he thinks. Somewhere shimmering like the steel rails just before they curve out of sight. Sky drops to meet gravel and steel at that shimmering point. The world is as thin as tissue paper there. You could poke your finger through it. He can't see streets beyond that flattened stretched-out place where the tracks are on fire. Those faraway streets are not inside him; they have no names.

Brother, he thinks, has no name. My man, my buddy, my ace boon coon running pardner Brother. No name. No color. No nothing if you think about it.

Carl calls over his shoulder, Hey, Brother. Hey man, you ain't nothing. And then Carl thinks how easy it is to be Brother. To have no color. No name. No job. No father you got to find.

Man, you got it easy.

Before they get to the platform they can see it's empty. Trains used to stop, but now it's nothing but a place where the men sit when they want to get out of the sun. A beat-up, slant-roofed shed, a brick wall, some

gray planks left from the floor where people once stood
waiting for trains, wooden steps down the hillside from
the platform to the cobblestones of Mulberry Way. Nobody uses the steps anymore. Beside them, cutting up
the hillside, a trail is worn through the weeds. A few
of the steps near the top still safe for sitting but the
rest so rotten you'd crash right through. Nobody is sitting where the men usually sit. No voices echo under
the slanted roof. His father is not sprawled there with
his long legs dangling over the crushed steps, his big
hat pushed back off his forehead so he can stare down
Mulberry Way as if he owns it.

Where is he? Where you think he is?

Carl wonders if it really is easy to have no color. No
answers. He's always asking Brother questions, questions like he asks himself, questions nobody could answer. He wonders what would happen if one day Brother
started answering. Brother could go for days, for weeks,
and never say a mumbling word. He wonders if Brother
likes having no words, no father, no name. Mr. Tate is
little and quiet. A kind of nice, washed-out, stuttering
little man. Mr. Tate never drinks wine or shoots crap
in the Bums' Forest or hangs on the corner outside the
Bucket of Blood loudtalking and singing and making
ladies cross to the other side of the street. The Tates
take care of Brother and take care of Lucy, but they
are not Brother's real father and mother. Carl wonders
if that's easy. Wonders where Brother came from. Wonders if there are two ghosts someplace, white like
Brother, who are his mother and father. Wonders if
Brother sees the Homewood streets like he sees them.
Like a job, like a book in his hand and Carl is turning
the pages, trying to find his father, trying to decide
where to look next as he dreams the streets, and dreams
himself and his shadow in another place.

What would happen to Homewood if he ran away?
What would happen to his mother and father if one
morning, a bright, lazy spring summer morning, he
didn't wake up and start the dream of Homewood? Carl
is suddenly afraid. More scared than he's ever been in
the scare games when a train shakes the earth behind
him. So afraid he does not close his eyes against the

roaring thing rushing up behind his back, but opens
them as wide as he can to take in all of the broad blue
sky. He digs into the gravel, stomping it, kicking it
onto the tracks. Quickly, he spins around to face the
pale, skinny boy.

Brother, you got it easy, man.

He hears how squeaky his voice sounds. But he's so
happy to see Brother he doesn't care. Brother answers
with his hands. They are saying the names of all the
Homewood streets. But his hands change the sound.
The street names are blurred like song words when
somebody hums or moans them. The white hands dance
up and down a keyboard. Play the blues. A fast-chug-
ging keep-up-with-the-train blues. Brother's hands are
playing: C'mon. C'mon. You moving too slow this morning, boy. Train gon catch you you don't c'mon.

Brother's hands play all the streets of Homewood.
He throws them down like dice and they come up seven.

Instead of saying it, this time Carl thinks, *Brother
you ain't nothing,* but he can't think the words without
grinning, grinning at the washboard ribs, the watermelon belly, the pink eyes and pink fingernails racing
up and down those black and white piano keys.

C'mon, fool.

And both boys break for the room-for-nothing-but-
trains bridge back over Homewood Avenue.

My grandmother, Freeda, is standing in the front
room of the house on Cassina Way. She stares down at
her hands as if she's trying to remember what they're
for. She had winced as she always did when the door
slammed behind her son, winced once and waited for a
yell from upstairs, a startled-awake holler of annoyance
from one of the girls, echoing the gunshot slam of the
door. It hadn't come but she stood stock-still anyway,
waiting, listening, wishing now for something to break
the silence. I'm trying to remember the inside of her
house, its shape, the furniture, the way things in it
would trap the silence and spin a dusty, beaded web
around her so if you peeked in from Cassina you'd see
a young woman draped by layers of transparent gauze,
a young woman standing up asleep, her eyes open,

threads stretched from the top of her head to all the
walls, the things in the room, the planes of smoky light
surrounding her like wash pinned on lines to dry. That's
what I see, invisible in the alley, trying to remember.
When I lived on Cassina Way I couldn't have been more
than four or five, so my image of the inside of the house
comes less from what I saw than from what I've been
told since. Yet the cobblestones are real under my feet,
slippery and cold from last night's rain, cold and damp
until the sun gets high enough to light the shadowed
stillness behind me. There must have been a curtain
at the front window but the glass is bare now as I peer
through. This is the window my grandmother smashed
with her fist. She watched a man sneaking down Cassina, a man with a gun, a skinny, pigeon-toed somebody
whose eyes were fixed on her husband's back, a sneak
with a pistol in his hand getting closer and closer to
where she sat with Lizabeth on her lap. Lizabeth was
smiling. She loved to hear her mother tell the caterpillar story. When the man in the alley raised the gun
her mother's fist punched through the glass, her mother
screamed, and Lizabeth screamed and John French gone
like a turkey through the corn and the gun blasted the
emptiness of Cassina Way twice before it clattered to
the cobblestones and the scarecrow man took off toward
the far end as fast as John French had ducked round
the near corner. All of that happened, but now the glass
wears rag stuffing in one shattered corner. A scar zig-
zags like a caterpillar across my grandmother's
knuckles. The hands she stares at make no sense, but
they are her hands and she doesn't believe either one
of them can save John French's life again.

Freeda looks round at the things in the room. They
are so familiar, yet they look strange this morning. As
though she's waking up in someone else's house. All
this rummage sale stuff that's been in the family and
the stuff John French won shooting crap and stuff he
"found" patrolling the alleys behind the white folks'
houses with Strayhorn, all of it strange as the hands
at the end of her wrists, hands that made her think she
might be waking up in someone else's body.

Once, washing dishes at the kitchen sink, in another

house, another world where the sun hit the second-story
window over the sink first thing early in the morning
and the tiny kitchen was the warmest, brightest room
in the house and nobody lived with the butt end of their
house pressed up against the nose of yours like two
dirty dogs in an alley, once, when she lifted her hand
from a sinkful of suds a bubble was trapped between
her thumb and first finger. She had been thinking of
all the new people arriving in Homewood. Colored people, they said. Ignorant, countrified niggers, they said,
from the South. Downhome niggers they said so black
and brown sounded nasty and she was thinking about
color when she pulled her hand up out of the water.
Her hand was brown as it ever got and that no browner
than a cup of milk mixed with a tablespoon of coffee.
Not even brown enough to hide the pink flush after it
had been sloshing all morning in a sinkful of soap and
dishes and pots and pans. A bulky mitten of suds had
slowly slid down her fingers when she lifted her hand
from the sink. She shook her wrist so it slid faster.
That's when she saw the bubble webbed between her
thumb and first finger, a long, jelly-bellied bubble with
see-through skin that held all the colors of the rainbow.

She had raised the rainbow to her lips. The bubble
quivered when she breathed on it. She thought of dan-
delions and wishes, of ladybugs who'd carry your whispered secrets to the Good Fairy when you opened your
fist and let them fly away. A little harder, if she gently
blew just a little harder, maybe she could loosen the
bubble from the arc of her thumb and finger, maybe
she could make a wish and set the rainbow free. Tilted
in a certain way the colors disappeared and the glistening skin reflected the kitchen, the kitchen made tiny
and funny-shaped like a face in a spoon. With one puff
she could set the room and the rainbow free.

My grandmother Freeda had been just a girl then.
In that other room, that other world, enchanted by a
soap bubble. She remembered its exact shape now. A
long watermelon blister of soap quivering between her
thumb and finger. Something had broken the spell, made
her look away and the strange bubble had burst. She'd
never been able to recall what had distracted her from

the soapsuds' little trick. But something had made her look away, and in that instant the bubble had popped. Gone before she could whisper her wish, set it free. She couldn't remember what had pulled her away, but it continued pulling, drawing her past the edges of her-self. Since that day, whenever she looked away from something, she was never sure it would be there when she looked back. Alone in the downstairs of the half a house on Cassina Way listening to dishwater gurgle and burp down the sluggish drain she was afraid they would never return, not the girls sleeping at the top of the steps, not the man nor the boy she sent to search for the man, not even the boy's white shadow or the shadow of herself, that dreamy part of herself just be-yond the edge, not afraid to look away.

Perhaps things happened, she thought, perhaps all the moments of her life had occurred not to make her somebody, not because there needed to be a Freeda French, but because living was learning to forget. The next thing happened because you needed to forget what was happening now because what was happening now was nothing but a way of forgetting what had happened before. In church they sang *Farther along we'll know more about Him. Farther along we'll understand why.* What did those words mean? Would there be a bright day, a clear singing day farther along when the dead ones, the lost ones, the ones hurt and suffering beyond tears, the ones who sinned and the ones who prayed would all come crowding back from Glory, a day farther along when you understood once and forever that He forgot no one, nothing, that He never forgot but always forgave, that He took his own sweet time but everything was all right, had to be all right and you understood farther along?

But if her life had a shape, if she was Freeda French, it had nothing to do with memories she could line up, not the babies, the nights with John French, not the golden Christmas turkey basting in the oven, not the snow on Bruston Hill, or the gray rain or the enemas and coughing in the night or the prayers or the songs. If her life had a shape, the shape was not what she could remember, but what kept tearing her away, the

voice which could look and look away, the voice beyond
the edges of herself making her lose what she had in
her hand, making her settle for whatever came next.

Sometimes the songs helped. If you loved God and
loved your man and loved your children you were safe.
The music would say that to her. Farther Along. Everything could be taken away tomorrow and still the music
made her feel how good it would be when He folded her
in His arms. The music could soothe her, quiet her, and
she'd see her worst fears were nothing more than a
child's cry in the darkness. He'd understand, He'd snap
on the light and rock her back to sleep. All that in the
music. A garden in the music where she could come to
Him alone, where the dew was still on the roses. And
the voice she'd hear as she tarried there, that voice was
in the music too. A place to rest, to lay her head, her
burdens, she heard it all in the hymns they sang in
Homewood A. M. E. Zion Church. But the same songs
that saved her could leave her stranded just short of
the promised shore. She wouldn't rise up new and shining on the far bank but slip into icy Jordan waters,
waters black and cold and still would close over her
head. She'd found in the songs a vast emptiness, a de-
sert of bones, rows and rows of caskets, moaning oceans
of tears. The songs taught her to fear death, to fear the
sky which could fall on your head like a hammer, to
fear the smothering earth, to fear the fire in thunder
and lightning, the rotting hands in the black depths of
the water waiting to drag you down. Tempest, trial and
toil and snare and miring clay. They were all in the
songs. You could die alone, suffer alone forever in those
vast, empty places where the songs carried you.

But she held on to her God, and held on to her family
and swore to herself she would cling as long as there
was breath in her body. And the oath was strong, and
her arms grew strong but never stronger than the voice
tearing her away.

It was Albert Wilkes scratching at the window last
night. Scratching and tapping like a cat. She couldn't
hear what was said after John French went out into
Cassina, but she knew that alleycat tap scratching,
hadn't heard it in seven years but knew it when she

heard it again. Knew it was Albert Wilkes again and
trouble again.

She had lain awake till her man mounted the stairs,
till he stepped across the landing and peeked into the
children's room, till the landing buckled again and
creaked again receiving his full weight again and he
snuffed out the wall-climbing flame of the candle and
pushed through the door of their bedroom. The last
thing she heard was the clang of his belt buckle when
he draped his pants over the end of their brass bed.

That was him at the window last night, wasn't it?

Him? Watchyou talkin bout? Him?

You know just who I mean.

If you talking bout Albert Wilkes he sure nuff got a
name. And you know it. He ain't no *Him* if you talkin
about Albert.

Then he's back.

Yes he is.

And couldn't wait to get hold of you. Had to come
here scratching like some alleycat in the middle of the
night. Couldn't wait till daytime. Couldn't knock at
people's door like a civilized human being.

You know that's his way.

Always sneaking around.

You know how he is.

I told him to keep his Devil self away from here. So
he sneaks round like an alleycat in the dark. Why won't
he leave you alone? Why won't he just go on about his
business? Why'd he have to come back?

He's my friend. Where else he gon go if he in trouble?

Albert Wilkes born to trouble.

Can't help that. Can't do nothing bout none of that.
But he's my friend. Ima do what I can, and that's all
there is to that. Now you go on back to sleep. No need
gettin all in a bother. I got that job over on Thomas
Boulevard to go to this morning. I got to go, but you
mize well get your rest whiles you can. The children
still sleepin. You go on back to sleep and don't be studying no Albert Wilkes.

I hated that whistle of his. And that scratching at
night. Because that's all he'd have to do. Stand out there

in Cassina and purse his lips and don't care what you
doing you're gone. You hear him whistling at you and
you're up and gone. It'd make my blood boil. I'd want
to run outside and strangle him. And it was worse at
night. You'd hear it in your sleep. Jump out of bed to
run the streets with that man. Now he's back again
and scratching again. Please don't act a fool with Albert
Wilkes. Albert Wilkes got nobody to answer to but hisself. If I don't matter nothing to you, think about the
children. Don't go getting mixed up in none of Albert
Wilkes's mess.

Hush now. You gon wake them babies if you don't
hush. I got that job this morning and you needs to go
back to sleep. He's my friend. Ain't nothing else to be
said on the subject.

Can't find him, Mama. Looked everywhere and he
ain't noplace.

Stop, just stop right there. First thing is how many
times have I told you two not to come running in here
out the street like a pair of wild Indians. And the second
thing is you left the door open like I've told you a thousand times not to, and every fly in Homewood be in
here and you know better. And the third thing is me
talking myself blue in the face and you paying me no
nevermind. You still talk like some field hand fresh
from Georgia every chance you get. You're going to be
the death of me, Carl French. Now wipe that sweat out
your eyes and put your shirt on your back and shut the
door quietly and say what you have to say like a human
being.

She hated the fat, buzzing flies. Flies in Cassina Way
had never been bad till all those people from the deep
South started arriving with their dirty boxes and bags
and spitting in the street and throwing garbage where
people have to walk. It was like having all those people
in her house when the flies swarmed through the open
door, those careless, dirty people lighting on her things,
crawling across her ceilings and floors.

We can't find Daddy.

You looked...everywhere?

Everywhere, Mama.

What's on your feet, boy? That's black soot from the train tracks.

We had to look everywhere, like you said.

I didn't say walk those tracks. I told you never to walk those tracks. You've been up on that crossing, haven't you? Doesn't matter how many times I say no, you're still going to be a hardhead. You still have to do it your way. That's all I need on top of everything else. A hardhead son. How hard's your head gon be when somebody comes here, *Mrs. French, Mrs. French. Oh my Goodness, Miz French, I'm so sorry Miz French but that Carl, that boy of yours been hit by a train.* That's all I need around here. One more fool in the house trying to get hisself killed. You get in the bathroom and clean yourself up. And pull off those shoes before you take another step. And you better not make a mess in there and those shoes better be clean and looking better than new next time I see them. You're through for the day. Brother, you go on now. Carl through playing for the day.

The albino stood slack-jawed, his eyes on the floor. This is when he's ugly she thought, ugly as sin. When he stops moving and humming and has nothing for his hands to do, Brother dies. He is lumpy, colorless pie dough. His skin is raw and wrinkled like a plucked chicken before you wet it and roll it in flour and drop it in the bubbling grease. If she let him, he would stand there, dead in that bag of white skin till Carl returned. She thought of the flamingos in Highland Park Zoo. How they tucked one leg up into the bag of their pink bodies and stood frozen, balanced on the other stick leg for as long as you could watch.

Go on. Find something to do with yourself. You need to take that shirt from round your waist and put it on, too.

She flinched twice in anticipation before the door actually slammed, and when it did slam she flinched again. Carl and Brother like two peas in a pod. They walked and listened alike. Her son handsome and Brother pug ugly but they looked alike. Both of them rolled their narrow shoulders to get the mannish John French weight in their steps. Both had those potbellies and bony arms. Though she'd seen them together a million times, she didn't know who was taller. Neither one looked colored. Carl tanned slightly by the middle of summer, but he was like her and the girls, the sun-brown tint of their skin never deepened, it was a goldish dust, a shadow which disappeared altogether in some kinds of light, a coating thin enough for the wind to erase. Both boys had that deep seam down the middle of their backs, and shoulder blades poking like spatulas under their skin. Those big, restless bones seemed out of place. Maybe both boys supposed to be something else. Maybe both of them missing a set of arms or wings. Maybe something else supposed to be stuck on back there and waiting for it was what made them so alike.

Strange and ugly as he was she had barely noticed Brother when he first started coming around. Now he came and went just about as he pleased. Part of her life, part of what she'd become. It had taken no time to live her life. It had taken forever. Hard now to recall when Brother hadn't been around. She wasn't surprised anymore when she opened the door and found him sitting still as a statue on her steps, part of Cassina's quiet, the peace she needed to taste with her coffee before the rest of the house was awake. She'd pat his bald head. Looked like it should be cold, like his whole body be frozen out there hunched on the bottom step so early some mornings the chilled air set her coffee to steaming, but when she patted him, patted that head smooth and bare as a stone, her fingers found warmth humming in the web of blue veins crisscrossing his skull.

Up and out early with her coffee cup because she wanted to be alone. Funny how Brother could be on his step and Miss Pollard already pulled up to her window but Freeda was alone anyway. Funny how being alone had something to do with knowing those two would be at their posts. They helped her find her peace those mornings she needed to be up before the others, out in Cassina before anybody called her name or called her Mama.

Brother almost like one of her own children. They start out so light you can carry them round the house in one arm. Then before you know it, they're carrying you. Mama do this and Mama do that and Please Mama and if one ain't calling your name or begging you for something or trying to steal that moment's peace you thought you had coming you're lost as a helpless little child. They're carrying you around and you're weak as a baby. You're light as a feather and their silence heavy as stones in your heart.

Brother came and went now as he pleased just like the other strange things in her life. Once in the middle of the night a terrible dream had driven her out of bed groping down those steep, treacherous steps and she'd found him at the oilclothed table eating a bowl of cornflakes and milk. Brother alone in her kitchen, at her table, in the middle of the night, munching cornflakes and glowing in the dark like some moony ghost. Well, it didn't faze her. She said nothing to him and he just kept working on those Kellogg's cornflakes. Sounded like mice playing in the walls.

She had been born and raised in Homewood and if there was a time in her life when Brother hadn't been around, she couldn't remember it. And one day I'll die in Homewood, she thought. One night he'll be at my table nibbling like some big white mouse. One night the terrible dream will come looking for me in my bed and won't be nobody there to scare. She could see herself disappear, see herself gone forever in the emptiness of Brother's pink eyes. Some days she knew she'd rather die than have to touch him. Yet Brother just a boy, a big-head, potbellied boy like her son Carl and she remembers Lucy Tate pushing the albino in a baby buggy up and down Tioga Street till the buggy rotted and Brother was bigger than Lucy and nothing left of the buggy but springs and frame and Brother clinging like a monkey to the skeleton. She had heard people talk about the Tates and Lucy Bruce who became a Tate after her mother burnt up in the fire on Hamilton Avenue. Brother had been part of Homewood for as long as she cared to remember. He was just a boy but sometimes he seemed older than she was. Sometimes he was older than old Mr. and Mrs. Tate who they say had found him and raised him in that big old house of theirs. Old Mr. and Mrs. Tate had raised half the orphans and

strays in Homewood in that big house of theirs. No
children of their own but always kept a houseful of kids.

If she let herself she could start crying this morning.
Get weepy and be good for nothing the rest of the day.
She could get her mother Gert on her mind. Her beautiful mama with furs and feathers and beaded necklaces
hanging to her waist and silver bracelets and turquoise
rings. Real diamonds in her ears she said and lifted the
curls off her neck to show anybody who wanted to see.
Her Mama Gert who went with white men and died
somewhere far away. Her Mama Gert who Isabelle Lewis
called no good, whispering *No good* loud enough for
everybody in the church vestibule to hear. And little
Aunt Aida waiting outside for Isabelle Lewis. Caught
Isabelle Lewis soon as she stepped that one step out the
church down to the street.

You put my sister's name in that nasty mouth of
yours one more time and you gon be spitting teeth with
your lies. This child standing right there and you bad-
mouth her mother. In church, too. Lucky it was church
too, or you'd be gumming your lies right now. Church
or no church I hear something like that again Ima snatch
you bald-headed and tongue-tied. Trifling wench like
you got the nerve to be talking bout who's good and no
good.

Hush now, Baby. Good and no good ain't got nothing
to do with it. Gert is Gert. That's who she is and what
she is and always will be. Always be your mama too.
Onliest one you gon get, onliest one you gon love like
a mama. And Gert love you long as she's Gert. Long's
she got breath in her body. Cause she's Gert. And that's
her way.

Gert's way was laughing like a bird. Laughing like
a bird and flying away like one too. Winter come she's
gone. Spring she pops up again. Here one day gone the
next. Then she come pecking at your window the very
day you thought the sun never shine in your back door
again.

Lookit my girl. Lookit how tall and pretty she's getting. Her way was perfumy hugs and lipstick kisses
and a soft-gloved hand wrapped round yours for walks
in Westinghouse Park. Gert lives in a fashion magazine

and because you're her daughter your buck teeth will straighten one day and the freckles peel from your nose and your knees stop knocking and your ankle bones start holding up your socks. Gert's way was chatter and coo and smile back at all the men who smiled at her, a picture-book lady in the Sunday rotogravure the men couldn't keep their eyes off, a fashion ad suddenly appearing on a bench in Westinghouse Park with her little girl beside her, the little girl they'd wink at and smile at too cause they knew someday, some bright spring afternoon, all her dumpy, ugly-duck feathers fall away and she'd shine like her mama shined when she landed in Homewood.

On summer Sunday afternoons they'd watch the other strollers, and Gert, who was her mother, would hold her little girl's hand while the sun went down and the park emptied out. They'd sit till they were alone and dusk falling cool on their shoulders. Sky turning to fire and her mother still as the dancer poised on one toe atop the gold music box when the song stops. Quiet as the wound-down, glittering box at night in its dark corner beside the bed with all the other precious things her mama had brought her. The stories of good times, of fine times, of Homewood's handsomest, richest, nicest men ending suddenly. Her mama quiet and snuggling closer on the slats of the wooden bench and pulling a handkerchief from somewhere in her fabulous clothes and the whole shadowed park lavender like the sweet scent of her perfume and Gert would sniffle and blow her nose and whisper, Excuse me, Darlin. Excuse me, Darlin Baby Girl.

Gert's way could make Freeda shamed of Aunt Aida and Uncle Bill, of the cramped rooms above the Fox Bar and Grill where they lived and she lived when her mama flew away again into those slick pages of the magazine. But as she grew older, Anaydee's way and Uncle Bill's way made her shamed of Gert. But Anaydee always said: She's Gert. And Gert's Gert. Ain't no good or bad about it.

Freeda had learned the streets of Homewood walking beside Gert's rustling skirts, her hand wrapped in Gert's. She had learned to call Gert her mama on those long

walks, those long afternoons in the park. She wouldn't
wash her hand when she bathed in the clawfoot tub.
She'd keep the perfume alive so she could sniff it again
in her bed when her mama was long gone, gone to
Louisville or Detroit or Cincinnati where she died one
day far from home. Her mama gone for days but Freeda
could find her in the hollows back of her wrist. Even
now she'd catch the back of her hand sneaking up toward her face, rubbing her cheek, her lips. Even today
with John French God knows where and Albert Wilkes
back in town, when she didn't need to be crowded by
no dead woman's perfume, no dead Mama's laughing
eyes. Streets treacherous enough without that distrac-
tion. Close to tears anyway, and she didn't need sad-
eyed ghosts reminding her to call them Mama.

My grandmother cleared the cobwebs of rainbow and
bubble and perfume from her mind, tied a scarf around
her hair and set out into the Homewood streets to find
her husband. Her face hurts this morning when the air
hits it. Feels like a toothache, swollen and sore to the
touch. She feels the whiteness of her face hanging out
this morning, something silly, a big ugly white pumpkin on her shoulders. Even though the streets are empty
and quiet, even though you could pretend at this early
morning hour they were still the old Homewood streets
before the black tide of immigrants from the South
changed Homewood forever, even though her footsteps
tapped out the silence into precise little icy chunks so
she could hear silence and see it, she couldn't forget
who the streets belonged to now. Dark faces and bodies
crowded three and four into every Homewood spare
room. Hordes of burr-head children knock you down if
you're not careful. Their mamas outdoors in next to
nothing, heads uncombed and uncovered. Summer heat
chasing them outdoors. The men in undershirts and no
shirts at all. Like roaches when you light the gas stove
in the morning, fleeing every which way from the cracks
and crevices where they hide at night. Running and
oozing into the streets. Their streets now. Brazen now.
Loud talk and nasty talk and country ways and half-
naked like children, like people in the jungle.

But the last block of Susquehanna before it ran into

Homewood Avenue was a nice street. Neat brick
row houses set well back from the sidewalk. Most had
porches and three or four steps, so you knew when you
mounted them you had left the pavement, which belonged to anybody, and you were entering somebody's
home. Brightly painted wooden porches and straight,
solid steps and trim flower gardens and here and there
a little knee-high white picket fence. No boarders
crammed into every nook and closet. No sweaty eyes
staring out the windows. No men draped like dirty laun-
dry over every railing and women spraddle-legged on
the steps. Nobody's Victrola playing for the whole block
as if everybody wanted to listen to nastiness about my
man done gone and left me and good jelly rolls and if
you don't like my peaches don't shake my tree. Bad
enough the children and any decent folk walk by the
Bucket of Blood can't help hearing that terrible mess
they always singing and playing round there. Now it
wasn't a question of detouring bad places like the Bucket
of Blood because the music was everywhere. If you
couldn't hear it you could see it. In those funky undershirts the men rolled down off their chests and let dangle round their hips like raggedy skirts. In the way the
young girls switched their narrow fannies and the old
big-butt ones stood wide-legged, hands on hips shouting
back and forth across the alley, putting their business
in the street like it was everybody's and nobody's.

The music was everywhere. Sneaks in like a stray
alleycat and hides in your house just waiting for a chance
to slink out and take over. Like the wine bottles John
French hid in the cupboards and drawers. And worst
of all, that low down, down home stuff had crawled
inside her. Messed with the way she walked and talked
and thought about things. As she searched for John
French this morning the nasty music dared her not to
listen. But she paid it no mind. Wouldn't give it the
satisfaction. She held her head high. The moon was still
up, looking lonesome and out of place, but still hanging
on. Not shining like it does sometimes early, early in
the morning when she blows steam off her coffee and
eases into the quiet of Cassina Way. The moon was a
pale, whitish blue now like everything in Anaydee's

china cupboard when she forgets to polish the glass doors.

The music in her own house now. One day last month here come John French and Strayhorn pulling Carl's old wagon down Cassina Way. It's rolling and bumping over the cobblestones and they got something big sitting teeter-totter up on the yellow rails of that little wagon and John French in front pulling and Strayhorn stumbling beside it supposed to be steadying the load but he's been in that dago red you can tell it before you smell it because he's bobbing and weaving worse than the big box they got sitting up on Carl's old wagon. *Who's holding up who* she had wondered as they bumped along and then she could hear the bottles rattling around in the wagon's bed. As they got closer she could see it was a Victrola. Dials and fancy trim and shiny wood panels without even a smidgen of dust. She had groaned inside and closed her eyes. Prayed she wouldn't hear a policeman's whistle or sirens or a crowd of angry white voices coming to take her man away. Then she could smell sweet wine and groaned out loud because when they were into that dago red they'd do anything. John French try to walk on water if you dared him, lift her and the chair she's sitting on by one leg in one big fist. Get down on his knees and huff and puff till he looked like he'd bust wide open and she's scared he will before he gets her up and scared he will before he gets her down again out of the thin air and she doesn't even breathe till she feels all four legs hit the floor. He'd try anything and die trying before he'd give up. So she searched up and down the block for a policeman or white men red-faced and huffing and puffing like John French when he did that silly chair-lifting trick.

Watch it, boy. Watch what you doing. Ain't come all this way for you to dump my pretty box on these cobblestones. John French grinning like a Chessy cat. The handle of Carl's rusty yellow wagon swallowed in one big paw while he pats the Victrola with the other.

Some fool throwed away this good machine. Strayhorn found it back of some white people's house out in the alley behind Thomas Boulevard. A shame, ain't it, honey? Some people's got nothing and some can just

throw away stuff as fine as this. Shoot. I ain't too proud.
No indeed. Take somebody's leavings and fix them up
and make do best as I can. Help me lift it off here,
Strayhorn, fore these stones tear it up.

She could hear the police coming and hear the shouting and hear her heart in her throat. Because when
John French and Strayhorn drinking wine they were
capable of anything, even marching into white people's
living rooms and loading a Victrola, which probably
cost more than John French earned in a year, on that
child's yellow wagon and pulling it through the Homewood streets, calm as if it were a watermelon from the
A & P they had picked out and paid for.

Why you doing this, man? Nobody throws away machines like this. Not those rich folks on Thomas Boulevard nor nobody else on God's green earth about to
throw away something like this.

Yes, Mam. Strayhorn said the same thing. Figured
something had to be wrong with it. Yeah. That's why
he didn't take it hisself. Probably don't work right.
Youall probably right. Probably wasted my good time
hauling it all this way in the heat. But it look nice in
that corner over by the window even if the damn thing
don't play.

But it did. Loud and perfect. Never had to do a thing
but turn it on and twist in a steel needle, a box of which,
sharp as pins, John French found when he lifted the
machine's lid, needles thrown away like somebody had
thrown away the Victrola. So the music wasn't only in
the streets. It was prowling inside her own house now
like something slinked in out Cassina Way. Shaking
peaches from trees and moving on down the highway
and lonesome train whistles blowing and hollering like
a mountain jack and See, see rider, gal, See what you
have done. Every time she lifted the lid and peered into
the well of the Victrola the stack of records was higher,
and one day she'd take a hammer to them all. Smash
the shiny discs the way she had crushed the nest of
Tokay bottles, snug in their straw bottoms hid up under
the steps.

In the streets, in her house, in the church. The music
everywhere now, even in her head as she waited a min-

ute outside 725, waited to see her husband's big hat
and broad shoulders ease round the block. But nothing
turned round the corner or filled up the sky, nothing
but a little bit of that music, a sigh of music dark and
slow as the shadow of her sauntering man would have
been if it was him instead of nothing meeting her eyes.

Anaydee's house was on the corner of Susquehanna
where Albion, the last street before Homewood Avenue,
crossed. The house was not exactly on Albion and not
on Susquehanna either but recessed in the far corner
of the vacant lot at the intersection of the two streets.
Like an extra tooth sprouting behind the neat smile of
row houses on Susquehanna. Uncle Bill Campbell never
allowed that the house was anything but 725. Not 725
Albion or 725 Susquehanna. Just 725 because that was
the number he had been playing for twenty years when
one day a white man, a stranger to the Fox Bar and
Grill had gotten drunk and friendly and whispered 725
into Bill Campbell's ear after two or three boilermakers
and the one on the house Bill Campbell always served
up to his best customers or people who seemed to have
plenty of money to spend. Seven twenty-five and don't
you know I got to thinking. Got to thinking about working every day of my life and them cigar butts and spittoons, and every kind of filth curled up in that sawdust.
Got to thinking about the stink of stale beer every
morning and shoveling snow so some drunk Irishman
won't slip and crack his noggin coming or going out the
Fox. Don't you know I thought about all the money I
had made for Mr. O'Reilly and how he give me a bottle
of brandy with a fancy label on Christmas and a dollar
on my birthday and give Aida a fur piece his wife tired
of. I got to thinking, man. All them years working for
O'Reilly, and me and Aida in them little bitty rooms
over top the bar and me spending most my time slaving
down there in the Fox and what we got to show for it.
And don't you know all the sudden something said to
me Bill Campbell get that little teapot from behind the
bar. Run your fingers down in there and get every red
cent. Teapot was where I kept my tips. Let them fatten
up a month or so and take the few dollars be in there
and put it with the rest me and Aida been saving so if

I wake up dead one morning she might have a little something to get along. And I says to myself you been a penny, nickel, dime man all your life, Campbell. You been breaking your butt and making the white man rich and what you got to show for it? What you gonna have the day they lay you out in Allegheny County Cemetery besides the suit you got on your back and the suit ain't really yours cause it's bought on time and you and suit both six feet under but Aida still be carrying payments to the man. Man, I said to myself, hear me out now, I said, Damn these pennies and nickels and dimes. I told Clark who tends bar in the afternoon so I can get me a little nap before the night shift, Clark, I says, man you come on back here awhile. I got to go take care of some business. Tipped on up the stairs (Aida be nappin that time of day) with what that white man had whispered still burning in my ear. Funny how wasn't nothing special bout him. A big head like a lot of them and that white fringe around his ears and bald on top. Red-faced like a lot of them get after knocking back a couple boilermakers but nothing special bout him. But when he whispered my number, my 725 I been playing twenty years, I kinda got loose in the knees and my heart beating 4/4 time and thinking all kinds of things to myself so I untied my apron and tipped up the steps and got that money we been saving and took it to the bank and had them count me out brand-new, crisp bills for the pennies, nickels and dimes and wadded up paper notes we had hid in the shoebox under the bed. When I took that money to Joe Westray who was numbers king then, I snapped them bills down one by one, nice and new and stiff. Popped them down like old Clarence Brown pop that rag when he's shining shoes and said to Joe Westray: When I comes to get my hit I want it all just like I'm giving this to you. Pretty new money, Mister Joe. Course, he laughed. And I laughed too. But I laughed again next morning and been laughing since.

Seven-twenty-five was that money Bill Campbell won. 725 was the house he and Aunt Aida bought the day after his big hit. Now, at least Bill Campbell dying between walls he owned, his big body propped up on the bed in the front room of his own house. Freeda's Uncle Bill the only father she ever knew, the man who had raised her in those tiny rooms over the Fox.

Yoo-hoo, yoo-hoo. Aunt Aida had taught Freeda to holler instead of knock at people's doors. Aunt Aida which everybody in the family said so it came out Anaydee said you should let the people inside the house hear your voice so they'd know who they was opening they door to. Wasn't so much the robbers or strangers or bill collectors you didn't want to open your door to as it was the Devil who could slip in unseen while you holding the door open and wondering if you really heard a knock or if it was wind or kids playing a trick or somebody in such a big hurry already gone before you could let them in. So at the door of the little house tucked behind Albion or tucked behind Susquehanna, after she waited and looked up and down the block one more time for John French, Freeda yodeled, Yoo-hoo, yoo-hoo, Anaydee.

Zat you, Freeda?

Better be. Don't know who else it might be, if it's not me.

The clapboard house was yellow with shutters, doors, and trim painted deep green. Uncle Bill had made a walkway of flagstones through the vacant lot to the front door. The scratchy heads of Aida's sunflowers had inched past the bottom sill of the big window beside the door. The garden Bill Campbell had staked out the year before with sticks and string had been reclaimed by weeds. After Uncle Bill's stroke nobody had fought back the jungle. You couldn't tell he'd hacked down the weeds and turned the soil. As hard as he had struggled chopping weeds and digging out rocks, it was a shame he never had a chance to seed the ground. She'd get Carl over here. Brother would help. Carl was big enough now to keep the yard looking decent. Time for him to start helping the older people who had always loved and supported her.

If it's something in that pretty skin that ain't you, Freeda French, it's gon get a hot welcome pretty quick. Just sprinkled me some fresh salt all out there this morning.

Nobody but me, Anaydee.

Yes it is you, you pretty little stranger you.

The door of 725 was cracked only wide enough for Anaydee to poke her head into the bright sunshine. A blinking, squinting moonface the color of the pages in the old Bible Anaydee had given Freeda when she married John French. The Bible with family names and birthdays penciled in a faded list on the front pages, split-seamed and tatter-edged, held together by a thick rubber band. Moonface creased and pitted, but not so dry you were half afraid to touch it, let alone dare to slip off the gumband and turn the leaves. Anaydee had always parted her thick, dark hair in the middle, and the curls, pressed flat against her forehead, curls accented with silver threads, were two wings framing her face. High cheekbones like Gert her dead sister. Eyes widely spaced and deep-set behind the flesh, which over the years had drifted against her high Indian cheekbones. A green sparkle in the depths, in the smallish eyes so when she smiled you saw the dance of jade and forgot the creased surface of the moon.

Mr. Bill, guess who's here? Guess who's come to see us, Mr. Bill?

It was black inside. Freeda heard the door slam behind her and Anaydee fidgeting with locks. The interior of 725 was as familiar as her own house, and she knew what she'd see when her eyes became accustomed to the niggling light. Yet some shapes were impatient. They groped toward her through the darkness. Uncle Bill in his bed, the white sheet pulled to his chin. When she thought of him he was always wearing an apron. Tending bar he liked it to ride high under his armpits so it looked like a giant white bib. How many times had she watched Anaydee tie the apron in the morning and loosen it at night? She saw Uncle Bill aproned again now, whiteness draping him and draping the bed in its folds.

Freeda gal. Come on over here and gimme some sugar.

He don't much like light no more.

Ain't no light no more for Bill Campbell is what she's trying to say. And she be telling the God awful truth, too. Can't see the hand in front my face. But that don't make no nevermind. Just come on over and gimme some sugar.

Freeda picked her way across the room to the bed where he lay, sheet to his chin, head propped on a mound of pillows. She leaned over him, into the sour cloud of sickness, pressing her lips against his cheek. He was fair-skinned like John French. Deep shadows made his face a skull. The mask of flesh was gone, his face bone and black emptiness.

That's light. That's sweet light. All I ever need to see.

She was stepping back as he spoke, *fleeing,* a deeply shamed part of her scolded, *fleeing* and she stopped and hugged his shoulder and rubbed the chilly cotton undershirt. He had been a big man. She'd ridden on his shoulder when it was a mountain halfway to the sky where he balanced her and toted the huge wooden kegs of beer up from the cellar of the Fox.

How do you feel, Uncle Bill?

Like a man just been kissed by a pretty girl.

You're teasing me. And not answering.

Don't he always be teasing. Like some big overgrown boy laying up in that bed, and I can't hardly believe a word he says. Don't talk nothing but teasing and foolishness.

You're something, Uncle Bill.

No gal. Your Uncle Bill ain't nothing special. He's just lucky is all. Lucky.

The last word, the *lucky* was almost a whisper. His voice trembled. Each word was a struggle. He coughed, and the springs of the bed squeaked, the top sheet jerked like dogs fighting under it.

Oh...Mr. Bill, take some water.

Cool Jordan water get me to the other side. But Campbell ain't quite ready yet.

Don't try to talk.

Who you trying to hush, little gal?

Let em be, honey, can't tell this hardhead man nothing. He's just like that John French of yours. So much like him that's why he got out his shotgun when he heard youall run off. Just leave him be. No sense in

trying to tell Mr. Bill Campbell nothing he don't want
to hear.

John French never was no bad man. A dangerous
man, but he ain't bad. I'd a shot him dead if he was
bad. Just didn't want my little sweet gal here to love
the kind of man be here today and gone tomorrow. Dangerous man ain't got no choice day to day.

John French done good by Freeda. Gave her beautiful children. And he works hard.

Never surprised me. Ain't never said he was a bad
man. Just a dangerous one. But he been lucky. Lucky
like me.

Freeda rubbed the scar on the back of her hand. Saw
her man loping down the alley and the phantom behind
him raise the pistol and point it at his back. Lizabeth
is in her arms. They are in the house on Cassina, staring
at the grayness as it settles between the row houses.
Their peaceful, end-of-the-afternoon time at the front
window, the only window on the bottom floor. Cassina
Way filling up with dusk. Her image, if she stared a
certain way at the glass, staring back at her. Wondering
if the babygirl ever saw herself floating in the emptiness over the cobblestones. John French about to die in
the space framed by the window. Freeda's fist slams
through the glass to shield him, to shield her child from
the black mouth of the gun.

Rubbing the luck of John French, the jagged lightning stroke behind her knuckles, the scar which had
saved him once and which, as she traced it with her
fingertips in the shadowed room where no one could
see what she was doing with her hands, she prayed
might save him again. Though the scar was nothing
but a furrow plowed by broken glass, nothing but the
shape of her fear, the shape of her pain, the pain of the
man in the bed who spoke even though each word hurt
him. She could walk for miles and miles along the zigzag path scarring the back of her hand.

Anaydee, I need to know where Albert Wilkes is. I
know he's back, but I don't know where in Homewood
he would try to hide.

Albert Wilkes. Oh, my goodness gracious. Albert
Wilkes done come back home.

That Albert Wilkes. Yes, him.

It's God's will. Bring him back home so he can die in peace. Albert Wilkes a doomed man. Once another human being's blood on your hands, ain't nothing you can do but go in circles till you come back where you shed it. What goes round, comes round.

Woman,... what you talking about? You don't know nothing bout it.

I know he shot a police, a white police, and they gon hunt him down till they get him.

Wasn't no policeman. Was a white man coming after Wilkes cause Wilkes been messing with the white man's white woman.

Found him dead in his uniform.

Wilkes knew what that white man was after. Uniform didn't make no nevermind.

Lord saith vengeance is mine.

Ain't no vengeance to it. Man come to kill Albert Wilkes. Albert Wilkes got his shot in first. Lord didn't say nothing about standing still and dying just cause some peckerwood decide he needs you dead.

He come back to Homewood to die.

He's a fool to come back. You got that right.

Where would he be? Where would he stay, Anaydee?

Him and John French like the hand in the glove. Wonder he ain't been round to youall's house. John French and Strayhorn and Wilkes. Three the biggest devils ever run these Homewood streets. Don't you be grinning at me, Mr. Bill. I ain't forgot you was out there with em. See one, you see em all. And see em all, you know they's into something. Know they just looking for devilment. But they could sing. Yes, Lawd, those boys could sing. Ain't gon tell no lie. Your Anaydee young once her ownself. Young and foolish and just half listening to the Lord out one ear and the other ear steady listening hard to whatever Devil music going around. They could sing. Hear them boys singing when you pass the corner of Hamilton and Homewood where they all hung out. Every kind of sing. Ask Mr. Bill. He know something about it. He'd play that guitar of his. Yes, Mam. Your Uncle Bill had his day out there with them hounds. But he ain't played that thing since you a little

girl and we was still over the Fox. Don't believe that
guitar made the trip to 725.

She sure was a pretty one. Twelve steel strings and
fancy work all inlaid on the neck and body. Called her
Corrine, but I ain't never told nobody why. Brought her
up here from Virginny. Only thing I had when I got
here. Just me and that box and all these hills and mean
white folks and smoke and coal mines and boys with
nothing just like me arriving every day. I been luckier
than most. Real lucky.

I remember you singing to me, Uncle Bill. I remember Corrine.

You's a sweet thing. You got me thinking bout good
old times and all my miseries gone. You like medicine,
gal. Just what the doctor ordered. Albert Wilkes ain't
gon come near youall and them children. John French
wouldn't let him. Wilkes probably over to the Tates.
Albert Wilkes used to work on old Mr. Tate's truck.
Albert work for nothing long as he could get at that
piano.

Tate the one give him money to get outta town after
all that mess. But not many people know that. They go
way back. Yeah, he was always messing on that piano,
and I bet that's where Albert Wilkes be hiding now.

Standing beside him, above him, she could feel the
man's will, strong as the cloud of sickness hovering
around the bed. His voice was weak. My grandmother
had to listen closely to pick out the words and between
the words were spaces unnaturally long, but he was
saying what he had to say, what he wanted to say. Yes,
she remembered Corrine. But never heard the instrument strummed so sweetly, softly as it sang in her memory this moment. *Ride a shiny little pony/Ride a shiny
lit til po o ny*. Rumble of the Fox beneath their feet as
Uncle Bill hummed and plucked at the strings of the
guitar. To her a fox would always be a monster with a
huge belly that churned and rattled, a belly where all
the people it swallowed argued and fought over how to
get out. And a *po ny* something blue, light blue with
wings and a warm, furry place between them to sit. She
would soar up into the air, and the tiny clouds bobbing
like bubbles in bathwater, would smell just like Gert's

perfume and the wings of the pony carrying her past the stars would rustle like her mama's skirts.

Thank you, Uncle Bill.

Nothing to thank me for. How's all them beautiful children?

They're fine...fine.

Don't get to see them much.

You know how children are. They stay on the go. But I'm going to catch that Carl and send him to see you and Anaydee. That big-head boy can cut down those weeds in your front yard.

Don't put him to no trouble on account of us.

I'll send him. And the girls too...Bye, Uncle Bill...

Bye, little gal. Don't you worry none bout Albert Wilkes, John French know what to do.

God bless, darling.

Bye, Anaydee.

Kiss the children for me.

Bye.

Gotta close this quick. Light hurts his eyes these days. Don't know who be lurking around here. Put down some fresh salt this morning...but...

The door slams. Uncle Bill is coughing again, rattling the wooden walls. A dead bolt rams home. Freeda is dazzled by sunshine. For a moment she is confused. She can't find the stone path Bill Campbell had laid from the street to the front door of 725. So overgrown now you could hardly even call it a path. But her feet keep to it. She brushes back the waist-high weeds and thinks how Anaydee, little as she is, would be lost in this jungle. Carl and his shadow, Brother, better get over here and take care of business. When they finish, 725 be a fairy-tale house again. The frilly white curtains open again and light flooding through the big front window and the window box full of gladiolas and the smell of gingerbread or a blueberry cobbler welcoming you at the threshold when you *Yoo-hoo.*

Meanwhile, Albert Wilkes had sure enough returned. If someone had asked him *from* where, the image of a deck of cards broken in half and riffling back together under a dealer's thumbs would have flickered

an instant in Wilkes's mind. The days away had passed
that swiftly. Days different as hearts and spades and
diamonds and deuces and queens, but they all disappeared the same way in a double-backed blur between
the dealer's hands. If someone had asked *to* where,
Wilkes would have gone blank inside, his eyes would
have picked something, anything, and stared at that
piece of Homewood, that crack in the pavement, that
tree, that brick, that shadow moving across a window-
pane, stare as if it was his job to keep it in place and
if he faltered, if he lost concentration for one split second, the thing would disappear and all of Homewood
with it. But nobody had asked any questions of the
pencil-slim man in the gray duster who had stood like
someone who might be lost, oblivious to his surround-
ings, consulting an invisible scrap of paper scrawled
with a name or address which would tell him the direction his next step should take. He carried no bags.
A black locomotive belched and snorted and wheezed
clouds of steam behind him. Passengers helloing and
good-byeing, the rumble of baggage carts trundling over
the cobblestones, the shouts of trainmen and porters
were magnified in the cavernous station and trapped
under the metal canopy arching over his head. He had
stood motionless in the din and steam and coalsmoke
till a conductor pulled the courtesy step off the platform,
boosted his blue-uniformed self back into a Pullman car
and chanted *All aboard.* Nobody had asked any questions as he walked across the city, and now as dusk
deepened to the gray of his long duster coat, Albert
Wilkes stared at Homewood, making it stay put with
the power of his eyes. Now he was no closer to knowing
the answer to the questions nobody asked than he was
seven years before when he glanced over his shoulder
one more time at Homewood then turned away again
and hurried into the darkness.

A darkness aglow with snow. Snow beginning in the
morning and still falling that night seven years before
when he had fled. White piling up in the darkness, the
darkness shining. Old Mr. Tate in his stocking cap.
Lucy's walleyed teddy bear in the rocking chair. They
were his audience when he sat down at the Tates' piano

and played those last few licks he had to hit before he left town. One more time. Somebody had named the notes, but nobody had named the silence between the notes. The emptiness, the space waiting for him that night seven years ago. Nobody ever would name it because it was emptiness and silence and the notes they named, the notes he played were just a way of tipping across it, of pretending you knew where you were, where you were going. Like his footprints in the snow that night. Like the trail he tramped that was covered over as quickly as he made it.

Through the deep shadow under the railroad bridge and he knew he was in Homewood again. Sure he had made it back. This was the exact place, this daylight after the dark tunnel, this door you pushed through to get into Homewood, this line you stepped over, danced over if you were the 501 Engineer Corps returning from the war. You stopped marching and started dancing because this was the edge, the very moment you knew you'd made it home one more time. Soon he'd be invisible again. His gray coat and black hat disappearing into the night just the way they'd vanished in the darkness of the tunnel whose topside held the trains passing over Homewood Avenue. If he hadn't pawned the gold pocket watch, now would be the moment he'd tug on its chain and note the hour. Just enough light to read its gold face and he'd announce to himself: On this day, at this precise hour, minute, second and a half, Albert Wilkes returned. He could hear it ticking, feel the knurled winding stem twist between his thumb and first finger. He would name the hour like they named the notes.

Who was the first one to see him? You could get a good argument going in McKinley's about the answer to that one. Which was why people called McKinley's the Bucket of Blood. You could get an argument on just about anything. And occasionally the argument got too deep and they took it to the street. Nobody necessarily won, you could get another argument going on that, and nobody necessarily got bloody, but somebody would shut up or be shut up long enough for the talk to move

on to other things. McKinley said the one man who died
in the Bucket of Blood and whose spilled blood made
the mess some people say gave McKinley's its bad name
was a stranger and the man who cut his throat a stranger
too, and neither one said a word to the other except a
woman's name nobody knew. So it wasn't dangerous in
the Bucket of Blood if you opened your mouth and fussed
at people. Never was bloodshed except that once,
McKinley said, unless you count Fricassee's bloody nose
when he went to sleep standing up and his head hit the
bar, or count Bump Mallory's piles when he sits on his
fat behind all day on one of my stools and don't even
order a glass of beer.

You listen to McKinley he'll tell you it's not even
about blood. He'll say blood is wine and niggers would
drink it in buckets if he served it in buckets and some
try to drink a bucketful anyway so mize well go on and
call it Buckets of Blood which cause niggers is lazy with
s's is Bucket of Blood after a time. Or tell you any fool
know niggers is bloods and you come in his place Saturday night look like somebody dumped bucketfuls of
bloods in there so it's Buckets of Bloods and you lose
the s's again, it's *Bucketablood* either way. Either way
ain't really no blood in it. Just baptized with a terrible-
sounding name. Just like all these niggers round here
got a bark worser than they bite.

You could get a good, loud argument about who was
the first to see Albert Wilkes when he came back. Even
long after Wilkes was dead and buried, even from people who should have known better, people who couldn't
have seen Wilkes first, second or last because they
weren't even born that day in 1934 he returned.

Course I seen him first. First thing when he push
through that swinging door. Sitting on the first stool
inside the door. How my gon miss him?. In that long
black coat and black cowboy hat looking like some Jesse
James outlaw train robber. Wilkes wasn't above the
average height, but the man thin as spaghetti. Wasn't
no *round* to him. Just shot straight up so he looked tall,
real tall even though his eyes come to just about here,
just about where my eyes is. If he be standing here next

to me wouldn't be a inch either way if he took off his goddamn ten-gallon Stetson.

That ain't nothing nowhere near first cause you see I was on my way out. Had my little taste and I was heading home. You know how you get. Feeling good but a little shaky. Just a touch on the high side, so when I goes to push the door and it swings away spooky fore I touch it, I kinda follow my hand a little ways, might even have stumble some, nuff to make old Wilkes smile and back up a little and hold that door for me so how's anybody gon see him fore I did?

Yeah. We seen you falling out the door. You so drunk you didn't even know I was behind Wilkes with my hand on his shoulder. I'm the one guiding him in. I'm the one said let's stop here Albert and lemme buy you a welcome back drink.

All youall lying. Wasn't nobody here but me and Fricassee and Lemuel Smart God rest his soul. And Fricassee sleep like he always is and Lemuel talking to that bottle so who's that leave? Who's the one seen him first?

Gon nigger. You wasn't even bartending yet. Mc-Kinley still tending bar then.

Now here he come with his lie. Here he come with that met-him-at-the-station tale.

Wilkes parts the swinging doors enough to see in but not be seen. Neither John French nor Strayhorn at the bar so he lets the doors glide back together. Nobody he wants to see yet. Nobody he wants to see him except John French or maybe Strayhorn. He feels the night ride up under his gray coat. Homewood Avenue nearly deserted. A moon. Narrow doorways and storefronts already deep in shadow. Two blocks away the faint light of the poolroom. He's hungry and his feet hurt. Seven years away but he had believed he remembered everything, every detail of the streets, people's names and faces, the sound of the doorbell in the little restaurant on the corner where Saunders could cook you a pork-chop better than you could ever cook it yourself. Hear the pan sizzling while Saunders talks bout Paree, the best days of his life and he's going back, sure nuff going back soon's he saves the passage. Wilkes had believed he held every detail of Homewood exact in his memory, but now he wasn't sure. This street was too small. If he shouted his name, they'd hear him on Hamilton and hear him at the bridge by Finance. No room on this street for what he remembered. He had remembered a song, a song too big to ever play through, to ever finish. For seven years he had recalled phrases, chords, runs, teasing little bits and pieces reminding him of what he was missing. And he had expected the song to dance out and just about knock him down when he returned. He wanted to feel happy, to feel good, to hear the music rushing through him again. Wanted it in his fingers and toes so he could reach up and snatch that pale moon and shake it like a tambourine.

Nobody answered his knocking so he called Tate... Mr. Tate. Seven years and old man Tate might be dead now. Dead and gone and somebody else in his house. Seven years ago Tate had shuffled down the steps in his stocking cap and night shirt. Half dead then. Wheezing and shaking on his spindly legs, legs no bigger round than the candle stuck in a bowl he carried to light his way to the front room. Shaky, old Mr. Tate on that night seven years before. The walls bending and buckling cause he couldn't hold the candle still. And his stutter ... Al ... Al ... Al ... Albert ... Wi ... Wil ... Wi ... Like he'd never get it all out so you had finished it for him. Albert Wilkes. Yes, it's me. Albert Wilkes. Shadows bouncing on the walls and ceiling. Following Mr. Tate's crooked, spidery legs, his mashed-back slippers wide and flat as a duck's feet. What ... wha ... wh ... Whasmatta ... b ... b ... boy? Wilkes remembers the moment when he was ready to scream, to shut his eyes and shut his ears because everything was coming apart, was falling to pieces in the dance and sputter of the old man's hobble and broken words and that candle had been like a sword chipping away at everything it touched.

Tate. Mr. Tate. If he could, he would have taken back the words. He was talking to a dead man. Mr. Tate nearly dead seven years ago so he's surely dead now. And dead people could answer. Could blow that cold, dead breath in your face, in your ear, tickle the bare skin back of your neck with those icy ghost fingers. Wilkes shivered in the dark vestibule. Peered through the Tates' colored front-door glass to locate the light he'd seen from the street. His hand dropped automatically to the brass knob and turned and pushed. The heavy door squealed then shuddered when it hit the high spot still not shaved after seven years. A job Wilkes had promised Tate he'd do. And Tate dead and still waiting for Wilkes to sand the buckled place in the wooden hallway floor. *Tate...Mr. Tate*. This time the words rise up the stairwell and bounce off the high ceiling, chiming fainter and fainter, till they echo inside Wilkes, till he's not sure if he's calling Tate's name aloud or just whispering it to himself.

He liked you, Albert Wilkes. And I did too. With that little monkey cute face of yours.

For some reason Wilkes didn't bolt and run but took three long steps toward the quaking voice, toward the light flooding from the living room. Like the door's squeal, the bump and rattle when it hit the humped floorboard, the voice startled him and reminded him at once. You've been here before, you knew this was going to happen. So rather than haulassing back out the front door he snapped to attention and strode toward the voice, ready for what would come next, listening for what he'd forgotten in seven years away.

Wilkes remembers how old she is. Old Mrs. Tate in her rocker. The bright light hurts his eyes. He fidgets, weight on one foot then the other, like little Lucy when she was too busy to go pee, back and forth like the wall-eyed teddy bear in the rocker Mr. Tate had pushed up and back in time with the piano that night seven years before.

Mrs. Tate doesn't seem much bigger than a teddy bear. Her wool-stockinged toes dangle above the floor. In the ladderback, cane-bottomed rocker she measures her words by the slow nod of the chair.

All you cute little monkey-faced ones. That's the ones come to our door, that's the ones we took in. Days when this house full of children. Didn't know all they names.

But loved all youall. Sorry to see you go when you had to go.

None my own. Nothing down in that dry place he called my pretty Pussy-in-the-well. Mr. Tate always worked hard. A good man. Loved children. Loved youall running round here. Had a little more than most folks so we took in the little cute monkey-faced ones with no place to go. Now you standing there Albert Wilkes with that face we took in and it's old as me now and why you hollering for my dead man?

Never looking at him as she spoke. Talking to the couch or the tall, fringed, pinch-waisted lampshade on the end table. Speaking at him, but not to him.

Mrs. Tate shrunken to doll-size, rocking in the high-backed chair. The old woman's voice stopped, but Wilkes could hear it playing on and on in the squeak of the chair, the slow, steady up-and-back beat changing her words into things he had seen, places he'd been. In that story she rocked out phrase by phrase, he was just as she'd said, older than she was, older than she'd ever be. He listened, forgetting her like she'd forgotten him. He remembers a dream about a piano. Big and black and greasy as a train hurtling down the track. A piano filling the sky. Gleaming just a few feet away and you catch the beat of the rocker and step in the footprints it carves in the floor and the piano bench scrapes a discord when you pull it from beneath the keys but that sound is in another world you don't hear it any more than you hear yourself settle and sigh, any more than you hear the snaps of the duster unfasten one by one or the swish of its skirt when you flip it away and it drapes the back of the bench and falls slowly to the floor. You push up your gray sleeves. Then you are stepping right dead in the middle of her story and you play along awhile, measure for measure awhile until the song's yours. Then it's just you out there again by yourself again and you begin playing the seven years away.

The night grows blacker as Wilkes plays. A moody correspondence between what his fingers shape and what happens to the sky, the stars, the moon. At some

point that night of his return he leaves the Tates' ram-
shackle brick house, and his feet carry him where they've
been wanting to get all day, all night, all seven years.
He scratches, as my grandmother said, like a cat and
whistles in the stillness of Cassina Way and waits for
John French. What he says to John French has my
grandfather rising earlier than usual and has him
creeping down the alley like somebody stole something
from his ownself as Miss Pollard thinks watching him
disappear down the dark tunnel of Cassina. John French
up and gone because Albert Wilkes is back.

John French is first on the corner this morning. The
night chill hangs in the air. He can't tell from the sky
what kind of day it's going to be. A changing day most
likely. A hot gold and reddish band, clouds bumping
and losing their shape, what's left of the moon, pale,
melting down like a chunk of ice in a glass of tea. Yellow
as a cat's eye late last night. A Halloween moon as he
stood in the shadows of Cassina Way. Too early, too
damp now to be outdoors sitting on a crate. The first
man this morning on the corner of Frankstown and
Homewood where the white men drive up in their trucks
with that little piece of work you might get if you're
lucky, if you're early and smile and act like Jesus hisself
behind the wheel of them pickups. Grin like the white
man gon carry you to Great Glory but you knowing all
along he gon take you to some piece of job and pay you
half what he pay one his own kind. John French stretches
and yawns and rubs the evil knot at the end of his spine,
the tight place sore from standing all day and stretching
all day too many days. His wallpapering tools in a sack
beside his knees. A canvas drawstring sack it takes a
good man to heft. From the breast pocket of his flannel
shirt he pulls his tobacco pouch and loosens its bright
yellow string. The tool bag and tobacco sack look like
different-sized twins. He pinches out brown shreds of
Five Brothers. Spits to make more room for a fresh
chaw. Like blood it splats and sizzles, alive a moment
where it lands on the pavement.

If he squats too long on this crate, in this damp, the
misery be in his back all day. Sometimes he can hear
the little drops of pain pinging into that hollow just

above his backside. Nasty-colored drops that harden
and ball up so it's like somebody rams in a fist back
there and knuckle grinds his spine every time he moves.
From hanging wallpaper. The stretching, the bending,
the ladders. He walks like a cripple old man, taking
those bent-over, short, tippy steps when he gets up out
his chair. Needs to walk the length of the house, from
the window on Cassina all the way back to the kitchen
before he can straighten up. Bent over like he's looking
for something on the floor, like he's picking cotton and
got a two-hundred-pound sack slung cross his back.

   The sky can't make up its mind. He chews and pulls
the high crowned hat tighter down on his skull. The
snub-toed brogans are a mile away when he stretches
out his legs. Only way he can tell they belong to him
is that twinge in the small of his back. They used to
put people on wheels and pull them apart. Pull the arms
and legs out the sockets just like a kid do a bug. Albert
told him that. Albert had seen pictures of it. Boiling
people in oil and slamming their heads in a helmet full
of spikes, and horses tearing men into four pieces and
that wheel with ropes and pulleys stretch a man inch
by inch to death. The rack, Albert said. Said he didn't
know exactly what ailed him till he saw the picture in
his white woman's book, and then he understood exactly. They got us on a rack, John French. They gon
keep turning till ain't nothing connected where it's supposed to be. Ain't even gon recognize our ownselves in
the mirror.

   The brogans were spattered with every kind of work
John French had ever done. Paste and paint and mud
and plaster. They didn't have a color anymore. He wondered if they ever did, because he couldn't remember
what it was if it ever was. The sky now. What was the
right color of the sky? The first color? Did it start one
color before it began going through all those changes?
Was it one thing or the other? Blue or white or black
or the fire colors of dawn and sunset the first day it
was sky? You could use a chisel on his shoes and never
get down to the first color. Carl's friend Brother was
like somebody had used a chisel on him. A chisel then
sandpaper to get down to the whiteness underneath the

nigger. Because the little bugger looked chipped clean. Down to the first color or no color at all. Skin like waxed paper you could see through. This early in the morning things seemed to be closer to the way they used to be, to first colors or first shapes, to the quiet before there was a city always snorting and roaring like some animal prowling these hills.

Lots of nights crazy Albert never went to bed. Gambling or playing that piano all night long. When Albert finished playing, no matter how tired they thought they were, they'd wake up, even though they hadn't been asleep yet. Wake up and stagger into the red dawn, the quiet time when anybody got good sense is sleeping. A rooster crowing somewhere inside Albert cause he gets wide-awake and shouting happy. C'mon. C'mon, French. You ain't tired, man. It's a new day. We own all this motherfucker. This fine bitch got her legs cocked wide open just waiting, French. Everything you see, man. We own it all. And he'd walk like he did. Jigger-legged, getting out those kinks from sitting all night at the piano. Gleam in his eye. Hat pushed back on his forehead.

French, you a family man. How come you a family man? You like it out here just like I do. Acting a fool. Running wild. Come and go like you please. How come you a family man?

Nothing to do but shake your head. Albert start with those questions you always be asking your ownself, questions that ain't got no answers. Just look at him so he knows you know he's crazy and you ain't paying him no mind.

Go on, boy.

No, French. You gon answer me this morning. You gon testify right here where ain't nothing but sweet light and you and me and the truth if it's in you.

Cause I got a family, fool.

Now wait a minute. That's too easy, ain't it? I mean you trying to say all I need is a family and Albert Wilkes be a family man too? That's too easy, French.

Ain't nothing if it ain't easy.

Then you telling me the truth? So help you Tokay?

So help me Tawny Port and Dago Red and all the wine in all the grapes ain't even wrung out yet.

Being a family man meant one day he caught Lizabeth standing in his work shoes. Tops of the iron brogans come to her knees. She can't lift them off the floor, and kinda shuffles along like a tugboat pushing coal barges down the Allegheny River. Only she can't get the brogans to go straight, the toes bump and skew off catty-corner. Nothing to her skinny little twig legs. She bends down to work the shoes back the way she wants to go. Her little butt pokes over the back of the uppers. She doesn't see him watching. She smacks the crusty toes, jibber jabbers and winds up mad as a wet cat. Standing again as tall as she can, hands on hips, cussing his brogans nastier than he thought she could.

Which meant his boots least as old as Lizabeth. But they were old then, didn't have a color then, when he caught her planted like a flower in his boots, in that polka-dot dress Freeda had made. His boots past old now, down there a mile away at the end of his legs. The seed gets planted. So course you gon water it and watch it grow. You gon see the first color and the first shape and watch the changes, and sitting here on a crate this morning you can't remember what anything looked like at first, but you know you know something about what's under there. Closer to knowing on this kind of quiet morning so what else you gon do but pull on your brogans and go to work and be a family man.

But you never could tell Albert Wilkes nothing. Not about family nor nothing else. You said on one those rooster mornings, Boy, you crazy, boy. White woman's got your nose open and you riding for a fall. Wagged your head and said your piece and rolled your eyes but you knew you mize well be talking to the wall as try to tell Albert something. But you let him hear it anyway. Then shame on him. He's grown. It's his behind. His neck. If he's bold enough to traipse up to Thomas Boulevard in the middle of the day and knock on the front door of that white woman's house and bold enough to stay long as he wants to and march out when he's good and ready like he's been fucking rich white ladies

and strutting down rich white folks' streets all his life
then more power to him. And shame on him.

John French stings the gray pavement exactly where
he was aiming. Wine color, blood color. He shoots the
tobacco juice between his teeth again. An arc from the
slatted crate, over the curb into the street. That be all
that's left of Albert when they catch him up on Thomas
Boulevard. Black splat where they squash him on that
white street. Wouldn't be so bad if he used the back
door and creep around at night like anybody with good
sense. No. Not Albert Wilkes. Albert gon play it like
he plays that piano. It's him. Couldn't be nobody else
but him you hear him play once and nobody else get
on them keys sound like Albert.

Gon do it, French. Mize well do it right.

Well, doing it right was not doing it like this. He'd
promised he'd meet Albert early. Early, early before
anybody else be on the corner. Still early but too late
if Albert didn't want to be seen by nobody else. Boys
be right along. Still half sleep. Evil and blinking back
the light. And Albert ain't coming. And that was Albert.
Have your ass out in the cold. Out before dawn and my
back hurting already and he ain't even bothered to show
up. And you know where old rooster butt was. Sure as
nothing was never gon be like it used to be, Albert back
up there on Thomas Boulevard laid up in his white
woman's bed.

John French remembers how Lizabeth had jumped
when he shouted: Hey, Little Sugar. Where you learn
to talk so mean? And where you going in my brogans?
Better git your hands off your hips and sit down before
you fall down.

Lizabeth had yelled Stoppit and Leave me alone, but
then he had snatched her out his boots and whirled her
round and round. He jiggled her at the end of his arms
till she stopped fussing, till the braids pinned across
the top of her head pressed the ceiling, till she giggled
and laughed his name.

Daddy.

Daddy.

And there is no color underneath that. He lets her
down from the ceiling and they rub noses and she's

squealing again as the walls spin round them. He is
Daddy. What else he gon be with her strong, tight, little
body wiggling in his hands, her big bird eyes popping
open wider and wider as the merry-go-round speeds up.

Sunshine. My only sunshine.

He stands and stretches. The crate is bowed from his
weight. Easy does it now. Little bit at a time. Locking
his knees and tensing his backside and letting that hard
ball of pain unravel slowly. His hands are empty reaching into the undecided sky. Reaching for her laughter
again. Her cries. In his empty fingers.

Lizabeth had swiped at his hat, tried to steal it off
his head. Her big eyes would swallow it. And swallow
him. And that's why he's a family man. And he couldn't
say more than that. Couldn't talk about what he thought
when he shut his eyes and saw pictures of Freeda and
pictures of Lizabeth. So he'd just snap hisself out his
dream and say: That's why, Albert Wilkes.

And Albert would say: Truth ain't in you, French.

And John French answer: Get your nose out that
white woman's behind you might see something true,
boy.

Can't think of no place I'd rather be. Nothing I'd
rather see.

You a dog, boy.

And you a family-man dog.

John French hears Rupert and Clyde. Before they
turn the corner he scratches the place badly needs
scratching that ain't none of their business. Scratches
it good then sits again on the crate.

How you, Brother French?

How de do.

Thought we was up early this morning. But you sure
beat us here, didn't you?

You sure up early this morning. You waiting for
somebody this morning?

Why don't you mind your business, Rupert?

You my brother, not my keeper. Seem like you might
have learned that after thirty-two years.

Damn. It's been that long. I been putting up with
you that long? Somebody ought to give me a medal.

Man told me he had three rooms needed papering.

Supposed to run me up there to see them this morning. Told me he had the paper and I could start today.

You lucky then. Little work as there is these days.

French is lucky and good. Can't nobody hang paper like French. Even these hunkies know that. They all want French if it's a particular job.

You right about that. French a paperhanging fool.

The corner is crowded in half an hour. Men on the crates. Men in the doorway. McKinley got the Bucket of Blood open and coffee boiling on the potbellied stove in the back.

John French rolls up the sleeves of his flannel shirt and plants his elbow on the bar. Nobody had cleaned the brass spittoons. McKinley was slipping. Place used to shine in the morning. Like ten miles of bad road by closing time but McKinley used to have it clean to start the day. He'd get one wino or another and stick a broom and some rags in his hand and promise him a jug and the place be nice in the morning. All day McKinley have steins and mugs in his towel polishing them clean as a whistle. Or wiping the bar or shining the mirror. Hey man, you gon rub all the niggers off that glass. But now when it's slow, McKinley just hunkers back against his counter. Keeps a towel over his arm but his heart ain't in the swipes he takes every now and then. Glasses don't sparkle like they used to. Spittoons full and nasty round the edges.

Nobody bothered McKinley about it. If McKinley slipping, he wasn't slipping alone. All Homewood coming apart. He'd have to ask Albert. Albert would see how things had changed. Seven years. Couldn't see it with Albert's eyes unless you been gone those seven years. John French loosens the straps of his coveralls. Wouldn't be needing the vest much longer. Let the straps and the bib hang down and pull off his wool vest before he went back outside. Stuff it with his tools in the sack. The white man had said eight sharp. Be on the corner at eight sharp. Like eight sharp the only minute in the day the white man be at Frankstown and Homewood. Like they don't take their own good time. They tells you one thing then come when it suits them. You could wait an hour, wait all day if you fool enough or broke enough to believe they mean what they say. Well, this morning they gon wait for him.

He wonders what Albert will see. Wonders if Homewood's really gone down as bad as he thinks. He could ask the men around him. Start a conversation with McKinley or Strayhorn when Strayhorn pulled in. But they didn't have the seven years. They were trapped like him. If Homewood falling apart they were falling apart too. And the blind can't lead the blind. Albert Wilkes had those seven years. And seven years be like eyes on his chest and his shoulders and behind on his back. He could push through McKinley's door and see what nobody else could. Albert wouldn't have to say a word. Be like a mirror in the middle of the floor and you could walk up to him and see what you been missing. When Albert on that piano it was like a mirror anyway. Not cause he went round with his silk handkerchief and flicked off every spot of dust before he'd sit down to play, not because he polished the keys and the gleaming wood like McKinley used to do his glasses. It wasn't him fussing and worrying the wood and ivory and brass of the piano like he was a janitor or something. It was after he got it just like he wanted it and the music started coming out that you could find yourself, find your face grinning back at you like in a mirror.

But if Homewood slipping, maybe everything slipping, maybe the whole world and Albert Wilkes too, so when you hear him play again won't be no mirror or nothing else. Just you feeling sorry cause he been away too long and his fingers clumsy and you feel sorry for him and sorry for yourself. And shame on Homewood. Damn, boy. Why'd you stay away so long? Why'd you have to go and lose it? Maybe he don't even play no more. Maybe he's back to say he quit. Maybe he forgot the way it used to be. The good old days when Albert be playing and Homewood hanging on every note.

John French thinks about silence. Not the silence before things get started, not the stillness underneath things you can hear when you're peaceful and the sky is spread out so you know you're just one little lump, one little wrinkle like everybody else under the blanket of sky. With a mouthful of Tokay in his cheeks he squeezes his eyes shut and rinses the tobacco taste from his mouth. He thinks about the silence after things end.

Albert will have something to say. He could talk to Albert Wilkes like he couldn't talk to nobody else. In the Bucket of Blood with the men waking up around him, with their voices filling the emptiness, he realizes how long the seven years have been, how long he's been waiting to speak to Albert. Not a word in seven years. You could be on one side of Homewood Avenue and your buddy on the other and the earth could split, could open up between you and the two sides of Homewood go blasting away in different directions till there's an ocean between you instead of a little strip of street. You could scream bloody murder but his side the street keep sailing away. That's what happened. Seven years nothing to do with it. That's what happened sometimes when a song was over. When Albert stopped playing you could look down at your toes and see that black pit start to open. See your crusty toes dug in at the edge of nothing. You could snap your fingers once and seven years be over. You could keep snapping till the skin breaks and the bones break and ain't even a raw bloody stump left to wiggle and seven years ain't even started.

He finds Rupert and Clyde. Four years apart but the brothers alike as two peas in a pod. See one you see the other. And Fricassee at his end of the bar and Lemuel already on his stool at the far end where the first thing you see is his narrow back when you come out the bathroom. All the men doing what they do so the Bucket of Blood like it is every morning of the week but Sunday. Could wake up in China or on the moon you still know what they be doing here. Shut your eyes and see them doing what they do. Nobody looking round like they worried, nobody forgetting what they supposed to do. You could hear them on the moon. If it be morning the men be in the Bucket of Blood and it be sounding like this, looking this way. Albert gone seven years. Never did see him here in the morning unless he had that rooster crowing inside and he's up cause his back never hit bed that night.

Albert's time late afternoon. When he strolls in it's four or five o'clock. It's a different time of day but it's

like morning cause you can count on it. It's a picture
you can close your eyes and make. You could roll over
in Hell and if there's a clock on the wall and it's saying
four-thirty in the afternoon you can bet they doing what
they always do that hour in the Bucket of Blood. Nobody
forgets, nobody worries, nobody gets tired. Look around.
Everybody busy, everybody in place. Albert Wilkes gone
seven years but if he walks through the door this afternoon he'll know who to speak to, what to say, where to
stand and nobody'd hardly notice. Like he never left.
Like he got a brother, like Rupert got Clyde, and that
brother could hang around in Homewood and save Albert's place till Albert gets back. Almost see him sometimes. Albert's shadow moving round in the Bucket of
Blood like a natural man. Nobody bothers him, nobody
gets in his way. Wouldn't be the Bucket of Blood if they
did. Wouldn't be Homewood if you couldn't hear Albert's music when you walking down the street.

So it wasn't so much a matter of missing Albert as
it was a matter of having him around when he's gone.
All those shadows and pieces of Albert moving through
the bar but you can't call him over, you can't tap him
on his shoulder because it's just that ghost holding his
place till Albert gets back. Albert Wilkes around like
that fine piano music around and it's not a matter of
being gone but being here and being gone both. Like a
tune you can start and hum some of but you can't get
the best part, can't hum it through and finish it like
Albert would.

Nobody this morning looks like they miss Albert
Wilkes and nobody believes they might be the one missing tomorrow. Nobody sees the grass and trees growing
up through the floor. Nobody knows how hot the fire
will be sweeping away these boards one Sunday afternoon. John French hears it crackle and sizzle. Hears
the timbers pop like matchsticks and the flames
screaming like all the mothers ever lost a child. A burnt
pit. Ashes and a few black bricks from the basement
and maybe the toilet burned white again, clean again
in the middle of the pit like a bone poking from a grave.
If you counted back, used your toes and fingers a couple
times to count the years, these bloods in this bucket all

be down home, all be in the cotton patch sweating for
Massa. If you counted ahead a short minute, touched
your fingers and toes two or three times apiece all these
boys be dead. All be lost as Albert's ghost haunting
these walls if Albert don't come back.

He can kiss my ass.

What you say, French?

Said I'm leaving here.

What about the man? What about them walls he
want papered?

Tell em I'm gone. Tell em I got business. Tell em
don't need no corn and lasses. Tell em kiss my ass.

At the very moment John French sidles out of the
Bucket of Blood and nobody speaks to him because his
jaw is set and his high-crowned hat slanted down over
his eyebrows and his tool bag stashed with McKinley
behind the bar, at the precise instant John French stalks
out with a jug of Dago Red in his fist, evil so high in
him the others can smell it and don't say hello, good-
bye or nothing else, not to him or to each other till his
broad shoulders bump through the swinging doors and
disappear, Albert Wilkes rises up on his elbows and
remembers he's late. He stares down at miles of satin.
Remembers the only words he can recall his daddy saying: Your black head ain't made for no satin pillow.
And his daddy's hand upside that black head and stars
and shooting comets because he was acting uppity about
something, about a bone he didn't want to chew, or
greens with cold grease caked on their ribs or wanting
a blanket or more room on the dirt floor between him
and the next farting pickaninny. Acting spoiled and
getting slapped from daylight to stars and red comet
tails flashing across his brain. No face. No body. Just
a growling kind of angry voice and a hand upside the
head. Did he forget the rest of his daddy because it was
worse? Was this the good time, the best time with that
man his mama said to call Daddy? *Kapow*. Black head
ain't made for no satin pillows. But here he was looking
down over acres of satin, and satin under his black head
sure nuff and his woman getting perfume sweet again
in a bathroom bigger than the whole shanty that his

daddy shook with his voice. And his fine woman whiter than his daddy's whitest dreams. So white she could be black if she wanted to. Talk like a nigger, act like a nigger. Treat white folks like a nigger'd like to. Be black when they played under these satin sheets. Black so he couldn't see her and she couldn't see him so they had to find each other with toes and tongues and fingers and breath.

Look here, French. You know how it is. Didn't know if she'd open the door. Didn't even know if she was still living there so she could open it. Seven years. Seven years, man. So when she was there and did open it ... ow whee.

You know how it is. So poke your lip back in. And don't roll your eyes at me. How many times I been waiting high and dry for you and you ain't showed? Yeah. So I ain't hardly gon apologize.

Wilkes can't hear her feet on the soft carpet. Doesn't know how long she's been standing there wrapped knee to shoulder in a baby-blue towel. Water still draining from the tub. The bright shaft of light from the open bathroom door doesn't quite reach the foot of the bed where he lies. She stands so one side of her is silvered and the other soft as velvet in the candlelit room. She hugs herself in the blue bath towel, loosens it and briskly dries her skin with big handfuls. She lets the towel fall to her ankles and steps daintily out of it, bending quickly to gather it from the floor as she steps backward deeper into the shadow.

I know what you're thinking. You're thinking how easy it is to come back.

She's in the glare of the light again. Her arms flash as she unwraps a second matching towel turbaned around her head. Red hair splashes down to her shoulders. Her skin is like snow, like ice in the hard light, her wet hair black against its paleness. Perfect and naked as a statue he thinks as she poses at him an instant before she shakes her head like a soaked dog and attacks the tangled mass of hair with the towel.

She is leaning forward so the towel drops like a hood over the muddle of hair. Her long pale fingers dig through the cloth into her skull.

You're thinking how easy it is. How easy this easy woman is no matter how long you stay away. I know just what you're thinking.

He didn't answer her. Even though he knew she was wrong. She had never heard John French's name let alone knew about his pouting, about his jaws getting tight because he's out there on the corner of Frankstown and Homewood waiting for somebody who ain't showing up.

Seven years ain't put a wrinkle or a ounce of fat on you, woman. Looking good as I left you. Looking better if you want to hear the truth.

Her face jerks from under the towel. She snaps loose ringlets of hair away from her eyes.

So easy you can go away and utter not one word in seven years but she's so easy she'll smile at the first lie you tell her.

If I'm lying, I'm flying. He feels a wet spot on his cheek. Waterdrops flung from her hair darken the satin sheet.

Well, maybe you should be flying. Maybe you just ought to get your black ass out of my bed and fly away from here.

You know you don't mean that.

Don't I? Am I so easy you can tell me what I mean and don't mean now?

The towel hangs limp from the hand cocked on her hip.

Am I one of your easy mamas now?

What you talking about, gal?

Gal. So I'm a gal now. I'm one of your gals now. One of your fast, little, red-hot nigger gals.

You always did look good when you got mad.

I ought to break your neck. I ought to whip you back out in the street. Stretching the ends of the towel apart, she twirls it till it's taut and pops it over the foot of the bed.

Whipping's too good for you. Ought to just let you lie there and choke on your lies.

Don't mind choking if you come on back under here and choke with me.

I'd sooner crawl in bed with a black snake.

Got one them too under here.

You devil. You damn fool.

Hurry up. Let me grab a handful while it's all wet and smelling like lemon pie.

Damn fool. She snuffs the candle flame between two damp fingers. Shivers as she crawls across the silky darkness to find him.

How long you been waiting?

Lemme see now. Long about seven years seems to me. Seemed like seven hundred years this morning with my ass out in the cold and my back stiffening up. Seems like too long to me with my butt sticking to one them crates on the corner.

Look here, French. You know how it is. You know I had to go see my woman. Didn't know if she'd open the door. Didn't know if she was still living there to open it.

Well, you found my door. And you got me out in that alley to open it. Like some damn alleycat scratching and whistling. Like something chasing you. Meet me in the morning, French. Got to see you first thing in the morning. Early before anybody around. Early so you can sit on a cantaloupe box and get stiff as a board. So I can lay up in that white woman's warm bed and laugh at French propped up like some damn fool Eskimo Kewpie doll out there in the cold.

You exaggerating now. Wasn't cold this morning.

Whose ass was out in it? Guess it wasn't cold where you was.

Seven years. Seven years, man, and I didn't even know if she still alive. So when she was...and when she opened the door...you know how it is.

Yeah. Ow whee and all that mess. But I don't want to hear nothing about it.

Got here soon as I could. How long you been waiting?

Bout a jug long.

Got anything left in there?

Ain't no more waiting left in there.

Many times as you left me up a tree and hound dogs barking and snapping at my heels. C'mon, man. You know how it is. Gimme a swallow that blood.

You back then? Back to stay?

If they let me lone.

You still wearing a horseshoe round your neck, ain't you? Already been in that white woman's bed. Already drinking my wine. Bet you been over to the Tates' on that piano, too.

Ummmm, that's good. Tastes like heaven. Tastes like three dozen pretty angels singing.

You think the police done forgot you?

Hell no. Motherfuckers never forget. Naw. That's what the man's about. Not forgetting. Not forgiving. Naw, they ain't forgot nothing, but they ain't got no special reason to start remembering today. It's been seven years. Whole lotta people come and gone in Homewood in seven years. And you know one nigger look just like the rest to the man.

Yeah but only one nigger fool enough to go marching back to that white woman's door in broad daylight.

It was dark last night.

Then you ain't going no more? You ain't gon be Albert Wilkes and strut right up Thomas Boulevard when you want to?

French, you on page ninety and I just opened the book. Got time to think about all that. I just want to be here awhile. Get used to the old place again. Thought I remembered it. Thought I could draw a picture if I needed to. Thought I had Homewood in my mind and could say it easy as saying the alphabet. Say the streets and people's names and talk that talk with everybody just like I used to. Like I could just pick it up and start again and never miss a lick.

Albert Wilkes takes the wine bottle again. Wine is black inside the green glass. Three fingers all that's left. As he tilts the bottle, it catches the sun and wine shimmers like wet tar. Wilkes stares into the glistening oval floating inside the bottle. It's blacker than a mirror in a dark room. He swallows a mouthful, then wipes the lips of the bottle with the heel of his hand. In the green glass he can catch a reflection of scraggly treetops silhouetted against the sky. He plays the light and shadow till French rolls across the glass, all head, then all belly, then legs flattened and curling around the glass like fingers. Then his own face. The shape of a spoon. Greener than the trees, the grass, the weeds of the Bums' Forest where he'd known John French would be waiting.

They sit on stones. French sprawled over three or four big ones which form a chairlike backrest and seat. Wilkes on a single rock, gullied in the middle as if all the behinds over the years have managed to rub their shape into the granite. A blackened space, bare except for charred kindling and a ring of small stones lies between the men. A smaller bare patch of earth is hard and flat enough for dice to roll true when you bounce them off the board propped along one end of the square. Shattered glass spits back the sunlight. Wilkes can almost hear the crap game. *Fever in the funk house looking for a five. Pay the boss, the poor hoss lost.* The singsong magic words chanted at the bones, the bones rattling in somebody's cupped hands, the bones talking back as they stare up at the faces staring down on them.

How's all your pretty babies, French?

Four now. One born whiles you gone. Another little girl, Martha. Lizabeth and Carl and Geraldine and Martha. The oldest one's getting grown now. Lizabeth more like her mama everyday.

My man, the family man. Wouldna never believed it.

No way round it. Man find a good woman he better go on and grab her. I got a good one, Albert.

Must be. Must be good and strong to haul you out the streets. You a big, ugly, fighting fish to land.

Still got the fight in me.

You still tipping round to see Antoinette?

She got three babies herself now.

Any them babies yellow and ugly and bald and chew Five Brothers tobacco and wear a big brown country hat?

She got a husband, too.

That ain't what I asked you. Asked you if you tipping, man. Husband ain't never made no nevermind if wife be willing. Cat's away, mama will play.

It's ole Jody niggers like you keep things stirred up.

I ain't the one sneaking over to Antoinette's.

You the reason niggers keep shotguns leaning up in the corner. Wonder as your backside ain't full of buckshot. Just ought to be if it ain't.

Seems to me the last time I remember hearing a shotgun I was on the far side of a fence and it was somebody else's posterior up on top, somebody else's britches caught and yelling for Jesus and thought he was dead when that shotgun blasted. Seems like I remember the alley behind Kelley Street and two sweet little chocolate sisters and their evil yellow daddy taking aim at Mr. J. Q. John French esquire couldn't get down off that fence to save his soul. Seems like I remember taking my own precious life in my hands and ripping some fool down off there and him leaving half his drawers stuck to the fence and walking down Homewood Avenue with his hat held over his bare behind where pants supposed to be.

Didn't know no better then.

And now?

It's a new day.

Things ain't changed that much. Couple babies ain't gon change Antoinette's big, pretty legs.

She's still a fine-looking woman.

And you still tipping, ain't you?

Seven years ain't changed you. Ain't said nothing bout yourself but trying hard as you can get in my business.

Legs like Antoinette's every man's business.

You still a fool.

And still thirsty.

Well, you hiding or what?

Tell the truth, I don't know. Seems like I should walk easy awhile. I mean maybe I ought to lay low. Find a place on the Northside or Downtown or the Hill maybe. Thought I'd do that. Thought I'd ask you what you thought. You know. About being here. About being seen. Thought you might have some idea how safe that'd be. Whole lotta new people. That means things is different. But I missed you this morning and been slipping round till now and nobody ain't said a word. Hello. Good-bye. Welcome back. You're under arrest. Ain't nobody been after me with no shotgun. Nothing. Maybe they have forgot Albert Wilkes. Maybe I can just settle down and mind my business and they'll let me alone. Call myself Tom Smith or Jim Johnson and nobody know the difference. Just one more ole country boy come to the city to slave for white folks.

One more country boy who makes love with rich white ladies in broad daylight. One more country boy who plays the piano like nobody before or since Albert Wilkes. How long you think this ole country boy gon lay low and mind his business? How long before he marches up to Thomas Boulevard or marches into the Elks after that piano?

Don't know.

Well, I don't know neither. But I know it take more than seven years for a leopard to lose his spots. I know if he's a leopard he got them spots till he lay down and die. And you ain't no ghost, is you? Got all the spots you ever had under that coat. Yeah, you under there all right, Mr. Wilkes. Got to be.

Shit, French. What you saying, man? Damned if I do and damned if I don't.

You sure nobody seen you?

They seen me. But didn't seem like nobody knew me. Got some strange looks. You know. Little warm out here for this kind of coat.

Ain't a whole lot of hats like that, neither. Strange kind of hat for somebody don't want people to see him. Mize well have a billboard on top your head. Mize well have smoke puffing out that stovepipe.

That's the whole idea. Folks see the duster and see the hat. Now nobody trying to hide be wearing nothing like that. Folks see the big hat and see the long coat and don't think about somebody trying to hide. They think well here's one more fool trying to show off so they ignore whoever's in the hat and coat.

Why don't you steal you a elephant from the zoo and hang some bells on his ears and ride up and down Homewood Avenue singing Dixie. Then nobody pay you no mind for sure.

I'm telling you people don't say boo. Like I was invisible. Had to kick a can a couple times to make sure

I was still alive. Niggers looking right through me like
wasn't nothing under that hat but air.

Less seven years changed your mind about white
pussy and piano playing they gon find you soon enough.
They gon notice you real good and blow some holes in
that coat.

That's what you think then?

I think that horseshoe's working overtime keeping
you hid till now. Think you better find you a hiding
place till I can check around.

Was at the Tates' last night. Old Mrs. Tate must be
there by herself. Didn't see nobody else.

Little Lucy is there and Brother. They must been
sleep. Never could quite figure out who's keeping who
over there. They take care the old lady and she takes
care of them. Since Tate died the three them been together and they gets along. Funny little Lucy and the
albino boy and Mrs. Tate, she must be a hundred. Must
be older than Homewood. She was old when I come here.
My boy, Carl. He's over there much as he's home. Him
and Brother like we was Albert in the old days. See
one, see the other.

Those were some good days.

Owned Homewood in those days.

Far as we could see.

Damn. We gon figure something out. Got to figure
out something. How they gon chase you out your own
briarpatch? How we gon let em? No way, my man. You
just cool it for a little while till I figures something out.
You lay low in your invisibility clothes and keep rubbing that horseshoe for luck and we'll find something
to do. Sure as my name's John French. Sure as you
Albert Wilkes with all your spots under that blanket.

Who told on Albert Wilkes was another thing you
could get an argument about. Except wasn't nobody
claiming to be the one who told the police Albert Wilkes
was back. Huh uh. Nobody bragged about being the one
who told like they all bragged about being the one who
saw him first. Nobody wanted to be the one John French
had promised to kill with his bare hands. But there
were plenty stories going round. People had their fa-

vorites and would shout down anybody didn't agree. Gather all the stories, listen to every tale and all of Homewood guilty. John French have to strangle every man, woman and child in Homewood if you believed what the stories said. Strangle every nigger in Homewood and most the white folks up on Thomas Boulevard too. Because lots of the stories blamed white people. Course everybody knew it was white cops who shot Wilkes. But what counted wasn't the murdering puppets in uniforms so much as it was the ones who pulled their strings. The ones who ran Homewood without ever setting foot in Homewood. The ones whose lily-white hands held Homewood like a lemon and squeezed pennies out drop by drop and every drop bitter as tears, sour as sweat when you work all day and ain't got nothing to show for it.

Was that white woman Albert Wilkes had. Course it was her. Give Albert all her loving. Giving him her money too. She was scared he was gon run away again. Scared he'd take all her money and run off with some other woman and there she'd be. Cause she couldn't say no to him. Couldn't hold him and couldn't let him go neither. Nothing worse than a jealous woman. Nothing crazier or meaner. Course she called the cops on him. She can't have Albert Wilkes, nobody else would. I can see her dialing the phone. Them long scarlet fingernails. And a silk handkerchief dabbing at the tears as she tells the police where he's at. Shedding a tear for poor Albert and feeling sorry for herself cause she knows she ain't never gon have that kind of loving man again. I can see her weeping and stirring the ice cubes in her drink real slow with one those bloody nails.

Wasn't nothing to do with white folks. Niggers dirty enough to do their own dirt. That's the way it's always been. We our own worst enemy. Always find one nigger who'll snitch on the others. Always find a Judas. Don't need no pile of silver. Just a dime. Just a extra slice of watermelon. Find one them sneaky-type Negroes sell you to the white folks for a dime. That's the way it always been. In slavery days it was niggers keep watch on niggers. It's your own people tell on you you try to run away. Wasn't for treacherous, back-stabbing niggers no way they keep all those people slaves. It's the same today. You watch. A brother try to make something of hisself, a blood rise up to where he can do something for his people, who it gon be that drag him down. You name the ones tried to rise up and lead us and I'll name the nigger dragged him down. Wasn't nothing white about it. Just one these trifling Homewood splibs dropped a dime on Albert Wilkes.

The Lord giveth and the Lord taketh away.

Probably one the children. You know how kids is. Let something slip. Didn't mean no harm but they said it and walls got ears. You know how that is. Little pitchers got big mouths. And walls got ears. Poor little things got blood on they hands and never even know it.

By the time John French returned home that day that everybody was looking for him and he was looking for Albert Wilkes, the early evening sky was salmon pink and streaked with fiery drifts, and still hadn't made up its mind. Steel mills down along the river belched up clouds of smoke so there was something for the sunset to hang on, to paint. If you didn't know the smoke could kill you, if you didn't think of it as an iron cloud pressing the breath out your body, the dirt and soot and gas coloring the sky made a beautiful sight.

When John French walked into the kitchen of the house on Cassina Way he saw my grandmother sitting alone at the table quietly crying. He was full of oranges, golds, purples, the knife-edge keenness of the light shaping the sunset. He wanted to share the sight with his woman. But if they didn't hurry outdoors the sky would change. The lavender boards of the shanties in Cassina turn gray again. The rivers of fire in the sky become ash. He wanted to take his woman by her hand and walk with her out the door and down the narrow corridor of Cassina. Walk far away where rooftops ended, where Homewood and Pittsburgh and anything else with a name or a shadow was long gone. He wanted to go to a place where nothing got in the way and the sunset touched the earth. Instead he stroked her shoulder and ran his thumb up and down the hollows at the back of her neck. Her hair was piled on top of her head. The scarf she'd tied that morning was still knotted in place. Her neck was long and slender, the smooth ivory color of piano keys. He massaged the taut cords beneath the softness. A neck long and delicate as Lizabeth's. So much of this woman, this Freeda his wife, he'd never seen till after Lizabeth was born. His daughter growing more like her mother every day. But it was like Freeda growing younger too. Starting over again from the beginning so he can watch her becoming a woman. Freeda a girl again in her daughter's skin and bones. Sometimes he'd spy on Freeda through the cracked bathroom door. Watch her step out the tub, watch her naked body, so he could remember how beautiful she was under her clothes when she came out dressed. See two Freedas at once, later when she puttered quietly round the kitchen. His woman moving naturally and unaware in nothing but her ivory skin. His sweet woman in a housedress working her magic on the food for everybody's dinner. As Lizabeth grew up in the house on Cassina he could steal secret looks back at the way Freeda must have been. The bony awkwardness. The little girl shadow that the years had dressed as a woman. He saw one in the other. Could see where one body was headed, where the other had been. When he touched one, he touched both.

He wished he could tell my grandmother all the good things he felt. Something to change the way her day had been. Words to take them both back to the morning when he'd awakened beside her and she cuddled closer, warming his side a moment before he eased away and hung his stiff legs over the edge of the bed. What could he say about the long day he'd been away. She'd needed him and he hadn't been there. What could he tell her that would make up for the hours of worrying, the weariness. He stroked her shoulders and neck. Like touching that hot sky. Like running your fingers up and down the razor light, like poking them in the fire. He'd been the one whaling her body with the whip and now the same hands trying to heal, trying to mend the broken places. He saw in his wife's slumped shoulders the certainty that one day even Lizabeth would get old. He remembered the night both of them never went to bed. Remembered Lizabeth's fever and terrible hacking cough, his helplessness and fear as his daughter sat on the side of her bed, shivering, barely able to catch her breath, her little girl's round shoulders huddled under the blanket he'd draped over her. Nothing he could say, nothing he could do would change what was hurting her. He had been with Albert or waiting for Albert all day. And now there wasn't anything he could say to Freeda, no way to give back the day he'd taken.

Albert's in trouble. Can't stay here and he don't want to be nowhere else.

I can't talk now. Don't want to think about anybody else now. All day it's been you on my mind. Wandering the streets and praying nobody'd come running up to tell me you were dead. And seeing you dead. And having to tell the children. Watching their little faces break up when I say Your daddy's dead. How am I supposed to say those words to them? How would I say something like that to my ownself? Worrying myself sick all day about you. Trying to talk away the worst that could happen. Putting the worst in words and saying the words so it wouldn't really happen. Worrying about you. About them. All day long other people on my mind and now it's just me. I need to think about me. I'm sorry for Albert Wilkes and sorry for everybody else but now I just need to sit here awhile and be sorry for me.

He'll stay at the Tates' tonight. He'll be all right over there.

And where will you stay?

Be right here with you.

How long? Till he comes scratching and whistling?

How you gon be a friend you don't help when there's trouble?

There's all kind of trouble, man. Didn't you hear what I said to you? Wasn't I talking about trouble? Ain't I been in the deepest trouble there is today? Just cause you walk in here and squeeze my neck and rub my shoulders you think my trouble's over? You think I care whether Albert Wilkes at the Tates' or burning in Hell? I have these babies to face, these babies to feed. And a man act like he ain't got wife nor child the first. That's

real trouble. Youall just playing games. And Albert
Wilkes the worst. He looks for trouble. He made all the
trouble he ever had. He don't belong nowhere. Don't
answer to nobody. He needs trouble. Couldn't find
enough wherever he was those seven years so he's back
here again. Back to stir up trouble and you just itching
to be out there in it with him.

The man needs to come home.

Man like that don't have a home. His home is trouble.
He tears up homes. Never heard a good thing about
him. Except he could play the piano. And what's he do
with that piano but cause more trouble? Playing nasty
music and driving a bunch of drunk niggers crazier
than they already are.

He's a man just like I am. Breath and britches. Walks
on two legs. He ain't got no horns sprouting out his
head. Ain't got no tail. He's a man like me, and I been
knowing him ever since I been in Homewood. Seems
like we go back further than that. Seems like I always
been knowing Albert, and if he's in trouble I got to do
what I can.

You have to be with him all hours of the night and
day so when the police come to kill him they'll kill you
too? Is that what you mean? Is that why you've been
gone since dawn and why you'll go running again when
he comes scratching tonight?

Nobody bother him over to the Tates'. Just old Mrs.
Tate there and those two children. Nobody knows Albert's there.

You send him to a house with children? He's at the
Tates'? And where do you think your son goes running
first thing every morning? Where do you think he spends
every day after school's out?

Nobody knows Albert's over there. Nobody's gon
bother the children.

How do you know that? Unless the devil granted him
wings Albert Wilkes had to walk to the Tates'. How
you know nobody didn't see him? How you know the
police ain't on their way right now?

Albert got this long coat and a hat. He...

He's a fool. He killed a white policeman, and he can
stay away a hundred years, they still be waiting to kill

him when he come back. You know that. You said that
to me. So how you know nobody ain't recognized him?
You know the police would burn down the Tates' and
everybody in there to get him.

Gotta help him. Have to figure out something and
till I do the Tates be all right.

Well, Carl won't set his foot outside the door tomorrow. And if it'd do any good I'd get down on my knees
and beg you in God's name not to go either.

Don't talk like that.

Talk's all I can do. Nobody listens but what else can
I do?

Where the children?

Lizabeth taking them for iceballs. Told her go straight
there and straight back and they better be home before
dark.

She's a good girl.

And I want her to stay that way.

People look out for Lizabeth. They know she's my
girl. Wish I could have seen them marching down
Homewood Avenue. They growing up too fast.

Carl better listen to his sister. Warned him he better
stay with her and come back with her. Started not to
let him go. Bad as my nerves was this morning, him
and Brother walking those tracks again. Told him a
million times to stay off those tracks, but his head's
hard as yours. Chased Brother away from here but I
bet they back together now. Brother and that fast little
Lucy too. He just better be back here before dark. He
better listen to his sister and they all better be home
in a few short minutes.

Won't be dark for another hour.

Be black in another hour. Just about dark now.

You should have seen the sky tonight.

Lots of things I should have seen today instead of
worrying over you.

So pretty it scared me.

Walking around all day with a ghost, you should be
scared.

I know you ain't wanting to hear nothing I got to
say but Ima tell you bout the sky anyway. Kind of sky
gets you to thinking. Looked up and saw it all streaked

up and thought about how it was this morning and how
the sky is always up there doing what it has to do just
like you doing what you got to do down here. Made me
think about things like that. Like everything got its
own life but you don't hardly never notice nothing but
your own. Too busy with your own business. Then one
day you look up and see the sky and can't remember
why you so busy doing what you doing.

Please stay here tonight. Please leave Albert Wilkes
alone, and if he comes whistling around here in the
middle of the night tell him to leave you alone. Say yes.
Say you will.

The sky colors are like bits of music. He can remember the oranges, the reds, the purples. They flash back
to him, he can see them, but he can't put them together
the way Albert puts together the chords, the phrases,
the bits and pieces into a whole song. He remembers
how good it looked, how it swallowed him and filled
him and just about took his breath away but he can't
picture the whole thing, the stretch from the earth to
the stars, from right to left along the horizon.

I'll stay.

She smiles across the table at him. The kind of smile
which begins as anything but a smile and can't make
up its mind till the last minute what it's going to be so
a little bit of everything's in it. Then she reaches across
the checkered oilcloth and lays her soft hand on his
hard one, her young fingers on his old fingers, her lit-
tlegirl, Lizabeth smoothness on his rough paperhanging crusty-as-brogan skin. She takes back her hand and
he stretches out his long legs and both listen for the
children returning.

II

THE COURTING
OF LUCY TATE

The strange thing was that nobody taught him. The stranger thing was that nobody cared. One day Brother Tate sat down at the piano and began playing. Lucy remembered the hours she had spent with Brother watching Albert Wilkes. In the daytime in the living room, at night hiding in the shadows at the top of the stairs when they were supposed to be sleep. And Carl remembered the funny way Brother would play the air, pecking at an imaginary keyboard with his pale fingers. Brother could always scat sing and he'd drum on the oilcloth tabletop in the kitchen of the house on Cassina Way till his fingers were a blur and my grandmother mad enough to stomp in from another room and think about the butcher knife in the drawer and ten bony little quiet white sausages and peace at last as she shouted at him to stop.

Nobody cared that Brother hadn't ever played a note before Thursday because what they heard Saturday was so fine you just said Thank Jesus a day early and paid every iota of attention you owned to what was dancing from the Elks piano. And it wasn't strange at all that somebody got happy and shouted, *Play, Albert. Play, Albert Wilkes. Albert's home again,* because good piano playing and Albert Wilkes were just about the same word in Homewood. You'd look for one and here come the other. If you shut your eyes that Saturday night like a lot of people did during the down tempo, bluesy parts, slow dragging with your baby or just sitting stirring your drink and thinking your own thoughts, you wouldn't remember who was playing. You wouldn't care. All you'd know is that you'd heard the music before and that was why it sounded so good, so right, right now. And you knew you'd need to hear it again. One more time.

Brother was three times seven the first night he played the piano at the Elks Club. My Uncle Carl said it surprised hell out of him. Scared him too. The three of them, Lucy, Brother and Carl, were out that night. Nineteen forty-one because the war had just begun. The three musketeers drinking and smoking a little reefer and it was round about midnight and the band on a break, circulating in the crowd and the crowd like it gets then, lots of people out their seats, ordering another round at the bar, visiting other tables, jawing with the musicians, hustling to the toilet before a line formed and somebody made a mess in the sink or used up all the paper towels. One minute Brother right there across the table. Next minute he's on the piano stool and the notes are like somebody coughing, clearing his throat and getting your attention at the same time because just about the moment you look up to see who made the noise it's not noise anymore it's somebody taking care of business on the piano and you squint through the cigarette haze and the clink of glasses and the seesaw mutter of talking and laughing and it's Brother up there, your main man you've never seen close to a piano before unless it's that imaginary one, that invisible one he plays in thin air.

Brother wasn't supposed to be up there, Brother wasn't supposed to know how to play. He was my main man, and I knew better than anybody else he wasn't supposed to be doing what he was doing. So not only was I surprised. I was scared. I mean if he could just get up and start playing like that then what else could he do I didn't know nothing about. It's like you been knowing a fella all your life, knowing him and knowing his name is Tom just as well as you know your own name is Carl then one day somebody says that ain't Tom, that's Chuck. And everybody else says, Yeah. That's Chuck all right, and they shout you down and

Tom is nodding too and laughing at whatever notion got in your head to call him Tom. So that's that. But where's it leave you? You know better but they say it's Chuck and he says it's Chuck so what you gon do?

Anyway I listened like everybody else and popped my fingers and patted my foot under the table and clapped and shouted like everybody else. Brother stopped three times and three times we hollered and whistled and stomped till he sat down again and played some more. Talk about a joint jumping. Man, Brother turned it out. All by hisself at the piano. The more he played the better it got and I didn't have time to be scared nor surprised. Tell you something though. I couldn't look over there at him. I could listen and groove but I knew better than to look over at the bandstand where he was playing. Didn't know what I'd see. Didn't know what I wanted to see. Cause it wasn't Brother over there. No way it could be him. And if it wasn't him I didn't want to see *who* it was.

Seemed like hours. Then it seemed like he'd only been gone a minute because there he was all sweaty and grinning at me across the table again. Like he'd only been gone long enough to pee, but there'd been that music for hours, for days. I didn't know what to say. If he was Tom I sure wasn't going to call him Chuck, and if he was Chuck I didn't know him anyway and wasn't about to start speaking, but Lucy understood and said:

Ain't you something. Then she said, I heard you messing on the piano. Heard you since Thursday messing around down there at night. Wondered what you were doing. Wondered what you thought you were doing. Sneaking around like that.

Brother still grinning like the cat swallow the canary.

Must of been Albert Wilkes taught you. And you hiding it all these years. Hiding it all this time then getting up on the bandstand and showing out tonight. Ain't you something, lil brother.

But Lucy knew better. Albert Wilkes dead seven years at least. And Brother wasn't more than six or seven when Wilkes ran away. So what's that make?

How's he supposed to learn when he just a baby? How he's supposed to keep it in his head and in his hands all those years? So I was scared again. Lucy just making excuses. And why she gon make excuses less she know something I don't? Unless they got a secret. And if they got a secret then I don't know what's happening. Brother's not even her real brother. Tates raised Lucy who was a Bruce before she was a Tate. Mama got burnt up in a terrible fire but the Tates took Lucy in and she goes by Tate, just like Brother's not really a Tate. They just took him in and he became a Tate like Lucy did. He's not her brother and not younger either. Lucy was with the Tates first and Brother was older than her when he came but because she was there first he was her little brother. Pushed him around in a baby buggy till the wheels wore off. Looked like a big spider in there. Legs and arms dangling and knees poked up in the air. Her little brother Brother twice as big as she was, and she's pushing him up and down Tioga Street till wasn't nothing but wheels and frame left of that buggy and probably still be pushing him around if the wheels hadn't broke.

Seemed strange then and still seems strange now, that nobody bothered about a thing strange as that. I mean, one day Brother was one thing. Hands dumb as mine or anybody else's. Next day he's got all that music in his fingers and nobody asks why. Or asks how he got it. Guess folks didn't care as long as it sounded good as it did. So the three of us at the table and the place still buzzing and Brother's fingers still burning. Half expected that glass of Scotch and ice somebody sent over to start sizzling when he picked it up. But it didn't. He just grinned and downed it and Lucy smiling too and paying the strangeness no mind so I decided then, neither will I. If people gon change overnight, if they're gon be one thing one day and something else the next and it don't bother nobody else why should I let it bother me? Drinks getting lined up on the table. Everybody setting Brother up and setting up his table so why not? Didn't spend one more dime that night and drank till dawn. Shucks. I've heard there was a time when niggers knew how to fly and knew how to tell the truth. And if people could manage all that and forget all that then I'd be a fool not to listen when the listening good and drink when the drinking's good. Nothing but a party anyway. Whole thing ain't nothing but a party so why should I be a fool and sit there and fret?

I was born about six months before that evening in 1941. So already I was inside the weave of voices, a thought, an idea, a way things might be seen and be said. I had heard them talk about Brother that winter and heard about the war and the harshness of the weather which wouldn't be matched till I was twelve years old visiting my grandmother's house and watched the Big Snow begin one morning and bury the garbage cans in the vacant lot by night. Seven feet of snow in two days. And weeks of stories about snow. How Aunt May saved my mother Lizabeth by dunking her in a snowbank. How they had to chip the ice off old Mr. Wilson when they found him in his shanty and how he moaned when he thawed in the undertaker's back room and you can still hear him some nights where his shack used to be, crying and groaning in the wind.

In 1941 it's quite possible I heard Brother play the piano, if there was a day nice enough for my Uncle Carl to steal me from my mother and bundle me up and carry me over to the Tates'. If I missed Brother playing between '41 and '46 then I missed him forever, because after Junebug died Brother stopped playing the piano just as suddenly as he stopped talking. His terrible headaches began and he never played again. One day in one of the stories I'm sure someone will tell me, I did hear Brother play. On such and such a day while the sun was shining and the wind died down and them trenches dug in the street so's you could get around I remember Carl getting you ready and your mama saying *No*, saying it's too bad outside, saying it while Carl is wrapping you in sweaters and a snowsuit so you looked like a bowling ball and Cold could have run over you with a truck and you wouldna felt a thing... One day I'll be in the Tates' living room listening. I'll hear Brother. I'll hear Albert Wilkes.

* * *

But it's spring now. Spring one more time in Homewood. I'm not born. Not even thought of, let alone born, as somebody would remind me if I needed to be reminded. Late spring and all the trees I've never learned the names of glow with new life. The big trees you still find on the nicer streets in Homewood grew everywhere then. Canopies and tunnels, arches heavy with leaves drooping over the sidewalks. After a rain you could drench the kids walking behind you by jumping up and shaking a branch and it's like a bucket emptied on the ones trudging home from school behind you. Brother Tate catches my Uncle Carl daydreaming, lagging behind, and jerks down a flood all over Carl's school clothes.

Shit man, why'd you do that dumb shit?

Brother had caught him real good. Soaked him to his skin. Water hit the pavement like a load of bricks. Wet leaves on the branch Brother jerked down still swayed in front of Carl's face. Behind him rain pattered in the tunnel. Brother was so easy to soak it had stopped being fun. Fool even acted like he liked it sometimes so Carl had given up on that trick, forgotten it almost till he stood dripping, wiping water out his eyes, mopping the back of his neck with his wet sleeve. Brother was already too far away to catch now, across the street, jumping up and down and showing all his teeth in a horsey grin. Carl searched along the curb for something to throw.

You got me you cream-of-wheat motherfucker. You got me good.

Brother sidled closer then stopped in the middle of Tioga threw back his head and with a puzzled expression searched the blue sky for rain. He raised his hands over his head and pantomimed a column of wiggly drizzle, avoiding it at the last minute by ducking away from his falling hands. Pointing at Carl now, the look of wonder broke into a grin and the grin to a titter and the titter exploded to snorts and whinnies.

OK. OK. You win this time. You got me and we're even this time.

But when he stepped toward Brother, Brother's gone. Flying back across Tioga and halfway up the next block before he checked behind to see if Carl's chasing him.

Hey man. Peace, man. How my supposed to go home now? Carl curls his little finger and flicks water from inside his ear.

Wait up, fool. I ain't gon home wet like this. My mama kill me.

Brother waits, doing a little skittish toe-dance shuffle on the far, treeless corner. In the time it takes to reach him, Carl figures it's no win. Either arriving home on time with wet school clothes or being late with them dry, he'll catch hell. So he decides to catch it for coming home late *and* being over at the Tates'.

Don't want you playing on those tracks and don't want you hanging around the Tates'. Nobody over there to supervise you children. Don't want you worrying Mrs. Tate. Got enough on her hands dealing with Brother and that fast Lucy.

Yes, she's said it a million times. And yes, he knows better. And yes, Mam. I'm sorry and I know Ima catch hell. Yes, Mama. Your hand upside my head. And straight home every day after school. Yes, I know you'll watch the clock. Count the minutes and tell Daddy if I don't do right and Daddy got that razor strop and I ain't too big for it yet. Never will get too big for it.

Beside Brother now he fakes a punch and Brother dodges not so much to get away as to get a better look at the damage up close. Brother raises both hands and crouches Joe Louis style, bobbing and weaving, circling Carl and popping holes in the air with his jab.

C'mon, fool. Go get dry over your place.

The air smells like the salve his mama rubs on his chest at night when he's got the croup. Rain had rushed in and out again barely giving the sky time to change. Lots of thunder and crackling lightning. Like night suddenly in Miss Petronia's classroom. Dark anyway in the little seventh grade room in the middle of the hall. People jumping and squealing and acting crazy like nobody never heard thunder before. Miss Petronia at the blackboard scratching the answers to long division. She jumped the first time. Everybody did even though you knew it was coming. Dark like when the shades pulled down but she kept doing the problems on the board as if nothing happening. Squeak and scratch and tapping that chalk and it's blacker outside and blacker inside, but she don't turn on the lights, don't look over her shoulder to see how everybody's fidgeting and pointing to the window or staring at the puddles of shadow getting deeper round their feet. When it got us all wrapped up and it was dark as the inside of a drum in that room, somebody hit it, an arm as long as Homewood Avenue took a tree in its fist and slammed it down on top of Homewood School. *Baroom.* She stopped then. Jumped high as the rest of us. Dark in there but I could see the whites of her eyes getting wide while she stood there with the chalk in her hand trying to add up all the little niggers sitting in rows behind her. Told everybody be quiet and act like adults and switched on the light and switched her fine little Italian behind back to the board. Miss Petronia was fourth period and by eighth the sky is blue again, the black clouds fluffy white, the air dead still and smelling like his mother's hands when he's sick.

He follows Brother's narrow back up Tioga. Rain is itchy and chilly under his clothes. His mama kill him if he catch cold. Carl wonders if Lucy is home yet. If she wasn't, she'd be there in a minute. She didn't mess around like they did, doodling like doodlebugs to stretch the time between school and home. Lucy didn't join the packs of girls who had their own female doodling way of taking lots of time to get home from school. Nobody told Lucy what to do so she told herself. She acted so grown-up sometimes. Acted like him and Brother were kids. Lucy cooked and washed clothes and kept her house clean like his mama. She'd nag Brother like his mama nagged him, fussing, wagging a finger in his face. Too grown-up for a little skinny girl Carl thought and wondered if his mother called her fast because Lucy did all the grown-up chores Mrs. Tate couldn't do anymore. *Fast little Lucy Tate with her fast ways.* When his mother said it like that she wasn't talking about chores. She was talking about what was between Lucy's legs. His mother meant *womanish fast* when she kind of shook her head and twisted her lips tight together. Womanish fast. And when his mother said *fast* like she said it about certain girls on certain streets in Home-

wood or said it to his sisters about a crowd that was too
fast for them to run with, he couldn't help but think of
the space between Lucy's legs and think of wings or
racing car wheels or the flying thunder of a whole posse
of sheriffs chasing outlaws across the screen.

He'd dreamed once of Lucy growing in a red crockery
flowerpot like his mother had beside the living room
window. Lucy grew *fast*. Faster than an onion. Nothing
but a little girl string bean but as he watched she
sprouted nubs on her chest and apple cheeks on her
behind. She was bare and smooth all over and it wasn't
like peeking at the woman parts of his sisters because
Lucy was planted in that pot and growing faster than
a storm just for him.

The Tates' house sat a short cement walkway, five
steps and a porch from the sidewalk. A three-storied,
gable-roofed, brick building, it dwarfed the adjacent
row houses and made old Mr. Tate seem a rich man to
his neighbors. Brother squatted on the top step in the
shadow of the porch roof. When you played on the Tates'
porch it was like being indoors. If you stayed on your
knees nobody passing by on the sidewalk could see you
through the solid brick porch wall, and the overhang
of the roof kept out rain and sunlight. A cave for them
where everything they did could be a secret. Inside the
Tates' house were high ceilings, bare rooms, unlit hall-
ways and creaking stairs, doors Carl had never opened,
an attic and basement he'd never enter even with
Brother beside him or Lucy waiting inside. The porch
was their secret place, but inside belonged to old, dead
Mr. Tate, old, stooped, stuttering Mr. Tate with his
giant ring of keys rattling and jingling like chains as
he shuffled from room to dark room.

Brother's face was saying, Stop here, sit down here
and do nothing awhile. Carl understood the look, understood how it felt to be used by older boys who wanted
to get next to his sisters. They said things to him about
his sisters they wouldn't dare say to Lizabeth or Geral.
Treated him like a rug or a highway. He'd come home
beat up then get yelled at because he wouldn't explain
the bruises, couldn't repeat the nasty words that made
the big boys laugh and made him mad enough to attack

them. He understood Brother's look but only stopped
long enough to pop his knuckle once on Brother's bald
head before he skipped across the porch, through the
vestibule and landed in the footprints of Albert Wilkes.

You looking for Brother?

Lucy said the *you* like you'd say *boo* if you were
trying to scare somebody. And she got him like she
usually did, caught him and sent him jumping six inches
out his skin. She was behind him, her back toward the
front door. He tried to make his voice cool, but they
both knew she'd caught him again.

Brother's out on the stoop.

No, he ain't.

Well, he was.

Well, what you looking for then?

Me and Brother just come from school. My clothes
wet.

You too big a child to be peeing your pants.

You know I ain't done that. Fool pulled a treeful of
water on me.

Too big a child for that kind of messing, too. You
sure not the one takes care of washing and ironing
clothes at your house. If you did, you'd know better.

She's got her hands on her hips and nagging and
smirking cause she knows she caught him again. Whenever he was alone in the Tates', he couldn't help thinking of dead people. That's what he was thinking in the
hallway when he busted in from the street and didn't
see anybody. Old dead Mr. Tate and dead Albert Wilkes
dressed up in sheets and wagging their clammy ghost
hands. Lon Chaney and hunchbacks and werewolves
and Dracula and anything else dead and bloody sneaking up to grab him. So when she said *who,* said it like
some goddamn moony-eyed owl in the middle of the
night in the middle of a cemetery, of course he jumped.
Nothing funny about it neither. Just cause her and
Brother don't know no better. Just cause they go to
sleep every night in a haunted house full of chain-drag-
ging, piano-playing ghosts don't mean he got to be crazy
too. Lucy glides past him. Still grinning, still quiet and
sneaky as a ghost. Like there wasn't nothing dead on
the floor, no spilled brains and vampire feathers and

no hands dripping cold gravy come out the floorboards to grab her bare feet.

You got any peanut butter?

Might be some.

Fix me a sandwich.

Boy, you better act like you got good sense and fix what you want your ownself.

Can I have some milk?

Gwan and get what you want. Know as well as I do where everything is. You and Brother messed up my kitchen enough times, you just ought to know, if you don't.

Want one?

One what?

Peanut butter and jelly sandwich.

Oh. You gon get in my jelly too. Guess you gon fry my bacon and scramble up my eggs on this peanut butter sandwich you're fixing. Boys ain't nothing but eating machines. And all that food goes straight to your feet. Seems like some ought to rise to your brains. Ought to get smarter or something, all that food youall be wolfing down.

Carl sits alone at the kitchen table. If he stops chewing, the peanut butter will cement his jaws together. He is not hungry. His stomach floats up to the pit of his throat and just lies there, a flat, gassy little bag, and there's no place for the food he crams in his mouth to go. When he's in the Tates' house he needs to eat, he's never really hungry but he needs to eat. It's work. Packing peanut butter and jelly and bread into the tiny sack, into the lump which makes it hard to breathe right till he leaves the Tates'.

That's half a jar of jelly you got on there.

He had been wishing for Lucy's voice. Wishing and keeping his eye on the door so she couldn't sneak up again and spook him again. He wanted to reply in a firm, steady, man's voice this time but his mouth is full of peanut butter sandwich.

Lucy is handing him a tall glass of milk. He wonders why he had forgotten to get one himself. He avoids her eyes as he takes the glass and says thank you and thinks of Brother's watery, milky color. The icebox door clicks again. She's after something for herself. She's chewing something crispy. One of her end toes is crooked. It curls up from the floor and hugs the one next to it. Her toenails are painted pale pink, almost the color of Brother's eyes. Painted nails and painted toes. That was fast. And her ankle bones and bare feet looked fast. Fast little wing-boned feet smacking against the linoleum when she brought him the milk. Naked feet slipping quiet as a cat when she wanted to sneak up on him. He could almost hear the fast hum of blood in the veins crisscrossing the hump over her high arches.

You counting my toes, boy? They all there you think?

The top part of her was string bean thin and the bottom half lost in a pair of man-size corduroys rolled at the waist and baggy and rolled again above her ankles. Her school clothes hung up neat on hangers in a closet somewhere upstairs. Out of them fast because she's grown-up and keeps her clothes clean. Growing fast as an onion. If he wanted to see her the way she was in his dream he'd have to pull down the green corduroy like you peeled the green shell of a buckeye. Peel green spiky layers and layers of brown skin and damp white meat and delicate membranes. At the buckeye's core it's green again, a tiny green seed with a tree inside if you knew how to plant it and make it grow.

Mrs. French die if she saw you now. Sitting up there all goggle-eyed and face full of sandwich and you know she don't allow you over here after school.

Lots of things she don't allow. But I ain't no kid no more. Got my own rules now.

My, my. Listen at Mister Man. Bet you wouldn't be talking that trash if your mama was here.

Say what I have to say. And do what I have to do.

Listen at this child. Since when you so grown?

Since I could walk on water and swim on dry land. Since I been Long John the Conqueroo and crossed seven seas and whooped seven tribes and carried my people to the promised land.

Git out my face, boy.

Too high and heavy for you, ain't it? If I ain't grown, grits ain't groceries and eggs ain't poultries and Mona Lisa was a man.

You been listening to them winos in the Bums' Forest. You been listening, but that don't make you grown. Grown is working if you the man and cleaning and cooking and having babies if you the woman. Jive talking nothing to do with being grown. I could tell you something about being grown. And show you something too.

Show me.

Not what you're thinking, boy. That's one thing you surely is too grown for. No more that doctor, nursey, playing house with you and Brother undressing me on the porch mess.

You the one said you had something to show.

And you better believe I got it.

And the something she shows first is the ladderback chair in the living room with one rocker raw and split down near the bottom.

Knocked it over. Spilled poor Mrs. Tate right out on the floor like a sack of potatoes. She ain't been in it since. Her favorite chair, too. Police carried her upstairs when the shooting was all over, and that's where she been ever since.

The next something Lucy shows him is the holes in the piano, and beneath the piano's rolltop cover Albert Wilkes's blood on the keys. You had to look closely, but it was there, a purplish stain on the ivory like the pigment showing through at the roots of dark people's fingernails.

The last something begins as Carl follows Lucy up the stairs to the room where she sleeps.

Had to go find Brother because I wasn't exactly sure. Albert Wilkes gone a long time. So when this stranger come here in a big hat and a long gray coat there's something makes me look real hard at him when he ain't looking at me, but I ain't sure what it is. I was just a baby when Mr. Albert left. So I found Brother and we ran every step of the way back here and didn't stop till we was looking the stranger in the face. I was sure then. Didn't even need to look at Brother then to be sure. He had on a long dusty-colored coat. Kinda funny looking to be sitting at a piano in a coat but he had the sleeves rolled up and the tail of that coat pushed off his hips so it draped over the back of the piano bench. A big black hat beside him on the floor. Smiling at us like he knew us but didn't have time to say hello or nothing because he was in the middle of something and he'd speak later when he wasn't so busy. Couldn't remember his name but I knew who he was. And Brother knew too. Brother start to fidgeting beside me and moving his fingers like he's playing a piano so I said, *Play*. And Mr. Albert Wilkes did. I couldn't have called his name if you paid me, but I knew he could play that piano so I said as nice as I could, *Play*. And you talk about playing. My oh my. The sweetest song a dead man ever played for his own funeral. Course I didn't know he'd be dead before he finished. Course he didn't know neither, I guess. Not so sure what Albert Wilkes knew and didn't know. Shucks, honey. While the man was playing I didn't care. His name came back to me right in the middle of the music. That sweet, sweet good music. Sometimes I think I'd be willing to die if I could play one time as fine and sweet as Albert Wilkes played that afternoon. Maybe he did know he was gon die. Maybe he didn't care. I sure didn't. Didn't nothing matter but the music. And poor old Mrs. Tate, God rest her soul, rocking all the while. Couldn't tell what she might be hearing or seeing or thinking. Probably didn't even know Albert Wilkes was back, let alone hear what he was playing or know he was going to die and she'd be in jail before he finished.

Lucy's butt is half on, half off the bar stool. One long leg dangles to the floor, the other is drawn up to her chest and she circles it with both arms, stretching it, testing her sleek, dancer's muscles. When she stops her story she rests her chin on her upthrust knee. Carl has seen her in a skirt or dress sit the same way, on the same barstool, talking slowly and exercising absentmindedly so anybody from her stool to the front door of the Velvet Slipper could tell you the color of her underwear, if it was a day she was wearing any. Lucy had a way of letting you look if you wanted to look, but letting you know that looking was your business and she had nothing to hide and what you saw wasn't her

business because her business was private and you could
stare till your eyeballs froze over and her business still
be hers and still be private. Carl thinks back to the
time he first knew he loved her. When he'd take pictures of her with his mind and carry them around. Lucy
never stood still. Always changeable as the weather so
he needed the snapshots in his mind to study, to figure
out who she was. Always changing, always a mystery
so he'd stop her trap her in those little white-framed
pictures like a bee in a bottle he could study without
getting stung.

No music like that ever before and none since. Music's spoiled for me. That crazy, lazy brother of mine
could have played if he wanted to but don't look like
he ever will. Shucks. Listening to Albert Wilkes play
the way he did that day spoiled all the rest of music
for me.

Rest of us ain't spoiled. Put a quarter in the box,
Cat.

Yeah, Cat. Drop some change in that thing. Play
something got that old-time swing to it.

Shot poor Albert Wilkes to pieces that day. And I
saved me one.

She had opened the skinny top drawer of the dresser
in the far corner of her bedroom. She unfolded a handkerchief, emptied it carefully into her hand as she
crossed the room again toward the door where Carl
stood.

Shut that door and come on over here.

Lucy had closed her fist and stopped abruptly. One
backward bounce landed her buttocks-first atop the high
four-poster bed. The swayback springs squeak as she
squirms to a comfortable position on the green chenille
spread.

You deaf, boy? Shut the door and hit that light beside
it and c'mon over here before I change my mind.

When Carl is on the edge of the bed beside her, she
wiggles away to offset his weight, scooting a little farther from the edge so her legs dangle. She chucks him
once under the chin, then uncurls her fist slowly, close

to his eyes. Her fingers almost touch his face. Carl can hear her bones unwind. Smell soap.

The bare bulb stuck in a ceiling socket cooks the dust gathered on its surface. Sounds like a moth circling above their heads. The blind over the room's one window is closed, so the bed floats in shadow. All the light in the room is drawn to the object in Lucy's palm. The third something she shows him that afternoon after school is white and hot looking. A pearl. A baby tooth. A chip of ivory. A piece of seashell. A rare, white pebble from the grimy hillside where the trains run.

Don't know what you're looking at, do you, Mister Grown-up? Well, that's a piece of Albert Wilkes.

Lucy grabs his wrist and sets his hand in her lap. *Turn over. Open up.* She dumps the object in his hand. It's light as a pigeon feather. And cold as ice. It burns a hole through the meat of his palm.

What you holding is a piece of his head. Albert Wilkes's skull the police blowed a hole in and scattered all over the living room.

I had to clean up after they was gone. They rolled Albert Wilkes in a blanket and carried him off. One run a rag or something over the real wet place and run it once down the piano keys. Looked like he didn't even want to do that much. Somebody probably told him he had to so he sopped up the wettest spot and wiped a little here and there with a frown on his face. Used Albert Wilkes's coat to mop the floor. They shot it clean off him. It was laying in a heap beside Albert, and the flunky stuck his toe in it and scrubbed it around after they moved Albert Wilkes off the floor. Held it down with his boot and ripped off a sleeve or something and ran it over the keys and made a little tinkle of music. He smiled then like he'd done something special and threw the rag down and followed the rest out the door. That's all the straightening up they done behind the mess they made. Except one dog stomped down Albert Wilkes's black hat. And oh yeah. They picked old Mrs. Tate off the floor and slung her upstairs. Poor thing didn't know what to think with all them police crowded round her. Sometimes I believe she thinks they put her in jail and she ain't allowed to move. Wouldn't move now unless me and Brother move her. Sometimes I think that's what's wrong with her. Poor thing thinks she's locked in jail.

So cleaning up was on me. I had to do it. Get up all that pretty glass from the door they busted in. Purple glass and green glass and yellow and blue. Pretty as a church window. Had to sweep and mop. Started to save a hunk of bullet. Didn't even know what it was at first, mashed up and everything. Thought bullets supposed to be pointy-nosed and long like sharks so I didn't recognize it at first when one slid up in the dustpan. Sent another one rattling out in the hallway when I swiped the broom under the lamp table. But I didn't keep none of it. No bullets, no little diamonds of colored glass. Just this piece of Albert Wilkes's headbone they shot away.

Carl knows it's just a seashell sliver, and she's trying to scare him. Like she does when she creeps up and hollers boo. Testing his manhood. The heat he feels is not in his palm but on the back of his hand resting against her thigh. Fast womanish heat from between her legs and he can feel it throbbing, follow its path, red and pushy like an army of ants crossing the sidewalk, follow it up through his hand and arm till it's burning in his chest with the smoke thick as peanut butter cementing his mouth shut.

This the biggest piece I found. Clean just like you see. No blood. No hair. White and clean.

Well, it is something. I do admit you showed me something.

Carl stares down at the seashell. He would taste it if he had the nerve. Run his tongue over it and taste the salt. He knew better than to believe what she said. Albert Wilkes a black man like him. Bones had skin. You'd see the brown of Albert Wilkes if it was really him laying there. Both Carl's hands resting on Lucy's thigh now. He had ventured his finger closer to the white object, closer so if it was chalk the white dust would come off when he rubbed it. But he couldn't touch it and his hand had dropped short beside the other in her lap. Double heat, double-time marching in his chest. He uses both hands, one cupped beneath the other as though he needed the strength of two arms to lift the something and return it to Lucy.

She has turned away. At first he thinks she's laughing at him. Her narrow shoulders are shaking. Then she faces him again, and he sees the tears.

He was playing so beautiful, and they just busted in and killed him.

Carl half tosses, half drops the skull of Albert Wilkes as he leans too far and gets twisted up with the soft bed sinking under his shifting weight. One hand brushes her lap again trying to catch the speck of bone and the other reaches for her shoulders, and wet-eyed Lucy collapses toward him. He loses his balance, and all that matters is catching her some way so they don't bump heads or tumble off the bed.

He remembers thinking something was wrong. Like now, of all the damnedest times, he had to pee. So much happening at once. Coming out his wet clothes and peeling Lucy out hers. Skin and hair and teeth and bones and smell and blood boiling and rushing. Little Lucy so smooth, so much naked Lucy skin he doesn't know where to begin, where to stop. She's not bare like his dream. Curly hairs down there like his big sister in the bathtub. And he pats it and she lets him. Then that locomotive heating up in his gut. Like needing to pee. But pushing harder and hotter than the fullest bladder ever did. Pushing hard and hot and loud like it means to blow out his eyes and ears. If that engine keeps coming, he's going to explode and Lucy feel the egg running down her leg. Beans and cornbread having a fight. Beans and cornbread fighting to get out and he doesn't know whether to holler or fart but knows he better not pee on Lucy, knows she'll jump up and never let him touch her again if he's not grown enough to hold his water. But it's good, it's scaring the breath out his body but it's so good. Shaking his eardrums and asshole and the ends of his toes. He hears her saying so too. That coffee grinder and those jelly eggs running down her legs. He thinks of his wet school clothes on the floor. Of those big, old baggy pants and the little skimpy ones Lucy wore underneath. You peel them down with your thumbs. And she wiggles. And you squeeze both buns and hold on and it's the scare game. It's that train flying like a giant black bullet at his back. And you can't run and you can't hide and you can't stand still. And he damns Brother for grinning, for laughing as the train smashes into him and shrinks to the size of a BB and roars out again full size through the end of his joint spewing black smoke onto Lucy's belly.

But it's not black and not smoking. A little sticky whitish puddle and scattered driplets, cool to the touch as he finally tests one with the tip of a finger. Not black, not smoking and thank God, not pee.

In the Velvet Slipper at the end of a Friday afternoon, listening to the jukebox take over the room, watching Lucy return from wherever her Albert Wilkes story had carried her, Carl wonders about love and if it's always so confusing. If anybody besides him was ever so sure something was wrong before realizing how right everything really was.

Hey, Bruh.

He knows his albino pardner is behind him. Doesn't know why he knows but would bet his life Brother hovers just behind his right shoulder.

Cat. Give this cream-of-wheat motherfucker an Iron City.

The music sucking up people's quarters could kick down a door. Loud enough to drown the noise of trains crossing Homewood Avenue. Like they fighting a war to see which instrument could kill all the others. And if your horn ain't tooting loud enough you scream and holler or blow a police whistle in your microphone. Mize well snap your fingers and tap your toes. Try to ignore it and it'd tear your head off.

You don't remember that piece of paper, do you, Bruh? No reason for you to remember. It was way back. We was just kids. Raining like a dog that day but you brought it over anyway. Member you sitting at the kitchen table soaking wet. My mama was up and mad cause she found you out on the stoop all wet and had to let you come in to get dry. I was scared she knew something. Scared maybe Lucy told you and you got mad and told my mama. Didn't know what to think finding you all wet at the table first thing in the morning. Had me a real bad case of guilty conscience anyway. Seemed like everything tattling on me. Wanted to burn my clothes. Wanted to be invisible so nobody could see what I'd done. Felt like I was striped or spotted and anybody look at me know I been doing something I ain't supposed to.

Can't even hear me, can you? I'm shouting but that goddamn music's too loud. No reason for you to remember anyhow. Was between me and Lucy but she did send you with the note so you're part of it even if you don't remember. Your jacket on the back of one of those kitchen chairs and a puddle on the floor where it been dripping. And you looking like a drowned rat. And my mama mad anyway cause I got home so late from school the day before and she had already laid down the law. A whole week of nothing but straight home and doing the dishes every night and talking about the strop next time I mess up. Sure didn't expect to see you or nobody else that morning. Didn't want to see nobody neither. I remember thinking how did this fool get so wet and keep this piece of paper dry. Do you remember how you slipped it on the table soon as Mama went upstairs? Grinning and laying it down and I just knew you had to be counting the stripes and counting the spots. Still don't know just how much you knew. I carried that paper around so long it shredded up in my wallet

Just because I showed you that bone don't make you grown-up. Don't you forget it.
                                        ME

The note was on Big Chief tablet paper, blue lined, speckled if you looked close. Lucy used a whole sheet and printed her message in the middle. Brother was soaked, the note was dry. On the drainboard beside the sink a bowl and spoon. The waxed inner bag of the Kellogg's cornflakes hadn't been rolled down into the box. Carl'd heard his mama fussing at Brother first thing in the morning, and he'd almost turned around and tipped back up the stairs to bed. Guilt like gobs of red paint sticking to his face. Like when he forgot to go potty and tottered round bowlegged like his mama wouldn't see the mess in his pants. But he's grown now. His business, his business now.

Don't you think I don't know where you were, either.

Called that over her shoulder as she left him alone with Brother in the kitchen. Then Brother slid the note across the oilcloth.

Carl leaned against the icebox and read the note standing up, paper in one hand, his other hand on his hip. *Just like John French,* people in the family would say if they had been there to see him. *His Daddy to a T.* A big spoon in one hand, the other hand on his hip. Like John French leaning up against the icebox taking his good time eating whatever he finds, with that big wooden-handled spoon. More like a shovel than a spoon. Shoveling food out the icebox. Carl's like a picture of John French as he reads Lucy's message the morning after they made love the first time, because he needs his daddy's footprints to stand in, needs to set his jaw and suck his teeth and thrust out his hip like he's claiming space beside the icebox, and if you got good sense you'll mind your own business and leave him alone.

Brother sat hunched over the table shivering. His tan jacket hanging on a chairback was seven shades darker than usual. Puddles glistened around each of the chair's back legs. The kitchen was bright. One of Carl's jobs was to keep three bulbs burning in the fixture over the table. Brother nearly as wet as the dripping jacket but somehow he kept the note dry. Why had he grinned when he slid it cross the table?

Just because I showed you that bone don't make you grown-up. Don't you forget it.
ME

Carl slowly refolded the note, carefully letting it close along the creases already in the paper, the creases which were the first places to rip later as the paper aged in his wallet. What did Brother know? Why'd his mama throw those words back over her shoulder? He needed to read the words again. He'd forgotten them because he wasn't paying attention the first time. He'd been saying words to himself and seeing Lucy and now he couldn't get straight which words had been his, which hers. He'd been thinking of Brother's grin and telling himself his mother couldn't know a thing and thinking of how his daddy saunters into the kitchen and pokes his spoon into the icebox and then he's there, solid as a rock slouched up against the icebox but gone too, in another place. The words of the note flashed by as Carl was dreaming, and now he could recall the dream but he'd missed the words. Lucy's words were in his pocket and he couldn't take the paper out again, not with Brother sitting there ready to grin.

Were the last words of the letter, *Don't forget me*? Didn't you say that to somebody when you were leaving? When you were going away? Did she say she wanted to *give* him something or had she said *show*? A million words in the letter. Why'd he only take a minute when he needed days to read them all?

He wanted Brother gone. Rain or no rain. Just put on that jacket and go catch pneumonia if you have to. Just go. Split. Nobody told you to sit like a dummy in the rain. So get up, turkey, and...

But Brother was part of it now. He had splashed five blocks through the rain to deliver the note. That's why Brother was smiling. That's why the paper was dry. Brother was part of it. Would always be. The three of them together in it now. Whatever *it* was.

Carl flips Brother's jacket to an empty chair. He plops down without noticing the wet spot spreading against his backside. He leans over the note as he smooths it open on the oilcloth.

Brother. She didn't say *me*. She said *it*.

Brother nods and smiles and begins drumming the table edge. And scat sings *Oppy Doop Doop Opp*. Softly. Background music as Carl deciphers the million words. It was all right. It was the three of them now. No secrets.

In the Velvet Slipper at the end of a Friday afternoon. Listening to the jukebox filling the room, watching Lucy return from her story, wondering about love and if it's always so confusing the first time. And if there's ever more than a first time. Because it's the three of them still. Brother part of it, always part of it.

Brother beside him sipping an Iron City. Nodding, yes. Slipping his hand in his jacket pocket and fondling something out of sight. And bringing the empty hand from his pocket to his lips, grinning, kissing it. Yes.

Brother at the table that first morning after to tell Carl that Lucy could take back what she'd given. That she hadn't *given*. She had *showed* him something. She showed it to him, but it was still hers, like that piece of Albert Wilkes in the handkerchief in her drawer.

Lucy could still scare him and amaze him. Even today she could do it. Pounce from the shadows of the Tates' house and yell *Boo*. Today climbing those stairs he'd still worry about ghosts creeping up behind him. And when he came down and shut the heavy door behind him and stepped down off the Tates' porch he'd wonder if she was writing another note, if she was taking something back, if she was writing good-bye.

Another Rock, Cat. Can't you turn that mess down some?

Turn it down and in a minute I got three asking me turn it up again.

Well, who's the boss?

The ones putting in the nickels.

Used to be a nice quiet place in here.

You getting old, honey. People like it noisy now. You getting old and set in your ways.

Just might be right, Cat. Be thirty soon and wasn't worth a good god damn at twenty. You just might be right.

Carl bolts the shot glass of Seagrams Seven and wets his lips with the last of his Rolling Rock.

Scored then, Bruh? Yeah, I can see it in your eyes. Got a scoreboard in your eyes, nigger.

He'll clear his throat with a fresh Rock and then get Lucy off her stool and it'll be the three of them, the three musketeers again and they'll walk back to the room where Albert Wilkes died and shoot up and dream.

Lucy and my Uncle Carl both thirteen the first time they made love. The next time was three years later and the next seven years after that. The second time was early summer. Brother and Carl had been sent to clear the weeds from Anaydee's yard. Every year they'd cut the weeds and 725 would sprout up again. Anaydee and Uncle Bill hanging on till they're rescued again from the jungle surrounding their little house. Lucy tagged along to watch and wound up raking the stone path and weeding the patch of sunflowers whose pointy-haloed black faces nodded in front of the windowbox. Carl had taken the long-handled rusty scythe Anaydee handed through the cracked door. The sickle, which meant squatting in the sticky weeds, he passed to Brother. From his bed Uncle Bill Campbell had grunted something Carl couldn't understand, but Anaydee chirped. Your Uncle Bill says they need sharpened. Three swipes through the waist-high weeds and Carl knew the tools needed to be pitched in the garbage because he mize well beat the weeds with a club as swat them with the blunt scythe. He whipped the rusty half-moon around again in a tree-toppling arc, his weight back on his heels, his arms taut in a Babe Ruth home run swing. The weeds leaned away, some even bent, but not one throat cut. Mize well lay down and roll over them because that's all his tool could do. Mash the weeds down a minute or two till that sticky green juice inside sprung them up again. Brother looked like he was cutting hair. Down on all fours, just about invisible except you could see the racket he was making where the tops of the weeds danced as he crawled around below. Snipping one or two or three at a time. Pulling them straight then sawing at the roots he'd slice them a hair at a time. Brother would get every weed if he stayed down there five or six years.

Carl chose a flattish, gray stone from the pile beside the house. He sat on the pile so he could sharpen the blade without the handle being in the way. He scraped up and back with the gray stone. The blade did look like the moon. Streaked, pitted. Its beveled edge chipped so it had as many teeth as a saw. How's somebody supposed to work with something like this. He stood up and pitched the scythe against the stones. Its clatter brought Lucy around the side of the house.

Mize well stomp on these weeds as try to cut them with this goddamn rusty banana.

She said sharpen it.

Ain't no sharpen in it.

Got to try. Lay it down on one of those big flat stones and then you can press hard down on it.

She must have been spying. She must have been waiting for a chance to bust in and mind his business. It's too hot to argue so he tries it her way, grinds the metal between two stones. One curved tip is crumbly and breaks off, but he scrapes enough of a cutting edge to try again and this time his first home run cut with Lucy watching topples a handful of weeds. He hacks at the rest while they're down and can't help grinning at the little cleared space and grinning at Lucy even though his back's to her.

He can't tell if she's still watching him or not. Doesn't matter because he's got her fixed, caught with the eyes in the back of his head so he can stare, can study without getting stung. Her bare arms and legs. The honey-colored skin sun-darkened now except where her shorts and sleeves begin. The skin lighter and softer in those places under her clothes she had let him see, let him touch once. The first time with Lucy crying and Albert Wilkes's skull grinning up from the bed seemed like a dream. Then the note taking everything back, then three years of remembering, of trying to tell himself it had happened, convince himself their lovemaking hadn't been a dream. How many times had he reached for Lucy, wanting to touch her the way he did on the mushy bed, wanting her hand on his, guiding him, helping him to all those places he was afraid to start after himself. He'd scheme ways to catch her alone in the big house, times when Brother was gone, when Mrs. Tate asleep like she always was. Lucy didn't seem to notice. The rocking chair became her favorite place. For rocking, for ignoring him. Once he started up the stairs by himself, nearly reached the first landing before he called down to her. Called again straddling two steps, poised, frozen, listening to the steady creaking of the rocker till his back leg got fuzzy and his jaw so tight he had to run down the steps and out the door to keep from snatching her out the chair and stomping it to pieces. He hated that chair anyway. Especially the pop of the cracked rocker, exploding like a gunshot in the silence. He'd always jump. Jump like somebody jagged him with a pin. Jump every time like some goddamn jack-in-the-box fool so Lucy'd have one more reason to laugh. One more reason to take back what she had shown him.

Crazy for six months after the first time. Was it him? Was each new pimple on his face, each spot in the crotch of his underwear driving her away? Did she know about *Doctor's Office,* spread-eagled under his mattress? Had she spied on him with his thumb in his mouth and his hand under the covers and his eyeballs sniffing the photos of the bare-tittied white ladies in *Pix*? Did she know he tried to peek under every woman's clothes? Young, old, sister, mother. No shame. Nothing but a spyglass or binoculars, looking anyplace, anytime he could. Trying to remember, to learn. Or was it her being a bitch, teasing him with this pussy business like she teased him about anything else? She was cold. She was Hard-Hearted-Hannah, pour water on a drowning man. Only she'd pee on him. Those baggy corduroy drawers pulled down and then the skimpy, silky ones and her perfect little buns, honey-colored, bright and creamier than the sun-toasted rest would hang there, bare and perfect and fringed with curly hairs and he'd reach out like he did before but they'd disappear, his dream wasn't strong enough to keep them still, they'd be hanging out bare to the world and he'd grab for them but they'd wiggle away and it'd be just like she was squatting to do something nasty on him.

When the scythe banged against one of the rocks Bill Campbell had missed in the yard of 725, the blade flew off the handle and buried itself in the ground. Carl had been chopping weeds an hour, hypnotized by the motion, by the hot sun on his naked back. Lucy was somewhere watching he was sure. He didn't want to see her sitting cross-legged in the weeds. Little Miss Muffet on that warm, soft tuffet, her long legs bare in the itchy grass. Sweat on her honey skin sweet as lemonade. Not like the sewer water rolling down his gritty back. Not like the boogery rolls inside his elbows where the sweat

collected. After a while he'd forced himself to stop remembering the first time. That or go crazy. But the
heat, the sweat, the singsong sway of his arms mowing
weeds, the dream of Lucy naked on the bed, her quiet
presence in the background, sitting cross-legged, pluck-
ing weeds from between the stepping-stones, digging
in the flowerbox at the window, weeding the patch of
lolly-headed sunflowers brought the first time back. As
he hacked the iron-necked weeds it was *she loves me,
she loves me not,* one then the other carved by the blade
swinging back and forth through its arc. His arms swung
faster and the words got closer together. She loves me,
she loves me not. If his arms whipped a little faster he
could be in both places at once, lovemelovenot one ripple
of sound, always yes and always no. Loving me and not
loving me all one word. The Lucy he kills on a down-
stroke made whole again as the pendulum rises. Faster
and faster till he hears his mother's warning *Youall be
careful over there,* hears it drowned by the clang of the
blade on an unseen rock. He hears his mother's voice
at the same instant he realizes it's not sweat running
down his ankle.

They go to the Tates' not because it's closer but because Lucy hovers beside him and inspects the gash
and takes his hand and leads him to Tioga Street, then
up the steps, across the porch, up to the second floor,
past the bedroom where Mrs. Tate has only a few more
years of her sentence to serve, the room where Mr. Tate
used to talk into the mirror while he undressed, speaking to the picture of his wife curled under the covers,
saying things like, How's my p...p...p...Pretty little
pu...pu...pu...Pussy-in-the-Well while he unbuttons
his shirt, tipping past the silence and darkness which
seeps from under the Tates' closed door to Lucy's bedroom where they had made love the first time three
years before. Carl wonders if he's left a trail of blood
spotting the floor, wonders why she is loosening his belt
and pulling down his pants to get at the cut she could
easily reach by rolling up his trouser leg.

Oh, didn't he ramble. Before they make love the third
time, Carl will travel round the world. On Okinawa
he'll push stacks of dead Japanese marines over the

edge of a cliff into the sea with the blade of his bulldozer. He'll carry dead GI's back across the beaches into the ships which had sailed them across the sea to die on that bloody island. He gains thirty pounds, broadens in the shoulders, and his skin gets as tanned as any of the red-bone Frenches ever get. His hunger for Lucy grows stronger, deeper as he learns the bodies of other women. All the sizes, shapes, and colors he'd been trying to imagine so many years led him right back to where he started. In the same space of years I'm born. Carl's sister Lizabeth's first child. John French's first grandson. John French my first daddy because Lizabeth's husband away in the war. By the time Carl and my father returned from the Pacific, I was big enough to empty the spittoon which sat beside Daddy John French's chair. Grown enough for that chore and for opening the yellow string of his pouch of Five Brothers tobacco when I sat on his knee.

Soon after Carl returned home Brother Tate caught me by my arm and tucked me into his chest and named me *Doot,* one of the scat sounds Brother talked with instead of using words. After the war Lucy spent lots of time in my grandmother's house on Cassina Way. Not as much as Brother who seemed to be around always, but I remember her from those days. Her eyes mostly. The teasing, sparkly eyes no one warned me away from but which I knew instinctively were more dangerous than steep basement steps and sharp knives and hot ovens and matches.

I remember. Partly because I was there in my grandmother's house, partly because I've heard the stories of Cassina Way a hundred times.

My grandfather's brown hat rests in the top of my cupboard. A sweat-blackened ring separates the high crown from the brim. The edging of the brim has worn away, leaving the cloth tattered in places. A mud-colored hat, soft as felt where dried sweat hasn't turned it brittle. A souvenir of John French. Like his razor strop my Aunt Geral keeps, hanging in her bathroom. Geral saved the hat and gave it to me. I don't know what to do with it. Clean it up? Get a fancy, feathered band to hide the stains at the base of the crown? Could the hat be cleaned, could somebody mend it without destroying it? Should I consider wearing it? Would John French like the idea of his hat reborn, his grandson wearing his swagger, his country-boy, city-boy lid? Damned if I know what to do with it. And leaving it sitting in the top of a closet is no answer. I can't decide what to do with the hat because it's not mine. John French dead twenty-five years now but his claim on the hat so strong I still can't touch it without looking over my shoulder and asking him if it's all right.

The stories of Cassina Way sit like that. Timeless, intimidating, fragile.

My Uncle Carl turns on his barstool. Doot. Doodle-doot Doot. Sitting up here grown as I am. You ain't supposed to be grown yet. And got the nerve to have children calling me Uncle Carl just like you was doing yesterday. Yesterday. My, my. That's all it seems sometimes. Just yesterday you was a baby and we was all over there on Cassina Way. Brother named you Doot while we was still on Cassina.

At the kitchen table. With the checkered oilcloth.

Yessiree. He sure did. At that very table. Seems like yesterday.

Shut up about yesterday, man. You starting to sound like Methuselah's granddaddy. Whole lotta yesterdays since this nephew of yours been a baby. How old you now, Doot? I know you got to be pushing thirty.

Thirty next June.

Shoot. You ain't even started the prime of life yet. You still a baby.

Who's talking old now?

I know just exactly how old I am, Mr. French. To the minute.

Bet you do. To the second, probably. Cause you was there directing traffic, wasn't you? Looked at your watch and told them Miss Lucy Tate's ready to be born.

Know how old I am and know I ain't old enough to be sitting around sighing about yesterday this and yesterday that. That's old people talk. Sighing and going on about the good old yesterdays. Brains turning to cream of wheat when you start talking like that.

Wasn't talking to you in the first place. I was addressing my nephew here before you butted in. In the second place you got what you half heard all twisted around. What I said didn't have nothing to do with old.

What's it got to do with then?

Just the opposite.

Opposite of what?

Yesterday.

You talking in circles.

That's right. Cause that's the way the world turns. Circles and circles and circles inside circles. Don't you understand nothing, woman? Doot don't make me feel old. Don't make me feel young neither, sitting there with children when I remember him in diapers. Point is I can see him back then just as plain as I see him now and it don't make no difference. Just a circle going round and round so you getting closer while you getting further away and further while you getting closer.

You understand that, Doot? Doot's a college man and I bet he don't understand that mess you're talking any better than I do.

Well, if people minded they own business they might give other people a chance to mind theirs.

He's always talking about yesterday this and yesterday that. If that ain't getting old, I don't know what is.

Told you once and I'll tell you again. Yesterday ain't got nothing to do with it. Boy, don't ever try and talk sense with a hardheaded woman. And they all of em got hard heads, Doot.

Go on with that mess. Only sense you got is the sense good women knocked into your thick skull and your nephew don't want to see me going upside your head, so just hush and tell him some more about Brother like he asked you in the first place. Your Uncle Carl getting senile. Poor thing begins a sentence then gets way off, you got to remind him to finish what he started.

I'm getting to Brother. Like I was saying it was in the house on Cassina Way before we moved to Finance and Lucy was teaching you to dance. You was a cute puppy then. Lucy saw you patting your foot to the Victrola and leaned over and took you by the hands. She pulled you on your feet and started swaying you to the music, side to side, but you jerked away. Wanted to do your own thing. She got you moving but she had to turn you loose. I cracked up. Everybody did. Hardly big as a minute and out there dancing by yourself. Count Basie playing. Basie with Jimmy Rushing on vocal. Think that's what it was. A new record Lucy brought to play on the Victrola Daddy and Strayhorn found. I remember that Victrola from when I was little, and it was still sounding good the night you got up to dance.

Daddy in his big chair with his big feet stretched out to the fireplace. Couldn't get out the room without tripping over his feet. Like a gate snoring in his chair. He wasn't really asleep. Just heavy on that wine, so he looked like he was sleep but he was just nodding. Didn't miss a thing. He slapped his knee and got to laughing when he saw you cut your little steps. Just about fell out that chair laughing, and the next minute he's nodding again. Brother scatting with the music like he always did. Everybody feeling good. Good music. Good times. Homewood was jumping. Lots of war work, so people had a little change in they pockets. Homewood different then. Hadn't turned ugly the way it is now. I mean now you take your life in your hands just walking down the street after dark. It was different in those days. No dope. No hoodlums prowling around looking for a throat to cut.

Yeah...I believe it was Basie with Jimmy Rushing. Lucy loved Jimmy Rushing. She loved you too. On your fat little bowlegs trying to get down. We were tight in those days. Me and Brother and Lucy. Called us the three musketeers. We did everything together, everything we were big and bad enough to do. Homewood was something then. Almost married Lucy. But didn't seem no point to it. Couldna been no closer.

Brother would have been your brother-in-law.

Brother-in-law Brother. Does sound kinda funny. That'd make him something to you too. Some kind of uncle-in-law or cousin or something.

Carl pats the empty stool beside him. The red vinyl cover is puckered by the shadow of Lucy's weight. Carl nods his head toward the ladies room door.

Make her your aunt.

Did Lucy really push Brother around in a baby carriage?

Rolled him around till wasn't nothing left but wheels and wire. That's what they say. She used to get mad when anybody'd tease her about it. Said it was serious business. Kept the top down so the sun wouldn't hurt his white skin. Just little doses at a time. That girl always had strange notions. Still does. Don't know why I didn't marry her. Still might. Cept now with Brother gone... with him out the picture, the picture ain't quite right. I mean living married together without Brother make us both think more about him. Like we had a baby once and lost it and see it every time we look at each other. We'd always be remembering what we once had. You know what I mean?

Carl. Why do you think he killed himself?

They kill everything.

But didn't Brother kill himself?

Found Brother dead on the tracks. Wasn't no blood so he was dead before the train hit him. It was something else or somebody else killed him, killed him just like they killing everything worth a good goddamn in Homewood.

They hear Lucy fussing all the way back to her stool: Bathroom's a pigpen. Just wait till I see that Conkoline head L.T. Riding his fat behind round in a Coup De Ville but can't pay nobody a quarter to keep the ladies room clean.

Lucy plops into the shadow she'd left. She makes herself mad at L.T. like she made herself mad at her hair in the cloudy bathroom mirror. A plucked chicken. Woody the Woodpecker. She thought she'd combed an upsweep, a neat pile leaning away from her face, soft waves brushed so they climb the topside of the pyramid. But a wild woman staring back at her from the mirror. Hair shooting every whichway. Mad anyway at the dirty bathroom, so she let herself get madder and didn't have to think about Brother. Who was everywhere. In the mirror. The music. In her hands smoothing the skin of her face while she stood in the tiny bathroom wondering where the time had gone. She didn't want to hear Carl's stories. Yet as soon as he began one she needed to get her two cents in. Help him say what she didn't want to hear. Brother was gone. Long gone. Past tears. Past the silly pause when her fingers wrap around the front doorknob and she thinks she feels warmth in the metal, the print of his hand so when she turns it and opens the door he'll be there in the wingback chair grinning at her.

Are you saying Brother could talk if he wanted to? How could he just stop speaking? I always thought he had some kind of handicap or deficiency.

He was ugly. That's for damn sure. And he loved sweet wine. But if drinking wine or being ugly's a crime half of Homewood be behind bars.

Did he talk to you?

Now you know better than to ask that. You know how tight we were.

I mean actual talk. Not scat sounds or gestures. Actual words.

He named you Doot.

That's a noise.

It's your name. Stuck all these years, ain't it?

But sixteen years. Not a word in sixteen years?

You listening but you ain't hearing, Doot. You keep asking the same question and getting the same answer. That what they teach you in college? Brother said what he needed to say in his own way. Be messing round in what everybody called the Bums' Forest, you know, over there beside the tracks before you get to the park. Course you know. Brother'd cut a fool for the winos and they'd hee haw and egg him on. Think he was feeble-minded and whatnot him being albino. Give him wine even though he was a kid like me. Brother loved sweet wine, and all the time they laughing at his monkey-shines he's sucking up that wine and laughing at them. I could tell you a hundred ways Brother got over. Didn't need words. People thought he didn't have good sense cause he was white and didn't talk much. Well, Brother had more sense than any five these Negroes sitting around here in the Velvet Slipper put together.

How old was he when he stopped?

Like I said he never did talk much. Week go by and then he'd say something to me and I'd think *Damn,* been a week since this nigger's opened his mouth. Bout twenty-six when he stopped altogether. Just after the war. Right around in there people started to notice and say Brother don't talk. Twenty-six cause it was right after what we used to call his birthday. Didn't know his real birthday. Brother never had one till Lucy said let's say January first. New Year's Day. Everybody needs a birthday so let's say Brother's is the first day of the new year. Brother least a couple years older than us even though Lucy called him her little brother. She had her own way of counting, but I know Brother had a few years on me. Brother about twenty-one that first time he played at the Elks. Make him round twenty-six when he stopped talking. Started playing like he been playing pianos all his life. Scared me, too. Like the music just moved in. Like Brother just reached out his hand and the music was there. Ain't heard nothing like it before or since. Then he stopped. Sudden as he started, he stopped. Stopped playing and talking both, right after the war.

Same year Junebug burnt up.

Lucy says the helping words. Can't stop herself even though she knows where they lead. She bites her tongue, but it's too late. Carl's heard and Junebug's story begins to open. Like a fan, she thinks. One of those tissue-paper and stick fans from Murphy's Five and Dime all folded so you can't see what's inside, but you roll off the gumband and spread the sticks and it's sunsets and rainbows and peacock tails. A fan she thinks listening to Carl lean on the helping words and begin to tell his nephew about Junebug. She knows already what the fan will look like, what's painted inside when the creases open and the picture hangs like a broken wing, before the dust-colored tissue rips and the bones snap one by one in the wind.

Poor little thing. You must of heard of Junebug. One of Samantha's children. Sam who lived back of Albion on Cassina Way. You heard of Crazy Sam. The one with all the children. They had to take her to Mayview. Little Junebug got burnt up on the Fourth of July. People say that's what pushed Sam over the line. She had a whole bunch of kids in that shack on Cassina. Must of been ten children and Samantha no more than twenty-five, twenty-six years old. A good-looking woman too. Long dark hair and coal black. Kind of girl with that velvety smooth skin. When I hear of beautiful African queens, Samantha comes to mind. She's the image. Black and comely. You know what I mean. Ninety-nine and forty-four one hundredths percent black. Yes indeed. Ivory snow black. You could set a glass of Chivas on top her head and go on about your business and come back a hour later not a drop be spilled. Long-legged, straight-backed, tall-walking woman. All them babies and she still looked like a sixteen-year-old girl. Walk by her yard and see them all in there you couldn't tell mama from the kids. All them kids black and beautiful like Sam. Except Junebug.

Carl's voice gets busy telling the story his way. A big man. Pale like all the Frenches. More like his daddy every day, she's heard Lizabeth or Geral or Martha say a million times. His belly pouts. She used to sit with Carl in Westinghouse Park and watch the young girls and boys courting. In spring when the leaves were coming back and the brown grass turning green again. They liked to spend those first few fine days together, days when you knew you could go outside without a jacket or sweater and toast on a bench in the park even though the ground still mushy from the last snowfall. Spring getting warmer and better till the park lit up like a garden, and Lucy would sit with Carl watching the squirrels and the kids acting like squirrels, giggly and teasing or suddenly quiet and checking out everything around them before pairing off arm in arm for a stroll around the path circling the park. Carl'd say, Be a watermelon up under that one's dress by summer. Lucy would shush him and think of squirrels and say they're just kids, just playing around. In October when the leaves turning and starting to pile up on the grass and the paths, he'd say I told you so when one the little spindle-legged, pigtailed girls shuffles by in an old lady's dress with the belly poked out. A watermelon under there is how Carl looked now. His middle a tub for all that Rolling Rock and Iron City he can't do without. She thinks of her man's smile and soft, pale hands. They

say his daddy, John French, was a gentle man. A loving,
generous man in his big hat and grizzly bear shuffle
down Homewood Avenue. Under the edge of the bar,
in the shadows, her man's heavy thighs flapping like
wings. When he gets excited some part of his body always shows it. Not his eyes or his voice. A part hidden
like his long thighs under the edge of the bar. Or a part
you don't pay attention to unless you're looking for the
telltale sign of something riling him, exciting him. Fingers drumming on the table. One hand worrying the
other. Her big man with the pillow under his Hawaiian
shirt. They may be kids he'd say and they may be playing but you watch, wagging his head and batting his
curly French eyes at me, you watch and see if that little
thing don't turn up wearing a housedress and slippers
and watermelon by fall.

He's settled back now. Into Junebug's story now. She
knows without hearing what he must be saying. The
parts unfolding like a fan. Sharp creases and inside
them, the sad gray story. Couldn't hear if she wanted
to. Doot between them, the music booming, rocking the
Velvet Slipper. She sees enough on Doot's face. Reads
the words plain as day. He's browner than his uncle
but French is there in his bones, in his eyes. Brother
named him Doot. Now he wants to name Brother. She'll
leave Carl's story alone. He doesn't need her helping
words, her amens, her reminders of dates, of names.
She's telling it to herself. Her way:

For some reason Junebug's story must begin with
water. With getting clean in the Tates' giant, clawfoot
tub.

Albert Wilkes is hot and mad. He's on his knees and
the floor is wet, but he'd rather get wet on his knees
than bend over to reach into the soapy tub. Funny how
those piano-playing hands, those long smooth fingers
begin her story not where they should be, not on the
keys playing the blues or like she heard them that last
time in the living room, playing sweet sweet before the
cops blew him away. No. Albert's in an undershirt. Albert Wilkes wearing suds up to his elbows and got a
washrag in his hands scrubbing her back. Standing in
the tub she's as tall as him. He's too wide to be so short.

Must have little midget legs or no legs at all like the bearded man she saw that time who lives on a board with wheels and scoots himself with long arms pushing on the pavement scooting faster than she can run because in her dream she knows he's going to catch her. Those growling skate wheels rolling up behind her and his long arms punching the street and his nasty breath each time he rows his arms *uhhh uhhh* closer and closer she can feel it explode hot and puky in her ear. Albert Wilkes's bare arms and sweaty face and mad eyes because bathing Brother like trying to wash a cat. Catching Brother and scrubbing him like trying to hold a bar of slithery soap. Brother looks like soap. The good kind they have sometimes. White and lean and sweet smelling. But Brother's a skunk. Won't hold still and nobody likes the job so he can go a week before Mrs. Tate gets tired of smelling him and goes to the living room and catches Albert Wilkes at the piano and hands him a washrag and a bar of soap.

Lucy stands so her butt and everything above it hits the air, and she shivers even though Albert Wilkes is sweating. Then he rubs her with his piano-playing hands and wrings hot washrags full of water down her back to rinse the soap and does it again and pats her drier with the balled-up washrag and picks her up and sets her down wrapped in a big towel. She shivers again, a warm, cuddly shiver this time because all the heat of the bath water is under the towel with her. Behind her, Albert Wilkes goddamns Brother again and it's a fight again like the time Mr. Tate bought live chickens and tried to kill one himself Sunday morning behind the locked bathroom door. Tried to slit its throat with his straight razor for Sunday dinner and a storm of squawking and flapping and cussing and then not a sound. Quiet as a grave and we thought the chicken had won and me and Brother scared to open the door. Old Mr. Tate was just catching his breath and the chicken getting hisself together too because they started up fighting again. I swear you could hear that razor slashing and feathers and blood flying all over the place. We ate that bird but he sure didn't die easy, and Mr. Tate sold the rest of the live chickens. Sounded like that behind

her, and she was scared to look till she heard the stopper
come out and the water start to gurgle down. Saw blood
for a minute all over the front of Albert Wilkes's undershirt and soaking his knees. Dark like blood for a
minute like Mr. Tate when he came through the bathroom door and you still didn't know if him or the chicken
had won, if him or the chicken doing the bleeding. Just
water though on Albert Wilkes and Brother wrapped
in a towel matching hers.

    Her story started like that. When she thought of
Junebug she thought of Brother when Brother was little. Albert Wilkes bathing them because Mrs. Tate too
feeble and tired of smelling skunk so she trapped Wilkes
at the piano and how's he gon say no sitting up there
in the Tates' house like he owned it and owned the piano
he was playing. Mrs. Tate probably said *Please.* Cause
that's the way she was. Nice to everybody. Wouldn't
step on a roach unless she caught it in the act. Didn't
blame nothing on nobody just let anybody come and go
as they please so she'd probably ask him with her eyes
and hold out the soap and rag and say, Sorry to inter-
rupt your playing Mr. Albert but could you please do
something with that stinky boy? She thought of Junebug then thought of Brother then Albert Wilkes kneel-
ing over the tub and his piano hands scrubbing her and
then she'd see Samantha. To tell Junebug's story you
had to be Samantha and it's wintertime and you shiver
at the thought of being naked. In a bathtub or anyplace
else. Even the thought of your bare skin under the piles
of clothes you wrap around yourself is enough to make
your teeth chatter. Wind twists up the winding drive-
way to the gray building on top of the hill. Always a
Sunday when she visited Samantha. The bus left you
off at the bottom of the hill. Many a time she almost
begged, Please Mister Driver, get me a little closer. Just
halfway up the hill if you can't make it to the top. On
cold, windy days she just about opened her mouth and
said what she was crying inside. A little head start up
the steep hill, cobblestoned just like Cassina Way. She
could imagine the tires sliding and popping up the broken road. The snarl of the engine finding a gear to pull
it to the top. And pretend she was inside, warm, watch-

ing out her window as Mayview loomed closer. Not so much a feeling of riding up as it was the sensation of watching the building sink, the whole gray mess settling slowly in the ocean or a river and her standing on the banks a witness. As she set down one foot after the other up the steep hill and the wind scratched at her face and tore at her clothes, she'd dream of riding, of arriving at the gate warm, her cheeks flushed from the one gust of wind she didn't mind smacking her as she scurried down from the bus to the curb and through the gate.

You had to be Samantha to understand. Sometimes Lucy thought that's what the visits were about. Being Samantha. That's why they had Mayview for crazy people like they had Highland Park Zoo for wild animals. You go to remind yourself you're not one of them. You go to see the bars that keep them in and you out. You need to make sure the bars are still there so you get as close as you can. You like the cages which are nearly invisible but you also like the low stone walls and the iron bars spaced almost wide enough for you to wiggle through because you can tease yourself, think about what would happen if you jumped over or squeezed in.

If you are Samantha you're waiting for Lucy. You know Lucy is on her way. Staring through the screened window which chops the world into little steel-framed cells you can see Lucy struggling up the hill. A scarecrow leaning into the wind. Shuffling one foot after the other on the frozen pavement like she just might not make it, like she doesn't want to make it to the crest of the hill and the heavy doors and the barred gate inside. If you are Samantha every day is the same and you pace back and forth in the emptiness of your room wondering where they are taking you, why the journey's so long. Nothing changes outside your window, just night to day and day to night and the seasons giving way one to the other just as monotonously, as grayly as dawn to dusk. There are days longer than seasons, days the color of the sky before snow, a blind white heaviness weighing on her skin, a prolonged stare she can't escape unless she smashes something the way she smashes the prying eyes of clocks. But she can't make a fist, let alone gather strength to drive it against the spying light. Days like that longer than seasons, and seasons flash by quicker than days. The pills they feed her could steal a whole summer or spring. Now I lay me down...and black dreamless oblivion till she awakens to find the wind howling and the snow driven in slants across the bars and then she catches movement, an ant crawling along the snow-packed sill or an intruder farther away, down the steep hill, inching its way raggedy and black against the swirling whiteness of gusting sheets of snow.

Lucy Tate trudging up the hill like she's bearing her cross and toting one for everybody else in Homewood on her scarecrow shoulders.

What you doing out there in all that mess?

Samantha watches for days, pacing, waiting for a sign of land, some humpbacked silhouette of island and trees to crop out of the mist, to break the monotonous ripple of gray sea.

Once, when she was blue-eyed and fair as once-upon-a-time and a golden braid wound like the tiers of a wedding cake atop her head she dreamed of a sailor calling to her, his voice bobbing clear as a bell: *Come Down. Come Down.* His voice curling through the iron bars of her tower's one round window. Let down your golden hair. Unfurling it in rippling bands, a golden snake thicker than her waist she fed it through the bars hand over hand, its silky weight plummeting through the emptiness to meet his song.

Lucy Tate bringing news and buttermints. What's she got to say I don't know already with her busy self stumbling like a roach got that Kills-em-Dead powder sticking to his legs? Carry that dust home on all eight feet and kill the rest his family he so busy bringing home the news of the day.

Lucy. Lucy Tate. You hear me, girl? Don't be coming up here bothering me, girl. I know he's dead. Knew before you and anybody else. Course he's dead. Been a ghost since I been knowing him. Ain't never been nothing but a ghost. So you crazy to love him and crazy if you think you lost him cause he ain't never been nothing but a ghost. Never been live in the first place so don't be coming up here bothering me and trying to make me feel bad. Ain't crying for no ghost. No tears left for nothing. Just go on back where you come from.

Once she had seen a tree outside her window, a tree with leaves flashing bright as mirrors. It was taller than Mayview. Samantha couldn't see the top and she was on the top floor, so the tree must be higher than the roof. You couldn't look long at it. All those mirrors turning and flashing burn out your eyes if you didn't squint and didn't turn away real quick. And the mirrors kind of banged a little bit into each other so they tinkled like the wind chimes Carl French brought back from the war. The chimes used to be on the French front porch and once she went as far as the steps with Brother but didn't go inside, didn't want to be away from her children too long so she said They're pretty and said Let's go back now, and Brother nodded and smiled and she could hear the chimes as they walked back to her house and the chimes made her think of faraway places like Okinawa where Brother's friend had been a soldier and paper houses and warm, sea breezes and giant flowers and tiny birds. The rectangles of cloudy glass were etched with black markings. Japanese writing, she thought, a message if I could read the designs, a message dangling from strings so the glass squares bumped and sang and she remembered Brother's skin that day. How you could almost see through it like you could almost see through the chiming glass squares. You see nothing for so long, for days and years longer than you ever thought you'd live, just the gray, nodding sea, but then for no reason you'll ever understand or try to understand, one day a tree grows up like Jack's beanstalk outside your window and dazzles you with its leaves flashing like mirrors. And next day it's gone.

Samantha. Brother's dead. He won't be coming to see you anymore. He's gone, Samantha. Do you understand?

Samantha, Samantha, let down your golden hair.

And she presses her head against the window and lets her braid fall through the bars. But it's not golden. Not syrupy sunshine. It's her black nappy wool plaited into a hundred pigtails and the bars dig into her skull

and she hears the scrape of a match against the stone
and her hair twisting like a vine around the walls of
the tower begins to burn. Black worms dancing and
howling. Then the fire is inside. Raging, consuming the
bones. She is hollow as moonlight. *Please. Please.* A
voice calling again. Pleading again. Fire climbs hand
over hand and the skin of her face is peeled by flames.
Her lover moans. He cannot touch the burning twigs
of hair. Ashes in her mouth. Fire licks between the bars.

Do you understand, Samantha?

Silly Lucy Tate reaches out to touch her. Same fingers she uses to pick her nose and wipe her ass. Naked.
Her fat mittens buried under the heap in the chair. You
could kiss the hand or bite it while it hangs there naked,
dripping snow from bloody fingertips. Sam shrinks away.
Lucy's touch would be like ice. Bringing the cold, the
news to her warm room.

Pipes gurgle and clank. Something hisses through
them. Rushing like seawater against the sides of the
ship. Metal sighs and hiccups again, and Samantha
can't help laughing out loud. She points at the radiator
and giggles. Somebody's guts frozen and painted pea
green like the walls. Maybe hers, maybe anybody's insides stolen, standing in the corner belching and farting. Somebody's loop de loop pig gut. Somebody's dark
cave filled with air. Sometimes she couldn't help farting
when she fucked. Nobody but Brother ever thought her
farts were funny.

Sam.

Lucy don't think it's funny. Lucy stares down at her
own silly feet in silly rubber baby booties. Wet. Lucy
studies the bars. The mountain peaks of ocean splashing the top of the tower.

No one comes to see me. No one asks me to dance.

Lucy stares at the gray sea. Hardly in the room five
minutes and she's forgetting Samantha already. Already scheming ways to slip through the iron bars. If
Samantha could, she'd help you escape. But ain't no
way out. Years on this same slow, gray trip. Nothing
changes. Brother dies again and again. And you keep
coming up that hill to make Sam cry. They gave me
pennies for my eyes. Doctor raised his Klu Klux hood

so I could see his pink face when he talked. You take
these, the dirty peckerwood said. Once a day. Every
day. You lay them on your eyes and count pigeons till
you fall asleep. Pennies heavy as this building. He had
yellow ga-ga on his crooked teeth and had the nerve to
be smiling, called hisself smiling when he handed them
pennies to me. For your eyes. For your eyes. Like I
couldn't hear the first time so he said it twice. For your
eyes and dropped them in my hand but Sam ain't all
kinds of fool. She crazy as a bedbug but she ain't everybody's fool. So soon's he turned his back I popped them
nasties down the toilet. Ain't about to lay up here with
them pennies on my eyes. No indeed. Can't tell where
they been. People suck on money. Don't know what they
hands been doing just before they touch it and give it
to you. You should be shamed treating Sam like a child.
Saying the same simple thing over and over when she
already knows. Knew before any youall.

Knew he was a ghost first time he come to my door.

He stands in the doorway. A white blackman. He
watches her dance. Kids out in the yard playing so she's
dancing alone, humming a song her feet follow. She'd
never seen a ghost before. Brother Tate had passed her
a hundred times on the street and he was part of Homewood like the storefronts and trees, but in her doorway
the albino was different. She knew his name and knew
he didn't talk much. She'd heard people say he was
feebleminded and crazy. Nothing she'd heard or seen
accounted for him standing silent as the moon grinning
in her doorway. If she looked away he'd be gone so she
smiled back at him and beckoned him into her dance.

I'm dancing. I like to dance.

She stopped humming. The music only in her feet
now, in her head, but she knew he could hear it.

When the kids outside playing I dance a lot. Dance
with them too. Got a little raggedy Victrola. They wear
out my records. Some of them fast rascals already dancing better than me. Put me to shame.

She stares at him. He was white, a color she hated,
yet nigger, the blackest, purest kind stamped his features. The thick lips, the broad flaring wings of his nose.
Hooded eyes with lashes clinging like blond ash.

Hey, white man. You come to stay awhile or you just going to stand there peeking.

He steps past her into the shanty. Cinnamon and bananas. A hint of sour wine. Then he takes his time sniffing around, the way a dog checks out a bush, little mincing, wary steps, poking his nose up and under and around, skittish and taking-over at the same time. She watches his narrow back. He'll disappear if she blinks. He turns, grinning at her again. She wonders why the kids aren't lined up at the door, why they don't swarm and buzz and follow him like they always do when a stranger crosses the yard.

You like my place? Don't allow just anybody in. Smells nice in here don't it? Baby stink and talcum powder and sweet milk. We're crowded in here. Eight bodies in this kennel. Barely room for all us to lay down at the same time. Spoon fashion. That's how we sleep. Have you heard of loose packers and tight packers, white man? Don't matter. But you mize well know before you get any closer. I'm a tight packer. Yes, Lawd. Going to build shelves round the wall after there ain't no more room on the floor. Build me some sleeping shelves around the wall and make a perfect black body for each one. Might lose some. No way round that. Some have to die. Ain't never enough food to go round here, but the strong will survive. When this old Ark docks be whole lotta strong niggers clamber out on the Promised Land.

What you think of that, Mr. White Blackman.

He takes her by the wrist. His grip is not cold, not clammy; the shudder she expected does not shake her body.

He leads her to little Becky who sits in the dirt sniffling, holding her big toe. The white man scoops up the child and carries her inside. Becky didn't fight him and Becky was evil to strangers. Her daughter didn't like anybody touching her. A snappy, mean little thing sometimes but she let the white man take her. She even snuggled into his shoulder and stopped whimpering. He sat her down on the drainboard. Becky the most private of her children, the one who shied from strangers, who'd treat her brothers and sisters like strangers, who'd rather suffer than say what's ailing her, little Becky

sat wide-eyed and still while the albino seared the tip
of his switchblade in the gas flame of the stove. War
when she combed out that child's hair in the morning.
Couldn't get her to hold still for the world, couldn't bribe
her or scare her or sweet talk Rebecca. Her little iron-
willed baby she almost strangled one time getting her
to swallow a spoonful of castor oil, that wild child raised
her ashy, black twig of a leg and let the albino slice
the pink underflesh of her big toe and suck out a splinter.

He spits out the splinter and it sticks to his finger.
He snarls at it and flicks it to the floor and stomps it
twice. Becky's eyes never leave him. She's smiling. Tear
stains like scars on her dimpled, dusty cheeks. He helps
her down. Two limping steps toward the door and she
bolts from the room.

You ain't no natural man come to Samantha's door,
is you? You some kind of hoodoo or trickster, ain't you?
Bet you'd jump right out that white skin I sprinkle some
salt on you. But I ain't scared. Samantha's an educated
Negro. Don't believe in youall. Buried you ghosts under
tons of reading, riting and rithmetic. I'se free, ghost.
I'se a free, educated disbelieving-in-ghosts enlightened
colored citizen. Wouldna believed what I just saw if I
hadn't seen it with my own eyes. My Becky says thank
you even if you didn't hear her.

Do you know how to dance, ghost? I'm going to put
on a record. Dance with my babies all the time but it's
nice every once in a while dancing with a body high
enough so I can rest my head on a shoulder.

He was the one kicked the door shut. She was the
one locked it. Watching Lucy Tate stare out the barred
window Samantha can hear both sounds. Hear the
scratchy drag of the needle hiss like a match against
stone before the music begins. Her door never slammed.
It was too shabby. More like a wing flapping with light
around the edges and light shining through the feathers. Lock was a hook and eye. You had to pull hard to
make the hook reach the eye. Lift and pull and get your
finger out the way quick. A tight fit. She remembered
her children playing outside. Barnyard noise like geese

and chickens after he kicked it shut and she hooked it tight.

Samantha slept only with the blackest men. Men black as she was because in her Ark she wanted pure African children. Then Brother at her door and in her bed that afternoon. Sure enough nigger nose and nigger lips, even nigger silence when he was finished and rolled his bones off her belly, but always that unsettling lack of color, like snow in July, and even though it felt good, part of her held back, part of her was aware it wasn't supposed to be this way. She could see through his skin. No organs inside, just a reddish kind of mist, a fog instead of heart and liver and lungs. She was afraid his white sweat would stain her body. On his knees, thrusting, he had begun to shudder and lose his seed. As he caved in on her breasts she grabbed his skinny backside. Gripping with both hands, gripping with her thighs, her shudders had spiraled into his and she thought of rivers of cool milk, of ice and snow and Ivory Flakes. But were the spasms shaking her body sent to welcome or kill what he spilled in her womb.

As soon as he left she inspected every square inch of her glossy, black skin in the piece of mirror hung on the bathroom door. Next morning with the three youngest children in tow she tramped out Hamilton Avenue to the Homewood branch of Carnegie Public Library. After setting her babies on a blanket in a corner and cutting her eyes at everyone who didn't have enough sense to mind their own business, she found the science books and pulled down the volume she needed. She moved the blanket so she could sit with one eye on her babies and one on the text and learned that:

Melanin is the brown to black pigment that colors the skin, hair and eyes. It is formed in the cytoplasm of the melanocytes by the oxidation of tyrosine catalyzed by tyrosinase, a copper containing enzyme...Melanocytes are derived embryologically from the neural crest. Before the third month of fetal life these cells migrate to their resting places in the skin at the epidermal-dermal junction, in

the eyes along the uveal tract, and in the central
nervous system in the leptomeninges…

She had read to herself in the tone of voice she thought
she had forgotten, the tone she would have heard if she
had asked the spectacled, lemon-colored lady behind
the desk for help, the tone of three years at Fisk when
she had believed crossing *t*'s and dotting *i*'s had something to do with becoming a human being and blackness
was the chaos you had to learn to whip into shape in
order to be a person who counted. In that tone of voice
the words meant next to nothing, because she'd buried
Biology I along with all the other trappings college had
prescribed to cure blackness. Why did that voice return.
She knew what it had to say about color, about her
children. She looked from the text down at her black
babies playing on the blanket and felt ashamed. She
read the words again, this time listening to their sound
and dance and understood that melanocytes, the bear-
ers of blackness, descended from royalty, from kings
whose neural crest contained ostrich plumes, a lion's
roar, the bright colors of jungle flowers. Even before
birth, before the fetus was three months old, the wan-
derlust of blackness sent melanocytes migrating through
the mysterious terrain of the body. Blackness seeking
a resting place, a home in the transparent baby. Blackness journeying to exotic places with strange-sounding
names. Settling beside railroad tracks, at crossroads,
the epidermal-dermal junction. She could see boxcars
rolling by. Black boys would awaken in the middle of
the night to the shriek of train whistles, learn to love
the trains' shuddering rhythm. Learn to hop the long
freights. Blackness would come to rest in the eyes;
blackness a way of seeing and being seen. Blackness
crouched in the shadow of the uveal tract would be a
way of being unseen. And of course blackness would
keep on keeping on to the farthest frontiers. Cross
mountains and prairies and seas. Boogey to the stars,
to Leptomeninges, that striped, tiger-colored planet
broadcasting jazz into the vast silence of the Milky Way.
Blackness something to do with long journeys, and eyes,
and being at the vibrating edge of things. Something

royal and restless in the melanocytes. What she had
known all along before she pulled down the bulky ref-
erence book and peeled back her skin.

C'mon, babies. Found what I was looking for.

Samantha lost her fear of Brother's whiteness because she also read under "Disorders of Melanin Pig-
mentation" what a bad case of albinism could do to
people and Brother showed none of the signs, no wrinkled skin, no photophobia or astigmatism or severe de-
fects of visual acuity. No. He was the healthy type. And
anyway none of it contagious. Enough blackness in his
body to counteract the runaway evil affecting his skin.
Nothing in Brother to rub off on her, to transform her
into one of those pinto-pony–looking people with white
patches on their faces and arms, the vitiligo and phen-
ylketonuria which were sicknesses, wars in the body
between the forces of light and darkness. She had been
surprised to learn certain kinds of albinos got darker
as they grew older. And that a condition the opposite
of albinism turned white people black. So when the
ghostly white fog crept over her body again and wrapped
its arms around her again, she had no fear. She enjoyed
the strangeness, the snow in July, the warmth where
she had believed only coldness dwelled, her ghost-white-
black man, royal and restless as the best nigger.

Then she was two again, carrying the seed her ghost
lover had planted. Lucy Tate. Lucy. Hey, gal. Let me
tell you how it was. How good it was getting all big
tittied and big behinded and knowing one day you'll
pop open like a nut and another beautiful one come
rolling out. You ain't never had no babies, have you,
Miss Lucy. Well, you missed something. You missed
the best. Ain't nothing like it in the world. Afterwhile
you get so big you feel like a boat. You stop walking
and start sailing. Hips roll and steer your belly. Ain't
no stepping to it. Just be floating along and things seem
to get out your way. Forget about all that morning
sickness and sore ankles and pains in the back. That
mess comes and goes, sure it does, but gal you the best
thing there is for them nine months you carrying. You
the Ark. You the shuttlebus and ferryboat over Jordan.

Lucy Tate sat on the corner of the bed, and Samantha

took her place by the window. A gust of wind blasted up the hill, shearing snow from car roofs and hedges and trees and drifts, then extinguishing itself against Mayview's gray flanks, against the bars outside the steel-screened window. A crack like sheets snapping on a clothesline. The building seemed to stagger, to slip on the icy concrete. A roar. A groan in the concrete bowels. Snow swirl blinded the window. Samantha could see the words, could say them to herself after all these years—*tyrosinase, melanocytes*. Remember how they marched across the pages of the medical textbook but she couldn't recall the names of her babies playing on the Kinte cloth she'd spread over the library floor.

A secret to remembering what you wanted to remember and forgetting what you needed to forget. She had begun to learn the secret, and that's when they stuck her in Mayview. When they pitched her in the tower and locked it and threw away the key.

They stole her children when she began to understand the secret. They killed Junebug because he was born with the secret and was teaching it to her.

Little monkey came here in a shopping bag.

Samantha teased Brother about the caul, the gauzy web clinging to Junebug's see-through skin. Old Miss Julia Strothers, Old Mother Strothers, nurse and midwife and baby-sitter and fortune-teller, had gathered every scrap of web and wrapped them in a handkerchief and stuck them deep into her bosom.

Got to be mighty careful. This some powerful stuff, child, Ima take this veil home wit me and do what have to be done. Don't you pay no mind to what I'm doing, you just keep your eye on this little one. He got the sign. Child born with the sign. Sign writ all over this child plain as day. Watch him. Watch him real good.

They came to see the newborn. All her nameless children lining up beside the bed after Mother Strothers put away the bloody rags and combed Samantha's hair and opened the curtain separating the bed from the rest of the one-room house. Samantha watched the older ones who had seen it all many times before, tugging and nudging till each black face could see their mama and the new baby. They stared like she stared when the ghost first appeared at her door.

This your new baby brother. Come and give him a kiss. C'mere and give little Junebug some sugar.

Nobody stepped toward the bed. She watched them clasp hands. Slow motion, the oldest two first, then on down the line, around the ring, like a secret whispered into each ear, her children silently joined hands till none stood outside the circle.

It's just kids. It's just children scared by something they ain't never seen. Junebug is a warm lump against her shoulder. A part of herself drained of color, strangely aglow. Her children don't understand yet. Perhaps they can't see him. Perhaps they look through his transparent skin and see only the pillow on which she's propped his head. She lowers her gaze to his pale, wrinkled skin, his pink eyes, then stares across him to their dark faces.

C'mon youall.

But as if a secret voice has whispered another command, they all step back.

They're scared, she thinks. They're just kids and scared. Like I got a ghost in bed with me, or a little white kitten laying here.

It's your babybrother. It's little Junebug.

When they burst from the room she can't tell whether they're laughing or crying, whether the door when it flaps closed behind them is shutting them out or shutting her in.

Oh, Lucy Tate. It hurt so bad. Learned I could hate my children. Learned I could hate the white one cause the black ones hated him. I blamed him, Lucy Tate. Blamed little Junebug and cursed his white skin and his ghost daddy cause I had to make a choice. If I loved Junebug I had to hate the others when they did those terrible things to him. I had to choose, and I hated him cause he made me build a fence around myself. I had to stop loving and stop hating altogether because it was tearing me apart. One day I just backed off. Put that fence up ten feet tall around me and just watched, watched it happening. Didn't take no sides. Just cried and tended wounds and let whatever had to happen, happen. Couldn't let my feeling for Junebug spoil what

I felt for all the others. Couldn't forgive them when I'd see him off in a corner by hisself, crying and them blue bruises showing through so plain on his skin.

For years, Lucy Tate. Dying inside for years. In the place meant for carrying life. Gave my black children another sister and brother. Thought that might even things. Thought they might forget. But the new ones sucked the evil at my titty. Soon's they could, they lined up against Junebug too. I talked to Brother but wasn't nothing neither of us could do. Brother come around and that make it worse. The other children got scared. They'd whip on June unmerciful soon as Brother left. And what was I supposed to do. Couldn't watch them all. Couldn't see what each one doing all the time. If I tried to keep June close by me, sooner or later he'd stray away or another one would need me all the sudden and that'd be the worst time, the times I thought they really tried to kill the child. So I just let it be. Stopped loving and hating. Junebug learned to stay off by hisself. Find a corner and play and hum that singsong way to hisself. Only sound he ever made. That singsong hum I still hear in my sleep. Play by hisself and forget the others and hope maybe the others forget him and give him a few minutes peace.

Told myself it would all be better one day. One sweet bye-and-bye day they was all gon be sorry and go to Junebug on their knees and he'd forgive them, and sweet bye and bye, things be like they used to be in Sam's Ark. Loving again. Brothers and sisters again. Some mornings I'd wake up and swear I could hear them talking to that boy and little Junebug answering and nobody studying war no more and I'd start to fling out my arms and kick off the covers and go running out in the yard and tell the world. Shout it loud as I could. Trouble don't last always. It don't last always. And all the children be laughing and dancing round me and I'd be light as a feather. That be the day I could fly if I wanted to. Me and all my children grow wings and go swooping round the world spreading the news. But then I'd hear somebody crying. And get the awful sinking hole in my heart and know I couldn't love and couldn't hate. Just crawl off my bed and watch and wait another day.

Before she told Brother Tate her dream Samantha had to tell him the facts. The facts were one thing and her dream another and she needed to tell him both but the facts first so he'd understand, so he wouldn't mix up her dream with what really happened. Because the facts were that Junebug got into the kerosene and fell into the fire and Becky screamed when she saw him burning. She told Brother Tate the facts first. His face turned to stone while he listened. Like a giant chalky stone and somebody had chipped eyes and nose and mouth in it and give it a name but it still ain't alive. Brother, she said, are you listening? Do you hear me, man? It was an accident. A terrible accident. June got in the kerosene and fell in the fire and I come running when I heard Becky scream but it was too late. Throwed myself at him. Look at my hands. My arms. I tried to beat out the fire with my bare hands but he was like a torch, a human torch and the fire like wind. I got close enough to beat it with my hands but then it blew me back. Knocked me off my feet. Poor thing gone anyway by the time I got to him. Wasn't Junebug no more when I grabbed the fire. So much going on, Brother. Kids all over the yard and I was trying to keep an eye on them and on the fire and the ribs I had soaking in a tub. I wanted it nice. It was Fourth of July and I wanted it special. Like I remembered old-time picnics when I was a kid. Plenty to eat. Everybody having a good time. So I was going all out. Had my sauce all made the night before, and stacks and stacks of neck-bones and ribs. People was coming by later. Grown-ups and anybody else on Cassina smell those ribs and want to come in the yard. A real party and I was jumping to keep everything going, to make everything right for my babies. Then he got in the kerosene when I had my back turned and he fell in the fire and first thing I know Becky's screaming and Oh my God I'm tearing through the yard but it's too late. June's gone before I get to him.

That's what happened, Brother. It happened that way, but I got to tell you the dream too. Not what happened but the way I dream it. Cause if I don't tell somebody it's gon drive me crazy. Cause in the dream I'm him. I'm little Junebug. And that's what makes it so hard, Brother. I know I'm him because I'm making one of those sad little *hmm, hmmm* songs like he used to hum. That's how I know the dream is starting. Everything quiet then I'm inside his song. I'm making the song. It's burning my lips and that's how I know the dream's beginning. Same way every time. Night after night, Brother. Can't get it out my mind. Like he's telling me his side of the story so I have to listen and I'm inside. I get caught and I'm him while he sings it.

It begins and it's the Fourth of July. I'm him. I know I'm him because nobody is talking to me and I can't talk. I'm off by myself watching things happen. I smell the tub of meat. Neckbones soaking in vinegar and pepper and salt. Stones around the fire to keep it in. Big pot of beans in the fire. I get up close cause it smells good and bubbles. Up close it's hot but I like it. A hot day too. Sun way up in a clear blue sky. I got that funny color so I can't keep my shirt off very long. Got to stay covered while the others run around black and shining in their skins. Off by myself. Nobody picking at me or bothering me. Mama Sam inside. The grill leaned against the stones so the fire can lick it clean.

I see it all. Every detail of the day. Like living it all over again each time. A dream but everything seems so clear, so real I feel like it's happening all over again. But it's happening to him. To Junebug. And I'm him. When I think *Mama Sam's inside,* she is inside. She's not me. In the dream there's no Samantha unless Junebug sees her or thinks about her. Then she's not me cause I'm inside June's white skin.

You got to help me, Brother. I know you're hurt too, I know I hurt you when I sent you away. When I had to try and even things. When I gave them a sister and a brother to make up for Junebug. I had to try everything, even hurting you if I could pull things back together. If I could make this Ark ride steady again. So I did what I had to do and hurt you and lost you, and now I've lost June and I'm losing my mind. A person can only take so much. The dream begins and I'm humming his pitiful music, his lonely little song and I know I have to be him because it's the dream again, the day again, it's the Fourth of July and he wanders around, seeing this and touching that and smelling things and liking the day and nobody speaks to him, nobody pays him no mind, but he sees things happening and the singsong humming is about everything he's feeling. He ain't mad at the others. Just sad when they're ugly doing ugly things to him. I watch the others playing. I smell the barbecue sauce simmering on the stones. I feel the heat when I get close to the pot of beans. I'm warm when I think of Mama Sam. A place on top my head waits for her to pat it. The others don't listen to me, but I like that. Cause when they let me alone I can like them. I can watch them playing and be part of their games. It's noisy when the kids running all over the yard and the Victrola in the doorway up loud as it goes, but what I hear is Junebug's song because that's what's inside his head and that's where I am, where I got to be till it's all over.

Something icy splashes my back. Like being high and dizzy all the sudden. I can't breathe nothing but kerosene. I'm tasting it, it's rushing up my nose. I see it shining on my bare feet. Then hands pushing. Becky screams and I fight the hands. I wonder why anybody wants to hurt Becky. She stops the others sometimes when they're hurting me, and now she's screaming *No no no* so I fight the hands and try to turn around and help Becky cause she's in trouble. I'm twisting to find her. The stones are wet and slipping under my feet... I'm fighting...

He never made a sound. Not a mumbling word. Not a peep from that poor child's lips. So when the scream comes I know it's me. I know I'm not Junebug anymore. Junebug's gone. That's how it ends. Me screaming and him burning up.

I know better, Brother. I know it couldn't have happened that way. I know the facts. None my babies could have pushed him in the fire. None them could have splashed kerosene on Junebug. Becky screamed afterwards. Started yelling when she saw her little brother

burning. I know all that. I know the facts. But when
the dream begins...when I'm him...

Out the barred window the sky is blue. Same bright
blue as July. Snow sparkles now where it's crusted on
drifts. The wind is still. Lucy Tate's track runs up the
slope, crooked like a beetle's. Lucy bringing the news
of Brother's death. Puddles where her silly rubber baby
booties touch the floor. What you doing on my bed?
What you doing on my chair? What you doing with your
mouth full my porridge? Your mouth full of old news?
Stale news? Old stinky fish wrapped up in *The Black
Dispatch*.

Never told Brother the other dream. Cause it was
worse. It was the same but it was different because I'm
not Junebug in it, I'm me. I'm nothing. I'm in the Ark
and it's pitch black night and I can't sleep. I'm worrying
and worrying that day it happened. It's like a bone
stuck in my throat, a sickness in my belly and I turn
and toss but can't get right. It's the middle of the night
and ain't no clocks in the Ark just my inside time telling
me I should be sleeping but I can't. I toss and turn and
ain't no use pretending I'm ever gon get to sleep, so I
pull on my dress over my head and pull the curtain and
slip out where my kids sleeping. Don't know what I'm
doing or why I'm doing it but I know I got to. I ask each
one the question. I whisper real quiet so nobody hears
me till it's their turn. Spoon fashion sleeping on their
mats all over the floor. I tip from one to the other in
the dark and whisper. Have to bend down each time
and each time I stir one I get that sweet child's breath
blowed up in my face. All them got long feathery lashes
and all them wake up easy and go back to sleep easy
after they answer. *Did you, baby? Did you, baby?* And
each perfect little face answers. *Yes, Mama. Yes, Mama
Sam.*

Then I know it got to be a dream cause I'm naked
as a jaybird and tearing down Cassina Way, and every
star in the sky is giggling and slobbering and saying
Yes Mama. Yes Mama.

Hello Samantha.

Hello Lucy Tate.

How you feel today?

Brother's dead, ain't he? You come to tell me he's dead.

You know he's dead, Samantha. Dead seven years now.

Sky's falling.

You feel all right?

If the kids out in all this snow they better be wrapped up good. Last winter the Ark smelt like a Vicks factory. Smearing a different one's chest with Vicks Vapor Rub every night. Sometimes three or four barking at once. Sore throats and noses caked in the morning no matter what I did. Didn't get no sleep and when I did nod off a minute be smelling Vicks Vapor Rub in my dream.

Sam, I got some cards and things for you from the children. From Detroit and Chicago and Atlanta and even one from California. They sure love their Mama Sam. They don't forget you.

Nigger's ought to stayed on board. Nothing out there in that Babylon. Just a howling wilderness out there. Ought to stayed on board till we got to the other side. Tried to tell em but mize well be talking to these walls. They said she's crazy. Said she ain't fit to steer no ship in a calm, let alone a storm. Fool can't even comb her nappy head or change her drawers no more. He walks around in his Klu Klux sheet talking about you got to eat if you want to get well. He say don't care how crazy you are you do that again I'll knock you down and make you lick it off the floor.

You want me to read you what the children say?

Dick and Jane went up the hill. See Spot run. See Dick run. See Jane run. See all the niggers run. Run. Run. Run. Run dog. Run cat. I got it all in this nappy head. All the books. Read more books than Carters got pills. Dick and Jane stone insane. I'm a scholar. I got the knowledge and you talking about some goddamn dog and goddamn cat. Like I don't know how dead he is. Like he didn't tell me first thing. Course he told me. Like I ain't got nothing better to do than stand here listening to you tell me what I already know. Go on off from here. Get off my boat, Lucy Tate. I'm tired. Tired of you and me and people minding my business. If they ain't got the sense to stay on board, it ain't none my fault. Ain't my problem no more. I'm tired. I'm crazy. Let me lone.

Two and a half hours getting to Mayview and back. And Samantha gone in fifteen minutes. Lucy remembered leaving the cards and two brown paper, string-tied packages at the desk on her way out. Not even a chance to read them before Sam went to pieces. Worse every time. Samantha losing the little grip she had.

Cat dumped too much water in her gin. Tastes like perfume when it's watery. No point in drinking gin it don't have that sting, those needles when you sniff it. Lucy in the Velvet Slipper now. Junebug's story over now. Yet she still felt it sticking to her. Like the bag Junebug came in. Like a thin, thin skin nobody but you could see. Like you could be one place and another at the same time, traveling in a bag of skin, like a Christmas ball hung up by a string and people see you shining and glittering but you ain't inside cause inside is somewhere else, is summer or spring, a whole world inside there with you and you can't get out and nobody gets in cause they don't even know it's there. She swallows the gin and shakes her shoulders. Should get up on her feet and wag her whole body, shake like a dog to get that skin off, those pieces of Mayview and Samantha still sticking to her. If you tell Junebug's story you have to be Samantha and you have to make that long trip. Buses and hills and barred doors and barred windows. Lucy was always scared in Mayview. Afraid one of the guards would grab her and sling her in a straitjacket and lock her in a room. What would she say? How could she prove she wasn't crazy? All the crazies claimed they were sane. She'd just be one more poor fool yelling what all the rest did. If she yelled long enough and loud enough they'd put her to sleep. If she fought them they'd strap her down. No way to get out. Once they had you things only got worse. If you weren't crazy to begin with you soon would be cause that's what you were supposed to be. Wouldn't be in Mayview if you weren't.

Like ice cracking. She hears the shell coming apart. Noise of the Velvet Slipper. Carl's voice, her own words scratching at the shell, then breaking through. It's down around her ankles. It's like stepping out her drawers and into the bathtub. A shiver as she stands there naked. A split second being two places at once. She could be standing in the tub. She could be waiting for Albert Wilkes to squeeze the warm water down her back. But she's not. Her buns are shivering and they're grown-up buns and she steps out of her underwear and it crunches like eggshell when she hears herself talking.

Cat. Don't you drown my gin this time.

And Cat smiles.

Sorry, Baby. Niggers got me hopping this afternoon. Ima do you right this time.

Lucy pats Carl's shoulder, and she sees the age on him as he turns from his nephew who's grown too and how time flies. How it flies. Yes it does.

He talked your ear off yet, Doot?

Uh uh. Just sitting here taking it all in. I could listen for days. Wish I'd paid attention before. When May and the rest were telling stories.

Well, this here child's had enough of the Velvet Slipper and Bucket of Blood and all these noisy niggers this afternoon. My behind turning to sawdust on this stool. Ima go home and put my feet up soon as I finish this poison Cat poured. Youall come on over when you're finished. Don't matter how late. I'll be there. Got some pork chops you can fix up.

You ain't all bad, sugar.

Know what you can do with your *sugar,* sugar.

Told you she was mean.

Doot, you come on over when you ready. Leave this old man on his throne. Pork chops ain't good for old folks' stomachs anyhow.

Lucy drains her stubby glass and slides down from the stool. A dancer's grace. A quick poke at my uncle's ribs then her hand rests on the watermelon bulge and her fingers spread to its shape. She pats him and winks at me and starts a smile which ends as a frown when he begins to grin back.

That woman's something, ain't she. Always will be. Look at how she walks. Still like a young girl, like her head's in a cloud and she's kinda lost and don't know the way out. Look how she uses her hands. Touching folks and stopping so they can touch her. Like she's blind and got to feel her way out here. Like Bubba Smith's a piece of Braille or something and she got to run her hand up and down him to see him. Both us old now, but to me she ain't never changed. I'm still trying to figure out why she did the things she did way back when we was kids. Old as I am, she's keeping me guessing.

Been looking at Lucy nearly fifty years now and still can't even finish her picture. Started one once. Don't know where in hell the rest of my paintings got to, but I keep the one of her I started when you was little. It's at the Tates' now. In the top of a cupboard with some of Mrs. Tate's old shoe boxes. Only thing right about the picture is one cheek and one eye. Got those right but a chicken scratching in dirt coulda done better with the rest. One eye, one cheek. Should have thought to do her from the side instead of straight on.

Drew her another time too. Don't you know that crazy woman showed up in my life-drawing class when I was in art school. There I sat with my sketch pad and charcoals. Doing charcoals that day, yeah charcoals, and the model was holding poses five minutes and we supposed to sketch fast. Catch what counted and not worry about getting everything down. Well, there I was daydreaming and playing with my sticks of charcoal and thinking if bones was as easy to break as these sticks we'd be in trouble and who strolls in the studio but Lucy Tate and struts up on the platform and shrugs off her robe like she's been standing naked in front of rooms full of white folks all her life. I didn't know whether to stand still or run. Whether to snatch her behind off that platform or go round slitting everybody's throat looking up there at my woman. Man, I didn't know what to do. Same old Lucy Tate kind of brazen trick I been dealing with all my life. Then I thought if she's got the nerve to pose butt-naked up there, then I got the nerve to sit here and draw her. So I did. Mashed up a couple sticks of charcoal, then wrapped myself round one and did just what the others doing.

You know what she said when I asked her why? She said it's good money and I wanted you to draw me and you never asked. That's Lucy Tate for you. So I started the painting. Put up my easel in the Tates' living room. She sat in old Mrs. Tate's creaky rocker. That was years ago, after the war, and I ain't finished yet. Just a eye and a cheek. People ain't easy to see. Can't see them cause half the time they ain't all there. I mean if you look, and look closer the way you have to do if you're trying to paint a picture, and you keep looking closer and closer, a person subject to go all to pieces and won't be nothing there to see. That's what they do with those microscopes. Get closer and closer and things come apart and the tiniest bit of anything is big as the world. I mean your skin under one them microscopes got mountains and valleys and trees like elephant trunks growing in it. And if there's all that, there's sure enough little-bitty people and animals living in those mountains and valleys. Like all of Homewood ain't nothing but a pimple on a pimple if you get far enough away and look real close. Looking down on the city with God's eye you can't see people in these streets, just bumpy hills and a little green here and there for a park and maybe a drool of spit which is the rivers coming together downtown they call the Golden Triangle.

Don't make no nevermind. I'm rambling like Lucy said. You want to know about Brother and the dope thing. Well, it was all us. The three musketeers. Me and Brother and Lucy. I came back from the war a mess. Couldn't settle down. Couldn't make sense of nothing. Like the Book says. A stranger in a strange land. That's how I felt. Nothing seemed right. Beginning with me. I tried a little of this and a little of that to keep myself going. Hung out with Brother a lot and me and Lucy started getting real serious, but I couldn't shit and couldn't get off the pot neither, you know what I mean. Betwixt and between.

I'd sit myself down and try to get myself together. You know. Say this is your life, Carl French, the only one you gon git. Now what you gon do with it? What you gon be? Seemed like I could always hear somebody laughing and giggling in the background when I tried to talk to myself serious like that. But I tried anyway till I had to laugh too. I mean, what was out there?

What could I do? What was I supposed to do? Finally I
started remembering. Yeah. I started listening a little
closer to the giggly voice. Wasn't giggling all the time.
It was saying you a nigger. You a blackass splib. I
started remembering and laughing too and things
started getting easier.

At certain moments Carl pauses. His eyes turn in-
ward and he's listening rather than telling his story.
The words stop. Nothing moves but his vacant eyes
searching somewhere for something that will help him
continue his tale, complete the frozen gesture. He's telling his own story, he knows his story better than anybody else, but in the long pauses between words as he
sits motionless on a barstool in the Velvet Slipper, he's
waiting for a witness. A voice to say amen. Waiting for
one of the long gone old folks to catch his eye and nod
at him and say *Yes. Yes. You got that right, boy*.

Yeah, Doot. I started remembering what I was. But
I'm not telling you nothing you don't know. Just needed
to be out here in these streets awhile. Just had to look
around me and remember what being a nigger meant.
Didn't take too long. They got us coming and going,
and it don't take too long to remember. You feel them
strings pulling and get them rope burns and you remember fast. I had the GI Bill, and like I was telling
you I tried some art classes at Tech. They let a few of
us in school. Veterans still supposed to be heroes then,
so a few of us got in college and what not, but I only
know of one or two who made it through. Times just
weren't right. You know what I mean.

But I could draw. I could really draw. Ever since I
was in grade school I could draw things, and they look
just like real. I knew I had a talent and drawing was
something I always liked to do, so I said hell. Go on
and try. And I was good. No doubt about it. Teachers
at Tech always using my work to show the others how
a thing could be done. One the instructors, a white dude,
shit they was all white dudes, probably still are, but
this one kinda tall and skinny with a moustache bigger
than he was, he said, *French, what do you think you're
doing?* Jerked my head up from my work. Thought he
was talking bout my sketch, and I sort of hid it with

my hands then peeked down underneath my fingers to see what was the matter. Always sat in the back of the studio. Far away from the models as I could. White chicks, of course, so I sat in the back so maybe they'd think I was a Turk or a Arab or some damned thing. So when this dude says, French, what do you think you're doing? I got uptight. He wasn't even looking at my pad. Wasn't even looking at me. He was standing there stiff and straight as the Statue of Liberty. Eyes front. Hissing out the corner of his mouth like that moustache too heavy for his upper lip. He said, Come to my office after class, French. So I do. And he sits behind his desk smoking the longest cigarette I ever saw: You're good. We all know that. Best student we have but you're wasting your time here. Can't earn a living with what you're learning here. Said he was telling me for my own good. Companies don't hire colored artists. He didn't say nigger artists but that's what he meant. Asked me to name a famous artist of my race. Name one artist or one painting by a black dude. Shit. Course I couldn't name one. Didn't even know the names of white dudes who was making it. When he was done speaking his piece he stood up and patted my shoulder real buddy-buddy like we just robbed Fort Knox and had the gold salted away and nobody but us knew where it was. Smiling and telling me I got talent and Ima decent person and that's why he was hipping me. The rest of the teachers hypocrites, he said. Leading me up a blind alley. Said he was my friend and didn't like saying what he had to say, but somebody had to.

And that was my graduation day. No way to go back to class after that. Shaky enough being the only spook at Tech. Wasn't like he was asking me if I wanted to quit. And nevermind it wasn't none his business. Shaggy-lipped motherfucker made it his business. Quituated me on the spot.

What do you think you're doing? Damn. I really didn't know. Not then, not now. So he made up my mind for me. Let me know I was making him uncomfortable so it was time to go. Put it to me so I'd be calling him a fool or a damned liar if I stayed. And shaky as I was I just quit. Gave it up. Those quiet bus rides in the morning to the campus. The leather satchel Lucy bought me to carry my supplies in. Cause part of what the dude said was the God's truth. No such thing as a black painter cept the ones on ladders painting somebody's porch. Not even many of those if you thought about it. Wasn't a damn thing a colored man could do when you got right down and thought about it. Every black man I knew trying to support a family had two or three pieces of jobs that never added up to one good one.

Carl is like his sister, Lizabeth. That fair French skin and a calm, dignified, assured manner. His speaking tone, like hers, is casual. He smiles a lot when he talks, breaking into the saddest stories with offhand, ironic remarks or whimsical details of people's peculiarities, and you can't help smiling too. Anaydee turning green under her nostrils when she cries. Aunt Fanny stuck in the funeral parlor vestibule because she can't get her umbrella down. How he said *Thank you, Dr. Weird* to the doctor named Strange who had tended my grandmother, Freeda, during her last days in Allegheny County hospital. And like his sister, Carl's outward calm is always counterpointed by some part of his body shaking fast as a triphammer. One raw nerve-end dangling, visibly vibrating a mile a minute, if you knew where to look.

Ain't changed that much, has it? Niggers still out here scuffling and hustling and ain't got a pot to piss in nor a window to throw it out. Daddy was a paperhanging fool. Be high as a kite on Dago Red and still measure out a room perfect. Drink enough Dago Red to drown an ordinary man, but he'd get up on a ladder and lay that paper so you couldn't find a seam. But laying wallpaper only a once-in-a-while thing. He was the best but couldn't do it steady cause none the contractors would hire him regular. He'd have to sit out every morning in front the Bucket a Blood with the rest of the men waiting for jackleg work. I know all about it. Sat there many a morning myself. Hoping a white man will drive up and mad if one does cause you know he'll talk down to you in that nasty cracker way and work you like a mule and pay you half what he'd pay a white boy. But you got no choice. You got to sit and wait for one them ragtag pickups to sidle along the curb. Then *Beep Beep*. The white man sits there looking you up and down like he's God Almighty. When times real bad, niggers scrambling and pushing one another so he can see em good. Man say jump and you jump. Hey you in the overalls. Step out here where I can see you, boy. And you take what the bastards give. Or take nothing. Hang around there the rest of the day with the rest of the trifling niggers cause you ain't got nothing better to do. I know all about it cause I been out there many a morning. Daddy dead and gone and me taking his place on one those boxes outside the Bucket a Blood.

It's a bitch. Niggers still out on the same corner waiting. Was a time couple years ago whiteys afraid to drive anywhere in Homewood. But they back again and niggers waiting again. You know the thought never even come into my mind that maybe I could make it where all the others failed. Carl French the first black artist. Michelangelo French. Your generation can think that way, Doot. Youall can see beyond your situation. You and the young bloods coming up. Not many get a chance, but a few is better than none, and it makes my heart feel good when I hear one these young brothers damn this and damn that and tell the man kiss my ass. We all going to hell, but it makes my heart proud. Sometimes I'd think that way, but when I was coming up wasn't no way I'd curse a white man to his face. Seems like a long time ago but I'm only talking about twenty years ago, the good old fifties in the good old U.S. of A. Your uncle did what the rest the jive niggers did. Let hisself be pushed down. Started sticking myself with needles. Put the world in a jug and held the stopper in my hand.

And we were the three musketeers, right. So all three of us, me and Lucy and Brother in that dope mess. Couldn't say now who was first. Don't remember a first time, or saying to myself, Go ahead. You ain't nothing. Ain't gon hurt you worse than you already hurt. Wasn't a matter of deciding to do it or not do it. One day you look round yourself and see these jive niggers nodding and sprawled out on the floor and you feel good, you grin at all these junkies in the Tates' living room and wonder a second what I got to be feeling good about but that thought's gone before it gets hold to you and nothing can get hold to you except you know you're feeling good, you got the shit whipped for a while and the wolf ain't at your heels and you're feeling good, real good, better than you ever thought you would.

The bar noise rises and falls. Somebody calls somebody else's name down the length of the bar. A woman squeals. A round of drinks is ordered for the fine lady in blue and her friends.

I ain't gon lie now like I'm supposed to and say how it tore me up to be a junkie. Nope. Cause it was better than being nothing. World was a hurting trick and being high was being out the world. Nothing wrong with that. If you find a way out the trick bag, you a fool not to take it. You take it and it makes you feel good and that's that. Why the hell not? I mean it's your body, it's your life. Shit. Who ever said you supposed to just stand still and suffer. No. You take the freedom train running through your veins. You get on board and couldn't care less where it's headed. Don't care nothing about dues, about the conductor coming one day to kick your ass off. All that's farther down the line. And down the line don't matter. It's the minutes that matter, the hour or the day if you can keep feeling good that long.

Always like Christmas at the Tates'. Like the good old days on Cassina Way waking up on Christmas morning and everybody done outdid theyselves buying presents and you're a kid and it's all for you.

Easy as falling out of bed. One day I looked in Lucy's eyes and saw junk. Lucy looked back in mine, and she musta seen the same thing. Junk. Like I said, Hello. Meet my monkey. And her monkey nodded at mine and then Lucy dead and Carl dead cause them monkeys didn't need us nomore. Get along fine without us, Thank you. Every once in a while I'd notice how bad Lucy looked or see her doing something Lucy Tate ain't supposed to. But then I'd see junk. Remember she ain't Lucy Tate no more. No need to yell or snatch her back from something or take her to a mirror so she could see herself, see for herself how low she was falling. Nothing in no glass to see. Just junk. Junk. Long as we could get it, wasn't no problem. Didn't need nothing else. Long as we had it, wasn't nothing else.

That was the good part. Being high was good. Bad part was you couldn't stay high. Bad part you still had to deal with that asskicking world to get high. You had to hurt people. Knew you hurting them just by being what you were. Stealing, turning tricks, lying. Taking from your family, messing over the people think they your friends. You had to go back out in the world so you could turn it off. Shoot it down. On a merry-go-round. Like a sick puppy on a merry-go-round. Chasing in circles after your own tail. Sooner or later you had to get off the floor, get out the Tates'.

Why? To get back again. Coming through the door you'd see yourself going. Coming and going like you got a ghost and you'd bump into yourself going in when you'd be coming out. Meet yourself in the vestibule and be half out your mind trying to figure whether you supposed to be leaving or just getting back.

That's when I caught the bus to Lexington. After I passed my ghost a few times in that doorway I knew I had to go. Tried to get Lucy and Brother to go but Lucy wasn't ready. She told me she wasn't ready after I got back to Homewood the first time. She wasn't ready to stop and I couldn't either. Had to go back to Lexington again. Then Brother quit. Like magic. The man just stopped one day and never touched it again. Brother was different, always was different from other people. Anyway, he quit and after he got hisself together he ran everybody out the Tates' and locked Lucy in her room and stayed with her while she cold-turkeyed. He stopped and made her stop. Just about killed her, and would have she said, if he had to. So by the time I got back from Lexington the second time they was both clean. I been at it again but everybody helped me and I go for my methadone now but I'm all right. And Lucy's all right. And Brother ain't got it to worry bout no more.

Old cream-of-wheat Brother. I know I'm supposed to be telling you his story. But how Ima tell his without telling mine. And Lucy's. Cause yeah. We was the three musketeers, all right. Woulda followed each other to Hell. And just about did. But that's all gone now. Broth-

er's gone and it's just me and Lucy now and it's time
to get off this stool cause I'm hungry. You ready, Doot?
You come over to the Tates' and it be three of us again
just like the old days.

III

BROTHER

1941

The week he turned twenty-one the train dream took Brother for the first time. Snatched him from sleep and twisted him inside out and left him sweating in the darkness. Where are my hands, my God-blessed hands is what he shouted that first night bolt upright in bed because he didn't know if the dream still had him or if it had turned him loose. He was alone in the black room, trying to find the parts of his body, but the hands running up and down his legs, hugging his shoulders, pinching the flesh beneath his eyes did not belong to him. They were not Brother Tate's hands. In the pitch and shudder of the train nothing belonged to anybody. The woman who had been hurled into his lap did not own the soft breasts which dragged over his thighs as she scrambled away. They weren't her fingers which mauled and grasped as she tried to find him and push him away all at once. A stew of bodies sloshed helter-skelter over the wet floor of the boxcar. Brother couldn't stand. He couldn't disentangle what belonged to him from the mass of bodies struggling in the black pit.

Brother Tate sat bolt upright, naked and scared on the mattress in the house of his dead father, trembling because he knew the dream could kill him, knew it could take him again and again until its work was finished.

His legs were wet under the storytelling quilt. His sister, Lucy, had patched and sewed the quilt, and Brother drew it over him every night, winter and summer. Some nights he'd hear the quilt talking story, chattering at him when sleep wasn't sleep, when he swam till dawn in a churning sea of Dago Red. Now it felt like all the people sewn into the bright mosaic of cloth had peed on him. Funky, blood-warm pee. He rubbed his eyes and fingered the parts of his body buried under the quilt. Everything was covered by sticky darkness. Everything was melting and running away.

No way he'd peed on his ownself. He was grown. He'd be twenty-one in two days. His birthday in two days and they'd party at the Velvet Slipper and the Elks. Carl be there and Lucy on her high stool and Cat behind the bar. He was a twenty-one-year-old man in his dead father's house, alone in the house of the old man he'd always called Father because nobody never told him not to. What he look like peeing the bed. His legs were drenched in sweat or blood from those bodies rolling haywire like marbles across the floor of the rattling freight car. Those bodies stink like horse shit or cow shit, and that's what was backed up under the covers with him.

Slowly the dream was turning into nothing as he remembered what it was about. In the dream he had been Albert Wilkes, long dead Albert Wilkes coming back to Homewood again. Brother remembered how real the dream had been, how clearly he'd seen the countryside flowing past the windows of the train. Because that's how it started. A train ride. Albert Wilkes on a train. And stayed that way until the lights went out and the doors slammed and the bodies began crashing into him and the screaming began...

He had seen Albert Wilkes's face in the window of the train. He is inside the train and the face running along on the outside. He can see through the face to the trees like broccoli heads lining the tracks. Can see through it to shanties and fields and red earth. The face is there always but parts of it come and go so maybe all he sees is eyes or a mouth or the cheekbone's shadow or maybe sees nothing but a stomped down shack and chickens scratching in a yard and a backside broad and round as two watermelons where a woman is on her knees in a vegetable patch. But the face is dimly there even then, and he's waiting for a time, maybe night-time, when he'll be able to see it all and clearly.

He's going home. He knows that. Knows it because the land and trees and air are changing. Even the sound of the tracks getting more familiar the closer he gets to home. The train is hunkering down, its wheels grabbing tighter. What sings and dances in the hurry of the train starts to get to him. He has been sitting a long time, watching through the face a long time, hearing nothing but the wheels saying I'm tired and still got a long way to go. He wouldn't listen because there was no play in the sound, nothing but a flat, lonely, almost moan like somebody telling the same sad story over and over again in the same tired voice and the wheels couldn't do nothing but keep on telling the tale. Now he hears a beat, a gallop. The steel wheels rising and set down one at a time so it's boogity, bop, boogity boopin a little different each measure.

More trees and rolling low hills. Everything in shades of green. So green the face looks back at him shiny-eyed and black. And for no reason he gets sad again. Gets more unhappy than he was when the land was flat and bare and the wheels moaning because they were standing still. Perhaps it's because home is just around the next bend. He knows there will be tunnels and bridges and a river deep in a valley he must fly over on a thread. Then he will be home again and the sadness comes because now he's sure he's gon make it.

Not just a tune now but words now between the mouthfuls of steel the wheels are chewing. They sing *seven years seven years* and he's Brother again. Ain't got no ticket then and plumb off the train and standing in the Tates' living room beside Lucy and she says play and the playing is *seven years, seven years* and the face out the window ain't even pretending no more it just goes on about its business and when he steps into the station he feels it slap him across the bare bones of his skull and it's Albert Wilkes in the soot and dirt and niggers in red caps and engines smoking and all aboard and steam hissing and people hurrying and people look-ing through him like he thought they never would. No fingers pointing, no sirens, no nothing but people getting down and people climbing up and niggers pushing boatloads of suitcases and trunks. Then he looks into the playing, looks past the seven years the way he looked past the face outside the window to find the countryside he was speeding by. He is Albert Wilkes all right, and he's caught somewhere in the middle. Maybe he is the window glass. Hot on one side. Cold on the other. Because he is Brother, too. Shuffling his feet and listening to Wilkes playing because Lucy said he's back.

Albert Wilkes steady humping on his piano. Playing honky-tonk and gut bucket and low-down dirty blues. He's playing righteous and deep in his song, but he is staring at Brother too. Trying to see something. Brother feels himself rushing like a river. Like the face on the other side of the glass. Albert Wilkes can see pieces of him. An eye. A mouth. The shadow of a cheekbone. But he also sees the gray sky, the gray water, the shaggy trees. Sees through Brother to all of that so his face is like a flag changing shape in the wind.

Play. And then he goes on about his business. He plays his piano song sad as train wheels when they standing still. He is beside Lucy and he is across the room, seated at the piano Strayhorn brought in Mr. Tate's truck. Mrs. Tate rocks up and back in slow time to something in the music nobody else can hear. Her song in his song. Like Brother hears his. Like Lucy beside him rocks on one foot then the other hearing what she needs to hear.

Like Albert Wilkes when he gets off the train and thinks *seven years*. Been gone seven years. The busy station paying him no mind when he had expected it to be all sirens and searchlights and dogs howling and pistols exploding. After so long on the train he can't stop moving. Part of him continues gliding down the track, sealed in a box so the world rushes past like scenery through a window. But the part of him which won't stop moving is hooked to the end of a rubber band and the rubber stretches as far as it can, then flies back like a boomerang upside his face. That wakes him to the beginning of Homewood. To his hands which have been waiting seven years. Piano-playing hands gone for seven years, gone so long, so far, he knew they were dying, knew he must bring them home. Return to Homewood to hear Lucy say. Play.

In his song like a window Brother could see way down the tracks. To now when he is dreaming. To the time when he will speak to a son. To the time he wouldn't speak to anyone anymore. To the lives he would live and the lives he would be inside. Albert Wilkes's song like a hand over the troubled waters, and then the water was still and he could see everything. Everything gone and everything coming not mixed up together anymore but still and calm. Albert Wilkes's life was hanging on him like a skin to be shed, a skin he couldn't shake off, so it was squeezing, choking all his other lives. It would kill him forever if he didn't shrug it off, so he ran from the living room and up Tioga to Homewood and Frankstown and said to a white policeman he'd never seen before that Albert Wilkes was back. That he killed a policeman seven years ago and now he's back in Homewood at the Tates' on Tioga.

And they stomped in and blew away his skin... and the lights went out and the boxcar rattling and the blood and the bodies. But then Brother bolts upright, the quilt shivers down his chest. He counts the parts of his body. He is remembering. Some parts of the dream still seem real, then all of it is real, then none as he remembers where he is, who he is. Parts of the dream real, then less real as he remembers.

The boxcar shrinks. Brother can see inside it now. It's smaller and smaller. It's a coffin now, silk lined, heaped with roses. Albert Wilkes in a tuxedo looking good like he always looked good in his clothes. A rose pinned on Albert's lapel. Albert smiling, winking as the box grows smaller, as it starts to rock and sing a lullaby. Then Albert's gone. The box is too small to hold a man. *S'a boy.* A tiny babyboy in a cradle rocking and a black hand tipping the cradle back and forth and it's a boy, a boy child white as snow and the black woman rocking the cradle is smiling. She's singing and the train's gone, and it's morning and light pours through the windows of the Tates' old house and birds are making a racket as they always did on spring mornings when there were trees in Homewood.

1946

The train dream returns. It's dark again and Brother is trapped again inside the rattling car. He knows he has been riding five years, trapped for five years, and nothing he believed was real is real anymore. There is only the ride, the darkness, the screaming. Everything else is finished, is made up like the music he plays, like the music he will never play again, like words he will never speak again.

This time he can't shake free. He's naked walking the floor. The storytelling quilt's a tangled mess half on, half off the bed like something somebody fought with and killed and left dying in its tracks. Brother hears the flat smack of his bare feet on the boards. He's marching. Like the Elks Band on V.J. Day under the bridge crossing Homewood Avenue. He doesn't know why. He doesn't care. It's a way of getting up and back, up and back, across the black space of the room. For days, for years, his poor feet wearing a path through the wooden floor. He hears the splat, splat rhythmless march steps going nowhere and tastes gritty, hot soot in his mouth.

S'a boy.

He's my son and it can't be no other way. Never be no other way. So I'm in his corner. Got to be. Always.

Sam is his mama and loves him and do the best she can. I know that and know she won't let nothing hurt him too bad. So I stay away except I'm always spying where they can't see me. I pretend they don't see me and

164

*they don't. Slip from behind Mother Strothers's shack
and cross the alley and inside Sam's yard and sidle next
to Junebug and don't none them see me coming. So there
I am beside him. I can hear him breathe and hear them
little songs he makes but he don't see me. If he sees me
the others will too and nobody's ready for that. He is sad
sometime and happy sometime. He is mostly like the
others. Not really knowing whether they happy or sad
because they got something to do and that keeps them
busy. Junebug busy with them songs he makes. Don't
say words yet but he's busy making things most all the
time. I watch him for hours. But it's hard to stay invisible
so nobody see me. Headaches. Got to split. Got to make
it on back and be with Lucy or be in the Velvet Slipper.
Or sit up by the tracks. More trains now. The kind Carl
went away to the war on. The kind got stuff covered up
on flat cars you know it got to be guns and tanks and
jeeps under there. Keep wondering why so many people
want so many people dead. Keep thinking you got a son
and it's never gon to be no other way.*

    *I see Junebug walking now. Like he got rubber bands
inside them bowlegs and sometimes they's pulled tight
enough and sometimes they get loose so he ain't walking
he's coming apart and falls down and picks hisself up
and puts hisself back together again one or two steps
closer to where he wanted to be in the first place. Either
way. Walking or coming apart Junebug gets off by hisself now. It's better now. The others forget him when
they don't see him. He can help them forget now. He can
find a corner and they leave him alone as long as they
ain't remembering. Samantha is the mother of all of
them. Samantha going to be the mother of more.*

    She said:

    *Brother, I can't stop. While I got life I got to give life.
They're killing us faster now. And beating down the ones
they can't kill. Our boys over there supposed to be dying
equal. It's a crying shame how they do us. So I can't
stop. When we cross over, I want a million, million black
feet to run up the bank and a million, million black
voices shout hallelulah in the promised land. So I got
to give life while I got it.*

    If you ain't felt it, don't think you know nothing about

it. Watch some nigger start to coming around Sam and know what she done picked him for. I watched it twice and second time no easier than the first. Worse than the first, to tell the truth. Like the first time a thing happens you can think well it's just a accident. Ain't never happened before, won't again. You tell yourself that shit. But the second time is always. Hurts so bad and you be so low you just know it's gon happen and happen and keep happening and ain't no accident to it. Had to work hard to keep myself this side of that curtain. Ain't no windows. You can't get out the bed except through the curtain. I had to make it a box. I'd seal Sam and the nigger in the box and make the curtain just as stiff and dark as the other three wood walls. I'd pack them in and pack the wood in steel and shoot it like a rocket someplace as far away as the moon. Then as long as I kept it there and kept them dark and silent in it, I'd be all right. Wouldn't have to think on it. No reason to think because the curtain is steel and far away and nothing is moving inside.

She told me she was going to do it, told me she had to and told me why and part of me would listen part of me would nod that ugly pumpkin on my shoulders but most of me be cooking steel and hammering and welding and getting that match ready to blow them to the moon.

Like it was when I watched all Samantha's black children playing in the yard. I loved them like she did. But loving them don't make it no easier when they evil to Junebug. Had my favorites like little Becky I carried in the Ark that first time when Sam dancing. Always thought of her mama dancing when I watched Becky playing in the yard. She the hardest one to fool. She the one would see me if I didn't keep thinking hard. Got my favorite but I love all them children. Any children. I can see little kids hanging on Carl. Half naked and dirty and got sores all over and nothing in they stomachs. Little brown kids like Doot. Halfway color between Junebug and the rest of Samantha's kids. They got slanty eyes and they crying. They ain't got mama nor daddy no more and Carl wants to be home. He empties his pockets and dumps the little snacks from his knapsack. But it's like fighting lions with a stick. Them kids gon

*die. Ain't nothing to do really but just keep on marching
and hoping you be home soon. When Junebug got a sister
I loved her. Loved his brother when he come. Love them
all but that don't make it no easier when I think of them
being evil to Junebug or Sam loving their daddies.*

She said:

*It's a river runs through me. Said it's the kind of river
never stops running. Always moving to the sea. She said
the water always changing. Said it's different every time.
Different water for them. Different water for you. Not
even the same water if you step in one minute out the
next and in again the next it's different water every time
that quick. It's a river and no one will ever touch me
where you touched me. Where you touched me is part of
the sea now and the sea is always. It's where we been
and where we're going and don't be sad, ghost. Don't
you be acting like no jealous natural man, ghost. Not
yet. Not yet. I need you different till we get through this
thing with Junebug. Just think of it in my way. Think
that now there's two more who are going to love him
that day we teach them all to love.*

*But Carl came back from the war and ain't been no
sign of love. Just less room for Junebug.*

*I take Carl by one day. I stop beside Sam's yard to
tie my tennis shoe which ain't untied. He knows why.
He knows my son and knows what I'm saying. Junebug
easy to pick out off by hisself digging in the dirt. Now
that Carl's back home I stay away a little more from
Sam's place. I think she might be ready to pick another
man and I might have to kill him. Kill him over Sam
for one thing. And kill him because he'll be stealing the
little breath Junebug's got left. It ain't me to think like
that. It ain't Brother being that way and I almost tell
Carl what I'm thinking so I can kill it in me. Stead of
talking we just walk. All over Homewood. Gonna walk
holes in the sidewalk or holes in our shoes and then start
wearing holes in our feet because the walking is instead
of talking and as long as the speech I need to say keeps
climbing to my throat I got to keep moving and walk it
back down again and Carl is beside me and I hear him
tramping on the words he don't want to say either. It's
Sunday morning and the bells in the white folks church*

on Penn Avenue is parading all over Homewood. Like somebody turned a hose on and said let's clean up this mess. The bells chase everything but theyselves out the streets. You got to hear them if you outdoors. No way not to hear them.

They chiming when Carl said:

Daddy used to say only difference between Sunday and every other day back in slavery times was they called you out the fields with the church bell instead of the conch horn. He teased Mama all the time about church. She loved the bells. Said they reminded her of the quiet days when Homewood was different. Daddy would say the day God put some black hands at the end of the ropes be the day those bells be beautiful. He said couldn't no white men play See-See Rider on them bells and that's what he wanted to hear.

Why do white folks run from us? Where do they think they're going? I seen enough dead bodies to fill two Homewoods. Brown and Yellow and White and Black. All the same. All stink the same. That was a job niggers got a lot. Cleanup. Just like over here. But in the war wasn't just garbage and spilled drinks and cigarette butts. War mess is dead people. So they brought over our brooms and mops and scrub buckets and put us on the same jobs they give us over here. You talk to fellows who was in the war and sooner or later they'll tell you about having to pick up pieces of white boy and bury them. That's the way it was for most. Except the ones they allowed to die fighting. The ones they let die so the rest of us be free to bring the shovels and brooms back home.

Carl talking and needing me to listen so I put everything out my mind awhile. Put Sam and Junebug to the side awhile so I could listen, so I could breathe, so I could get the razors out my chest.

Then it was summertime. Days got long and green. We'd drink sweet wine and sit on benches in the park. Half the time it be Carl talking and half the time we be sleeping or spying on the people messing round in Westinghouse Park. Kids out of school hanging around the swings and the tracks. Boys waiting for the girls. Girls strolling by in twos or in little packs so they can sass

back when the boys say something ignorant. I watched
and listened and tried to make up songs about it all.
With the sweet wine in my blood and the warm air on
my skin I felt like those tinkling chimes Carl brought
back from the war and hung on his front porch. Breeze
took pieces of me and knocked them together and I could
feel it floating through me, hear it playing me when it
moved the leaves and pushed the long shadows across
the grass.

June was the month he told Sam he was inside her
belly. And she told me and sure enough he came nine
months after in February but he was Junebug always
and I didn't think of snow and wind and standing in
the alley freezing and old Mother Strothers skating like
a beetle across the frozen middle of Cassina Way. I
thought of summer here to stay like it is when it's finally
June and you can lay out all day and let the sun melt
you to pieces. So he was always there in the back of my
mind those early summer days, but I didn't go around
except once or twice to peek in Sam's yard. Then it was
July and everything growing thick on the hillside. They
still had engines that smoked then and black soot clouds
would roll down from the tracks and trains would stop
at the water tower and drink. That smoke could get in
your throat and you'd be all right one minute then
coughing and spitting the next. You'd say, Got Damn.
You'd pick up a rock and throw it at the tracks even
though the locomotive long gone and couldn't reach it
anyway from where the smoke caught you standing there
sneezing and rubbing your eyes and can't do nothing
but holler Got Damn.

I remember cause the state store closed on the Fourth
and me and Carl had to go to Bows to get a jug of Dago
Red. Bows was the house looked like it's made out yellow
mud, on the corner of Tioga and Cassina Way. Bows
was where you get your throat slit good you cut your
eyes at the wrong nigger but if you want something to
drink and everyplace else shut like they is Sundays and
holidays you got to go on over to Bows, so me and Carl
was on our way when the smoke swooped off that hillside
and I could taste it all the way to Bow's back door.

Youall see that ambulance come through here. One

*them little childs got burnt up over to Samantha's. Say
the poor little thing ain't nothing but a cinder, time the
ambulance got there. It ain't been gone more'n a minute.
Come right through here. Thought you boys might of
seed it.*

*And the smoke taste on my lips and the smoke burn-
ing my eyes and ash is everywhere inside me. I die then
and remember the cold. Only it's colder than it ever was
when I was standing in February waiting for Mother
Strothers to come back across the alley and say, S'a boy.
So cold if anybody touched me I'd crack and be a million
broken pieces all over Bow's back step. Carl asking questions and Bow talking to hisself the way he does till
maybe he comes to what you asking him. And I'm freezing. Colder than February. Colder than ash.*

*Nobody needed to tell me nothing. I knew it was June-
bug. Knew he was gone and nothing to say, nothing to
do. Nothing bring him back. But he was mine. And
always would be and no way around that, so I went on
home and started to making that box.*

Sam said:

*I'm sorry ... I'm so sorry. Sam said, Have mercy. Have
mercy on us all.*

*She took the wood box I made for him. And took the
top to cover him. And Mr. Tucker laid him in it and
brought it back to the Ark. And Junebug slept one night
more in his mama's house and the house was empty
except for him and me. They took the other children away
when they took Sam to Mayview. She couldn't hold together so they took her to the hospital and the neighbors
that could took a child or two into they homes till Sam
got better. So it was just me and him in the Ark that
night. His last night home.*

*That's when I sang to Junebug. Sang to him to save
his life. Because he was just a baby. Because he didn't
know a thing about leaving or coming back again. So I
had to tell him what I knew. Where I had been. I was
his daddy and always would be. Just like he would
always be my son. I sang to him about crossing oceans.
About being on one side of the water and the sun sets
in the west while it's rising in the east on the other side.
And night one place is day in the other. And the sky's*

BROTHER

171

not full of stars but one bright star we only see pieces of because the darkness is a raggedy curtain pulled across it till we know better. I told him his Mama Sam would be better in the morning and that she and his brothers and sisters would come to get him at the first light. And they would sing the old songs to him. And take him out in the daylight and drive him through the streets of Homewood and carry him up the hill which is the quietest place they know. And sing over him again. And promise to meet him bye and bye and scatter ashes over his ashes and one long, green day would pass, a day to be alone, but then he would see the curtain pulled away and the great star reveal itself. Its shine a kind of singing. Its shine warm as their bodies when they gather around him in the dawn.

I told him he would feel all that. I told him to rest peacefully because of all that. But then I told him the secret. That there was more. More fire and pain and singing. That I been through it before. That nothing stopped. That I had crossed the ocean in a minute. That I had drowned in rivers and dangled like rotten fruit from trees. That my unmourned bones were ground to dust and the dust salted and plowed. That I had been chained and branded like an animal. That I had watched my children's brains dashed out against a rock. That I had seen my mother whipped and my woman raped and my daddy stretched on a cross. That I had even lost my color and lost my tongue but all of that too was only a minute.

I sang to him. I let him know I didn't understand any more than he did. Except I had been a witness. I had been there so I could tell about it. And that was all my secret. My magic.

Listen, son. Listen, Junebug. It all starts up again in you. It's all there again. You are in me and I am in you so it never stops. As long as I am, there's you. As long as there's you, I am. It never stops. Nothing stops. We just get tired and can't see no further. Our eyes get cloudy. They close and we can't see no further. But it don't stop.

Brother tasted soot. He wondered if that was the taste of a lie. Had he lied to his son? What bright, shining day ever came?

He looked down at the cracked pavement. His feet were there. Those were his raggedy sneakers sure enough and the pale chips of his big toenails where they'd chewed through the canvas tops. He'd thrown his clothes on. Hadn't taken time to dry his sweaty body or clean his teeth or find a pair of socks. He was running from the dream. He was one of those screams trying to tear through the darkness.

He could see one part of Brother Tate anchored to the busted sidewalk of Finance Street but he could also see the sun-dimpled bubble of his bald head floating miles up in the sky, so high the string attaching it to his feet disappeared before it reached the pale balloon. Brother Tate wondered what it would feel like to cut the string, to snip the cord and watch the balloon jet away. Would the sun pop it, would the air rush out and the balloon zigzag, crazy as a chicken with its head cut off, across the sky? Would he be able to hear it sputter and hiss and squeal? Would it finally fall back to earth, land somewhere on Finance Street and some little kid pick it out of the gutter and stretch it and poke it and maybe put his mouth on the dirty rubber and blow it up again?

Brother could be in both places at once. A Brother in the sky. A Brother humping down Finance Street. In one place he had no color, he could not speak or play. In another place he watches and waits.

He knows he should tell someone the train dream. The dream will return again and again if he doesn't. He had tried to tell Junebug the dream but different words came out and the taste of soot clogged his mouth and it was too late to say anything more now. His son gone and there would be many years of silence. Nothing more to say. He knew as he stepped off the fat-lipped curb of Finance down onto the cobblestones of Dunfermline, knew at that very instant, poised in the air over the broken intersection of street and alley, that he had said enough and wouldn't say any more.

1962

Brother Tate sank deeper and deeper into the neck of his tan jacket. The upturned collar reached as far as the puckered ridges at the base of his bald head. The seams there were like another face, another face staring back at the world as he passed by, a face hiding its eyes in the fleshy folds of skin when Brother tilted his head backward to laugh at something funny enough to get his whole body jumping and twisting and turned inside out. Laughing like a million invisible grinning monkeys tickling him all at once. When his head jumps back like that and his mouth full of laughing the loose skin creases and anything could be hiding in the pie-crust folds of neck. When he really got high on laughing you knew sooner or later he'd melt, all his strength laughed away and you'd have to catch him when he turned to rubber.

Get up from there, fool.

Brother collapsed sometimes when nobody around to break his fall and there he'd be, a puddle in the middle of Homewood Avenue, a dead man till you saw his shoulders twitching or his hind end wiggling then you'd know breath was still in his body and he was just lying there like a damn fool cause he couldn't stop laughing and couldn't get up either.

But this particular moonless night, double dark in the shadow cast by Bruston Hill, Brother had no reason to laugh or cry, no reason for doing anything except to try to lose himself in the skin of his tan jacket. For a

while he'd watched people moving in the other direction, toward a huge, lighted tent pitched on the vacant
lot just before Bruston started its steep rise. In the
shadow of an apartment building, in the darkness of
his own shadowy form which he felt enclosing him like
a black eggshell, from that invisible wedge between
brick walls, from that little patch of nowhere stinking
of pee and carpeted with broken wine bottles which
crunched like cornflakes if his feet made the slightest
move, Brother had watched them parading toward the
bright tent. Yes Lawd. They'd get it on tonight. Shout
Hallelujah and shake dance in the aisles. He could hear
rows of folding chairs crashing down as folks leaped to
their feet. Yes. Yes. Something's got a hold to me. They'd
party all night long. The old folks and children nodding
off, dreaming, farting in their sleep till a cymbal
snatches them back from wherever they been to sweet
glory. Some were singing softly when they passed. The
old-time, get-down, sorrowful songs you couldn't hear
nowhere but church or in the morning, Lucy ironing
his pants and humming like she had heard Mrs. Tate
when Mrs. Tate ironing one of Mr. Tate's white shirts
for church Sunday morning. Singing or humming softly
and it sounded good to him as he listened to the music
pass. Almost good enough to make him leave his hiding
place and follow them through the darkness to the shining tent where the singing would be loud and clear,
where all the voices get caught up in the old songs
whether they knew the words or not.

The collar tickles the back of his bald head. He wishes
he could draw it up like a hood. Cover the nakedness
back there, the bare white hanging out like a street-
lamp begging the kids to stone it. If the skimpy man-
darin collar was a hood he'd pull it down over his face,
close it so wouldn't be nothing showing but a slit for
his eyes. Like that slit between brick walls. And him
nothing but an eye. Not an eye that buzzed like the
streetlamps, not an eye with no business being out there,
spying, signifying in the Homewood night. Not an eye
somebody wants to stone. He just wanted to watch. Be
an eye that watched and listened. An eye nobody would
ever see or hear peering from the folds of darkness.

He almost slipped in line with the people moving
toward the empty lot where the star burned. Reverend
Somebody's somekind of Holiness and everything else
you-better-believe-it Revival cause-the-end's-coming
tent. He'd seen the posters all over Homewood. Funny
cause he hadn't seen anybody tacking them on the telly
poles or leaning them in storefront windows or pasting
them on walls, but one morning they was there, everywhere, like snow falling all night, and course you don't
hear a thing while you sleeping but there they are,
blam, covering everything in the morning. That sudden
and that surprising, the posters all over Homewood one
morning. Then people starting to talk. Sure. I heard of
him. My cousin told me bout the man. He's a famous
preacher. He's Moses and Jesus and Haile Selassie and
Billy Eckstine all in one. He can light a fire, yes he
can. Don't care if you got a hole in your soul. He can
fill it up. Yes he can now. Put a dip in your hips, a rock
in your walk and a glide in your stride. He's a preaching
man. Don't care if the Devil got Homewood in his bulldog jaws. This man snatch it back. Had him round in
them olden days wouldna been no Babylon, wouldna
been no pillars of salt and Sodom and Gommorahs.

Brother thought hard about trekking with the rest
of Homewood to that candle flickering in the middle of
nowhere. Woulda done it too if there was someplace
inside the tent he could hide, something he could pull
over him like a hood, an edge of canvas he could wrap
up in like Lucy used to curl up in Mrs. Tate's wide skirt,
sucking her thumb. All you could see of her in that
rocker going back and forth was one big Lucy eye cause
she's wrapped in the skirt and the other eye's behind
a corner of skirt she's rubbing up against her nose while
she sucks her thumb. If he could be an eye watching
and listening to the good music he'd make the trip, but
they got a wire or something connected up to a pole in
the tent and it's bright as daylight inside there. So he
waited till everybody passed and gone on about they
business. Then he stepped out from between the funky
walls and walked in the opposite direction.

Because not everybody in Homewood was going to
no salvation tent. They could bring the Sealtest Bigtop

and Barnum and Bailey and plant them in the middle of Homewood Avenue and let everybody in free, and half the niggers in the Velvet Slipper wouldn't see it and the other half wouldn't care. So Reverend whatchmacallit and his Everlasting Fire and Grace and whatever-else Revival wouldn't hardly be getting certain brothers and sisters out their set ways, out their set paths which was straight to the Velvet Slipper from the place they lay down they heads at night. Less the Rev serving communion wine by the gallon jug. Less he turning water to sweet Dago Red, these brothers and sisters patronize the Velvet Slipper ain't going noplace else. Not to pray, not to sing, not to get happy on weeping Jesus. Not to see the Rev close the wounds or sweep the floor with the hem of his milkwhite garment and suffer no corruption there. Not to watch him heal the sick or raise the dead or jump higher than Jesse Owens.

Brother had seen God once and that was enough. When Junebug died, Brother had to crawl through the needle's eye and the kinks still worrying his back so he wasn't about to get down that low no mo. So he watched people slipping past. Little groups on their way to hear the word. Brother had cat eyes. He could see in the dark. See a little group a block away gliding silently toward the black rise of Bruston Hill. But not their feet. Not even cat eyes could pick their shuffling feet out the darkness, but he could see round heads bobbing when they cleared the last houses and made a shape flat as paper against the night. Tall ones and little ones and heads in between, just enough darker than the night air so he could pick them out, clusters of folks moving silent, pressed together like they were in little boats, like there was a river beneath them where their feet all came together in blackness not even Brother's eyes could see. Raggedy boatloads of Homewood people sailing for the Promised Land.

Brother hunched deeper, pulling his shoulders up around his eyes, like he'd pull that hood he didn't have. Seemed like Homewood drained. No cars. Nobody out on the streets. All the houses dark. He knew the Slipper'd be the one place jumping if nothing else was. Seemed like he wanted to get there more than he wanted anything else in the world. Seemed like Homewood had dried up and blown away. Seemed like he could feel the hot wind in his face. Hear it. The dry hot stale wind of thousands of trifling souls, old souls stuffed in drawers. The graves in Allegheny Cemetery opening, a wind flood floating them through the streets so the streets are crowded and empty and everywhere he steps, his feet crush somebody's dry bones, somebody's body busted wide open and dry as a broken wine bottle. He's tramping on Kellogg's cornflakes but it doesn't matter because nobody's left to hear but him, and Brother thinks about lying down right there in the middle of the pavement. Not another step forward or backward ever. Just let all the strength run out his body and crumple here on the pavement and listen while the sidewalks die and the bricks tumble down and the sky cracks, and rain dry as talcum powder buries everything.

It is a Saturday night in Homewood. Brother remembers Carl's story of Japanese human-wave attacks against American machine guns on Okinawa. The Homewood night is unseasonably mild, the streets deserted. Through some odd circumstance of atmosphere and temperature, a peculiar alignment of planets and mysterious, incorporeal essences, Brother hears the screams of dying Japanese, hears the thump of bodies piling up against each other, the rip of thirty caliber machine gun bullets burying themselves in the flesh of those who hurdle a moaning barricade of dead and half-dead comrades in khaki suits and tennis shoes. The dead men look very much like cords of wood, like the bodies Carl pushed off a cliff into the sea with the blade of his bulldozer. Brother smells death in the air. Another war coming. But perhaps he is confused, smells one thing and thinks he smells another. Perhaps it's just Homewood dying. Perhaps Homewood's gone already.

His head pops out like a turtle's from its shell. As bald, as wrinkled as a turtle's head from crown to neck. But white. Pale as a baby bird. Naked as birds look before they get feathers. He scans the immediate area. A turtle's cautious, blinking reconnaissance because Brother needs to pee. For a second there is the crashing

of waves, wind or human voices roaring, but once free
of his collar, once his shoulders have settled again where
they belong and he can breathe freely and see three
hundred and sixty degrees around himself, a blessed
silence descends. At its edge the faintest hint of singing,
of voices in a blazing tent blocks away in the shadow
cast by Bruston Hill, but that sound becomes part of
the silence, its freshness, its cleansing quiet.

Then the gush of himself. Brother thinks of old John
French spitting tobacco. How it danced like popping
grease. The blood sizzling on the pavement or exploding
in the dust. Brother remembers the time on the corner
of Finance and Dunfermline when he felt like a balloon,
when he held the string in his hand and a balloon with
his funny face bobbed closer and closer to the sun. He
wondered if it would pop. Wondered as he made a little
river along the curb why the air didn't rush out when
the water rushed out. You pulled the plug and the water
drained, and why didn't the air leak out too?

He feels his body going limp. All the air hissing away
so his cheeks sink and his chest caves and his navel is
folding into his backbone and his potbelly shrivels and
the faucet in his fingers shrinks till it's nothing but a
string, a string attached to the flat kite he's become.
Then he starts to rise. The dry wind lifts him. Homewood spreads out below, a patchwork of tiny streets and
houses. But as he rises, as the string gets thinner and
thinner and his shoulders in the tan jacket become
skinny and powerful as wings, even his cat eyes can't
penetrate the darkness. Homewood is black as coal.
Nothing visible but two winking pinpoints of light. One
is the tent. The other must be the Velvet Slipper. But
as he rises on the wind and feels his bones swallowing
the thin air and the thin air swallowing his bones, as
the lightness and giddiness of a height he'd never
dreamed overtakes him, the last two lights disappear.
First one then the other blinks out. He can't tell if that's
what happened exactly or if as he rose the lights merged
and became one and then died together or if they died
in sequence one after the other and it doesn't matter
because he has even higher to go and stops looking

back, looking for Homewood or anything else in the black sea beneath him.

Brother shakes once, twice, neatly as if someone is watching and remembering his performance. As if someone will talk about it in the Slipper so he does it just right. One, two shakes so it's not dribbling when he tucks his joint back inside his pants and zips up his fly.

He's in an alley behind Dunfermline. And Dunfermline's not much more than an alley its ownself so if somebody got nothing better to do than spy on him peeing, well shame on his soul.

He walks right past the lights of the Velvet Slipper when he finally reaches them. He almost laughs outloud. Almost gets started and knows he won't stop till he's laid flat out on Homewood Avenue and will stay that way laughing deep inside hisself till somebody comes by to help him up.

Get up from there, fool.

It's the same way he felt when he was peeing. Let it rain. Let it come on down and take me. His laughter poised overhead inside a cloud looked like a balloon with a funny face painted on it. His laughter ready to drown him and drench the dry Homewood streets if he just peeked up at it. If he gave it half a chance, half a nod the cloud would burst and down it'd come. But he didn't laugh then and doesn't laugh now because he had something to do first, someplace to reach, a duty he'd forgotten till he passed the Slipper and crossed Homewood Avenue and started up the path worn through the weeds to the Bums' Forest.

He wanted to play the game one more time. He wanted to teach it to Junebug. The scare game on the tracks. He needed to teach his son to play so Junebug never be afraid of anything again. Because they were all afraid. All of them and him too. And Brother was tired. So tired he knew he better get on with it. He'd teach them tonight.

So he slogs up the path, picks his way along the hard-packed corridor through the broccoli trees. He cuts up the hillside just before the rotten steps, the steps nobody but Brother could see because he has cat eyes and he

remembers the steps and remembers the men who used
to sit there. Remembers Carl's daddy John French, the
king with his hat slung back and his bald head gleaming in the sun.

Just kids. Just kids playing games.

He sees the steps even though the last rotten board
has returned to the earth and nobody would ever know
that steps once climbed the embankment to the ruined
platform unless they happened to sit down in just the
right spot and get a rusty nail in the ass.

This is where they sat. John French and the rest of
them drinking that sweet wine and gambling and singing and making little boys feel foolish if they was foolish
enough to bother the men here, where they sat minding
their business cause they didn't like nobody else minding it for them.

Here's where Carl stood about to pee his pants cause
Mrs. French told him he better find his daddy and say
thus and so.

Here's where I got me a taste of blood, of wine sweet-
er than sweet Jesus.

Here's where the white men waited for the train.
The train that stopped here special cause they owned
it.

Mr. George Westinghouse. Mr. John French. Mr. Albert Wilkes.

Here's where Brother needed to get, and he squats
down where the platform used to be. In the shadow of
the one wall and treacherous overhang that someday's
gonna fall on somebody's head. Brother waits in all
that's left of the station for all that's left of the trains
which used to fly through Homewood every other minute it seemed. Now just a handful a day. And none
stopping. Not at the ancient water tower. Not at the
ghost of station. Brother peers across the tracks, which
even in this darkness retain enough light and heat inside themselves to gleam back at him. Long yellow cat
eyes reflecting the shine of his. Brother never could see
all the way across to the other side. Something always
in the way. The broad rows of tracks themselves. The
trees, the factories like a screen cutting him off from
what lay beyond Homewood. Carl always lying. Saying

he can see far as the track goes. See Ohio and...and
...and everything way over there yonder. But seeing
down the tracks was easier than seeing across. Than
smashing your eyes against that wall running along-
side the steel rails.

But Brother can see past the wall tonight. Through
it, around it, over it and under it. He'd been up under
that skirt. Seen the drawers and what's under the
drawers and what's under what's under the drawers.
He'd seen it all. Watched the last two lights go out and
wasn't nothing else to see. Just like wasn't nothing else
to say. Except one more time. Play the scare game one
more time. Teach Junebug wasn't nothing to be afraid
of. Teach them all.

Brother strolls closer to the tracks. Scuffs his invisible footprints in the invisible rocks of the track bed.
They sound like cornflakes crunching under his feet.
He hunkers down. He's almost tired enough to go to
sleep. But he has one more thing to do. One more place
to go.

He touches the icy metal. Icy even on this warm
night. He puts his ear to the steel. It glows in the dark
like fish in the ocean supposed to be able to do. If lightning bugs can shine in the dark, then probably fish can
too, so he thinks of the rails like long fish and leans
down and listens for the hum of their cold flesh. A hum
always there, Carl said. And Lucy believed him. She
swore she could hear it too. A train's always on the
way. Just coming or just going so the rails ain't never
quiet. Another one of Carl's lies, but Brother paid them
no mind. He knew that sometimes you couldn't hear a
thing unless you count the blood boiling between your
ears which you subject to hear always less you dead.
What you hear in them seashells in Mrs. French's bowl.
What you hear you bend down and put your ear to a
rail and ain't no train coming or going. You hear your
own blood boiling between your ears.

But now Brother hears more. First his blood, then
the hurry-up, hurry-up push of a train purring like a
cat inside the steel rails.

He'd taught Junebug how to get ready to sleep.

He crawled out Samantha's bed in the corner. Long

glowing legs first, then his pants pulled on, then quiet
as a ghost out through the curtain and into the dark
sleeping room where all the babies growing like weeds.
Junebug off by hisself. Or as off by hisself as he could
get in that crowded place.

Now I lay me down to sleep.

I pray the Lord my soul to keep.

Brother whispered in Junebug's ear so's not to wake
anybody. So quiet he might not even waked Junebug.
But he knew Junebug was listening. Junebug breathing so there's little spaces for the words to fit and Brother
whispering in the spaces.

Now I lay me down to sleep...

Four or five times. That was all. The little rhyme
Brother liked and wanted Junebug to know. It was
something nice. Something you could hum to yourself
or say outloud if you needed to. Say it when you closed
your eyes and left here. Like good-bye. Or hello. Same
difference. Cause you going either way. Brother liked
how the words sounded. Liked what the words *Lord* and
soul and *sleep* and *keep* sounded like. So he whispered
them in June's ear that night and knew June was listening because June was like him. Junebug didn't miss
nothing even though he never said nothing about it.

Something purring in the sleep of the tracks. Something whispering like him in Junebug's ear.

Brother straightens up. He rubs the hard back of the
rail. Strokes it one last time gingerly like it's sharp as
the edge of a straight razor.

Nothing to be fraid of. It all starts up again.

He hears John French and the rest of the men laughing over his shoulder. One throws an empty wine bottle
and it explodes on the tracks. They'll probably be singing before the train gets here. Or arguing or signifying
which is the same thing. Only different tunes.

Listen here, boy. Listen to me. Watch me. Cause ain't
nothing to be fraid of. Ima win this one for you. Ima be
the best for you. I ain't gon back down.

Watch me play.

1970

Lucy steps into the vestibule and stomps. She stares down at her feet and stomps again. No snow on her hush puppies but she stomps anyway. Stomps for the company of the noise. Stomps because Sam's still clinging, and Junebug and Brother and all the rest like the snow on her galoshes those winter days she had climbed to Mayview. She thought she'd gotten rid of that envelope of skin, shaken it off in the Velvet Slipper, but now as she hangs her jacket in the hall closet and crosses to the living room she sees Sam's long, dark fingers slipping from the edge. Samantha losing the last of the little grip she had. Black fingers letting go one by one like threads popping when you rip a seam.

She'd never really known Samantha. Lucy went to Mayview because Brother couldn't. She took up that duty and many others because Brother was no longer around. Seemed like the right thing to do. The only thing to do. Seemed like a way of holding on to Brother, too. Doing what he'd done, going the places he'd gone. She'd walk in Brother's footsteps and there he'd be beside her, grinning, as real as his business she was taking care of.

Carl would be by in a while. Carl like a mirror. She could see all her years, everything that had made her Lucy Tate, in his face. Her lover man, Carl. The first time and every time. Her prince charming with his beer belly and partial plate and bad feet.

He had courted her. If ever a woman was courted,

she'd been courted. By his hungry eyes, his silliness, his stories, the bloody hands he brought back from the war, by the deaths of his father and mother, by the dope, by Brother who was his brother too, and tea on Sunday and painting and dancing. Courted right off her feet by the years and years, the years heavy as his big body stretched atop hers, years as light as balloons, rising, floating, sailing them both away.

Courted by this big old empty house and Albert Wilkes dying at the piano. And Mrs. Tate fading behind her closed door. In jail where the cops had planted her. Lucy climbs the stairs thinking of their courtship. The bannister slides smooth beneath her palm. She grips it tighter, a ship's railing and will it hold her, can she hang on when the storm begins to pitch and buck? She's in the dark. Padding up the ancient stairs in the dark. Can't see her shoes behind her where she kicked them off at the foot of the steps. Old people stumble in the darkness, fall down steps and crack their brittle bones and nobody finds them till they start to stink. Eyes go sooner or later, so Lucy is teaching herself to see without seeing. With her ears and hands and nose she mounts the steps or slips from room to room at night with the lights out. The bannister is soft but firm. It ends a little ways, three steps from the top. Solid wall on both sides of the stairway at the top. The bathroom is to the right, follow the curve of the cool plaster.

She snaps on a light and the bathroom shudders, flickers unreal as a star. A cave of light. Bathrooms make her think of John French and the house on Cassina Way where he died wedged between tub and toilet. But all the rooms at the Tates' are big. This bathroom larger than the room where Carl slept on Cassina Way. She twists the brass faucets and water bursts into the clawfoot tub. Time to get clean before Carl arrives with Doot. She unbuttons and unsnaps dreamily, eases out of her clothes so she won't be ready before the water is. She kneels on the fuzzy oval rug and leans over the tub to test the temperature. Her breasts dangle against the chilly porcelain. Her nipples constrict but the tingle of goosebumps rising over her bare skin feels good. She pours bubble soap in the jet of water squirting from the faucet. Rich mounds of foam begin to form and shudder, break away and spread across the water.

She is up to her neck in suds. Her toes find the faucet and shut it off. The bathroom is suddenly quiet, silence thick and quivering like the blanket of foam stretching from her chin to the far end of the tub. Lucy touches her body to make sure it still sits under the suds. She shuts her eyes then slowly opens and closes her legs to make a gentle current, a submerged ebb and flow over her hidden parts.

She daydreams her men, lined up beside the tub, ready to do her bidding. All her men. The real ones and the ones who come only at times like this when she summons them. One will scrub her back. Another will lean down and do her breasts. As he lifts them, they'll be firm again, ride high and pouting on her chest while he kneads them and rinses away the wrinkles. One good at feet will wash hers so it almost tickles but not quite because laughing out loud would break the stillness, disturb the concentration of the others busy at their tasks. She'll roll over in the water and get up on her knees for the backside man. His hands are large. When he's done she turns over again, sits again, opens her thighs so Carl can do her legs. From ankle to groin he rubs, up to his elbows in warm water, a beard of suds on his chin. One hand washes and the other laps water between her thighs. He makes the same slow motion ebb and flow she had made by opening and closing her knees. Carl is the best. He takes longest doing his job. She can watch his face. He smiles above the silly foamy beard. Then he gets serious. She squirms and sighs, a big fish twisting in a warm pool.

No fool like an old fool. Lucy thinks it, then says the words aloud to herself. *No fool like an old fool* as she pads barefoot down the steps. The Tates' house is drafty and full of echoes, but with a towel turbaned around her head and the terry cloth robe belted tight she is snug and soundproofed. In the kitchen she pulls a package of Swiss cheese from the refrigerator. So much paper for these three pitiful little curled up slices, she thinks when the shiny Isaly's paper is undone. Big as a tablecloth spread out beneath the dried out slices. But

that's why she shops at Isaly's. They go ahead and wrap
your baloney or cheese like it means something even
if you only buy fifty cents worth. Put all that nice paper
on and jerk a strip of red Isaly's tape from the machine
to seal your package. She likes their attitude and their
chocolate chip cookies, but they don't keep their meat
as fresh as they once did. Always got to tell the girl
don't give me the end. Slice off that brown before you
start. Then again where you find fresh food anywhere
in Homewood these days? Don't mop the floor but once
a week in the A & P. Can't find nothing you want on
the shelves no more. Trouble is no white people shopping in Homewood. Not even the hippies anymore who
moved in all those big old houses up past Thomas Boulevard.

Lucy nibbles at the grainy ends of the Swiss Cheese,
then breaks them off and gobbles the center of each
slice. Old fool sitting in the tub playing with herself
like some hot blood young gal. And her man be here
any minute. But she had that telephone in her bosom
and had to use it once in a while. Ring him up on her
time, when it suited her. Call Carl and the rest of her
men round the tub. Ring them up with that telephone
in her bosom the old folks sang about. If she's getting
to be an old fool mize well be a happy one. No reason
to be lonely in this big, empty house by herself. Truth
was she could never be lonely here. Truth was she's
always tripping over ghosts and shoving them out the
way so she could have a little peace and quiet.

Grown man that he was, the house still scared Carl.
In all these years he never stayed through the night.
Even passed out on dope he used to wake up enough to
stumble home before morning. Found him and Brother
laid out on the porch once. Frozen so blue she was afraid
to shake them. As close to staying all night as Carl ever
came. Blue as an icicle curled next to Brother asleep
on the porch. Closer to dead than sleep and that's the
only way he ever stayed at the Tates' all night. Mrs.
French long gone but Carl hotfoots it home like she's
waiting for him with one eye on the clock and the other
on John French's razor strop.

She crumples the waxy paper and tosses it toward

one of the brown bags beside the refrigerator. Garbage needed to go out. She'd get Carl to take it when he left. And tomorrow she'd clean the house top to bottom. Even the rooms nobody used anymore. Because old was letting your filth pile up around you. Was living on cat food and wearing the same nasty clothes every day so you stink up the aisles of the A & P, rattling by with your cart full of cans. Old was too many brown paper sacks to count. A wall of your mess higher than your head and one day it crashes down and buries you. She never let the line of bags beside the icebox get longer than three. Old was losing count and not giving a damn. Old was people busting the locks on your door after nobody's seen you for a week and your lights burning all night and a stink worse than garbage seeping out from under your door they got to bust in when nobody answers the pounding. In Homewood people used to watch out for you when you got too old and feeble to take care yourself. Now they ship you to the Senior Citizens High Rise over on Kelley Street or Mayview all the way out Frankstown Road. But plenty old people dying alone in rooms full of garbage. And young ones dying alone in alleys.

She pops the top of one of the Iron Citys she kept in the icebox for Carl. She didn't really like beer but sometimes it was just what she wanted. Its bitterness, the foam blotting her lips, the bubbles up her nose. Had to drink it sometimes for the simple reason it was her man's drink. How you gon understand Carl French unless you know a little bit about Rolling Rock and Iron City? One beer late in the afternoon would make her drowsy. Not going-to-sleep drowsy but she'd start to feel the mellow, beery soft edges of things. How things swam together in the easy old gold color of beer. The voices in the Velvet Slipper. The music from the jukebox. She'd watch Carl hold his beer glass against his lips, letting it rest there while he peered into the golden funnel. Beer slowed everything. The way Carl smacked foam from his lips. The way he elegantly swallowed a belch, his hand cupped in front of his mouth, pinky pointed at the ceiling, then the slow trip of the flat of his hand down his chest and over his potbelly, guiding the belch on home, taming it as he swallows its sound.

Old was what happened to poor Samantha. She looked like somebody'd blown her up with a bicycle pump. Hard to believe she was the same woman who used to stride through the Homewood streets like a Zulu queen, turning the men's heads even though she always wore those loose, old-lady dresses. Everybody's getting old. Everybody changing but somebody had pumped Samantha full of air. Her skin splotchy and split like it's ready to bust open. The green Mayview dress like the dresses she used to wear, but she's not a racehorse under a blanket now. Sam is lumpy and puffy like a frog. Half the buttons on her green housecoat don't close.

Old was seeing Doot, taller than his uncle now, sitting on a stool in the Velvet Slipper drinking beer with Carl. Little Doot with children of his own listening to Carl tell about Junebug. Lucy walks to the brown bags, drains the Iron City and drops the can. Her knees crack when she stoops for the balled Isaly's paper which had bounced off the lip of one of the rolled-top sacks. Carl will be at the door any minute. And Doot who likes to get them talking about the old days. He likes to hear silly things like how she pushed Brother in a baby buggy. Plenty more Iron City in the fridge. Enough for her to have another if she wants it. She thinks she probably will, thank you.

Lucy closes her eyes from the kitchen to the living room. The bowed arm of the rocker floats out of the darkness to greet her. She feels its color, runs her hand to the round upright where the tall back begins. She gives it a little shove and there's a Lucy in the chair, rocking up and back, a Lucy snug and wise as the little pig in the story Mrs. Tate loved to tell. The Lucy in the chair shrinks to child size and burrows deeper in the old woman's lap as Mrs. Tate rocks and the wind howls at the house and the wolf huffs and puffs, but the little pig is happy. Little piggy laughs and laughs cause him got him brothers in there wit him and that pot of water boiling in the fireplace under the chimney and the big iron bolt's cross the door.

When Lucy sits down and her weight pops the cracked

rocker, the sound is like an old pain. It's part of the mellow gliding up and back, up and back, like the swings in Westinghouse Park, like the rope turning and spanking the pavement each time she bounces on her toes to miss it. The sound is familiar, even welcome because it's part of the glide, the turning. She wouldn't be Lucy Tate if it didn't hurt just when it did, just how it did.

Play. She commands Albert Wilkes again. Play. She hums his song. A song so full of Albert Wilkes the pieces of him falling around her, drifting lazy and soft like huge, wet snowflakes and she can see the shape of each one. Falling like snow or rain or the names in the stories Carl tells Doot.

Albert Wilkes's song so familiar because everything she's ever heard is in it, all the songs and voices she's ever heard, but everything is new and fresh because his music joined things, blended them so you follow one note and then it splits and shimmers and spills the thousand things it took to make the note whole, the silences within the note, the voices and songs. Lucy rocks up and back and hums quietly to herself. She wonders how such a gang of folks can keep so quiet, can go about their business and get in other people's business and stay so quiet you'd think she was the only one in the Tates'.

The chair again, like a gunshot in the silence. A trick of the damaged wood, the wounded rocker splitting apart as the chair tilts up and back, the sound of that afternoon they killed Albert Wilkes stored in the rocker. The chair popping like that used to scare Carl. Probably still did, he was such a funny, skittish, little boy grown man. With his peculiar ways and talk and belly hanging over his belt. Carl and Brother both sported those pickaninny watermelon bellies when they were kids. Their ribs like fingers reaching for the bowling balls pushing out their belly buttons. Carl pale. Blue veins like a spiderweb on his tight bubble belly. Sometimes looked white as Brother. From a distance, looked like two white boys playing with a bunch of colored kids. Closer you would notice how Brother's skin was soft cellophane you could see through and Carl one of those light, bright, pretty Frenches like his fabulous sisters. When Lucy

pushed Brother in the buggy she kept the canopy down.
No sun allowed on his delicate skin. He needed a hat.
Only one she could find to keep the sun off his face and
neck was an old one of hers, all frilly-edged with bows
and ribbons pink as his eyes. Brother was a boy and
would never live down such a silly bonnet, but to save
his skin she clamped it on his head and tied it under
his chin every time they left the house. Then she kept
the top down so nobody could tease or start stories when
she pushed him up and down Tioga Street. So she
wouldn't have to kick butt, so Brother could come into
the world with no sissy rep or tales people whispered
behind his back. Kids almost bad as the sun. Mean,
signifying devils give her brother hell anyway just because he was white and ugly as a frog's tummy. And
he was her brother. She decided he would be from the
beginning. Her baby brother even though he was a foot
taller and twice her weight. He'd be her baby brother
and then they'd all be a family. The Tates. All of them
Tates even though she knew she was a Bruce and knew
Brother was from the moon or wherever people with no
color and no names came from, all be Tates if she was
his big sister and old Mr. and Mrs. Tate loved them
both.

Lucy unwraps the turbaned towel, leans forward so
her bare feet rest on the floor and the rocker stops. Her
fingers dig and massage her scalp down to the roots.
Mrs. Tate taught her about hair. How to shampoo and
oil and comb and braid. When she could do her hair
herself is when she stopped sharing the tub with Brother.
Washing her own hair took time, took privacy. She
needed to be alone, so she let Brother bathe first then
she soaked as long as she wanted, as long as it took.
She never felt any shyness about her body's being different from his. And nobody ever told her she shouldn't
climb into the tub with him or play with what made
him different or let him scrub her places she couldn't
reach, scrub her with the same light dancing touch she
remembered in Albert Wilkes's piano-playing hands.
Nobody told her anything she did with Brother in the
bathtub was wrong, but she learned to wash and oil
and braid her own hair and then she needed space, then

she had to tell Brother, *Gwan. Go first, boy.* She'd supervise him sometimes but mostly went about her business till he finished, and then she checked the places kids were lazy about and sniffed him when he wasn't looking and made sure he hung up his wet towel. Then her turn. Alone, taking as long as she needed. Funny how Albert Wilkes returned just about the time she started needing to sit and soak by herself. Funny how, shutting the bathroom door behind herself and hearing Brother go off to mind his own business and running the water till suds bobbed at the curled rim of the clawfoot tub and stepping in and splashing the floor, she had thought of Albert Wilkes returning and Albert Wilkes dying while she drained off enough so she could settle into the steamy, fragrant water. Funny too how the first time she bled was in the water and the ghost of Albert Wilkes there again, his bare arms and smooth, strong fingers helping her stand but chilling her also as she rose frightened from water to air. She remembered how he had leaked on the ivory keys when the handfuls of suds she scooped away from the center of the tub revealed a crimson blush twisting and spreading in the water.

Young girls today learning again what Mrs. Tate had taught her about hair. Patterns of light and dark, twists and plaits following designs which spoke if you knew how to listen. Mrs. Tate named some of the designs. A Garden, Darling. This your Garden, child. Humming while she rocks, while her fingers weave and dance the strands of hair. Some designs took many hands to make. Lots of hands and lots of time when women could be alone, together. Quiet time like everybody needed. Time to comb and oil and braid. Time to clean your body.

Lucy loved Carl because he allowed her that time. He had learned she needed it and had learned to give it. After she showed him that piece of Albert Wilkes's skull and pulled him on top of her, inside her, she taught him the space she needed. Taught him with years so he could understand inches. Like she had to teach Brother. At first he pouted and sulked outside the bathroom door with his lip poked out. Finally she had to shout *Shoo, boy* through the closed door and hurt his feelings, but then everything was all right. And she had to clean up after Albert Wilkes and save his white skull bone to teach herself what she had to teach her lovers. Yes, her lovers. Carl. Brother. Albert Wilkes. Her men.

Yes. Like rain. Like rain. She'd heard it sung sometimes that way. Blues falling down like rain. But love rained too. When the rain starts to falling my love comes tumbling down. The songs Albert Wilkes played. And Brother. Her love, her men, her blues in this room, in this chair where she sits in an old woman's lap and listens to a story about pigs and wolves and listens to a dead man play everything she's ever heard, play it so it floats and hangs and she's inside one those little crystal balls you buy at Murphy's Five and Dime, those balls you turn upside down so they fill with snow, lazy floating warm suds of snow. Falling down. Falling down.

So you loved them. And cleaned up behind them. She sees Samantha finding one of Junebug's toys in the yard. Sam has to stoop way down, low down through the needle's eye. She stoops down and picks up a three-wheeled truck. Something broken with most of its paint gone. Just enough yellow or bright blue to catch Sam's eye and make her remember whose toy it was and kneel to dig it out. The other kids have left it alone. Yard dirt's begun to cover it. The toy leaves a little hole after Sam plucks it up. And the hole is a black pit opening at her feet. She wants to bury her face, her weary body in it. The earth rises and spins. She needs to stay on her knees or drop down farther, flatten her belly on the hard-packed belly of the dirt. Let it take her. Fall down and cry like a baby and say You won, you won. You got the best so go on and take the rest. She wants to give up and let the dirt win. Because you can only clean up behind somebody dead so many times. Then it gets you. In your mind, in your bones. Twice in this life enough for me Lucy says to herself or to Sam or to the emptiness of the Tates' living room where the rocker teeters through its arc.

Lucy remembers a broom in her hands. Remembers how she had swept the fragments of colored glass into a pile. All that was left of the pretty front door window after the cops busted in. Old Mrs. Tate upstairs in her room. Albert Wilkes dead somewhere. The white men smiling as they pulled off his bloody clothes. Lucy remembers how hard it had been to clean up after they killed Albert Wilkes and how much harder it had been when she was alone in Brother's room cleaning up again. Another one of her men gone, and there she was again, pulling Brother's sneakers out from under his bed, stuffing Brother's things from the closet into shopping bags. Emptying the pockets of his pants sprawled across the dirty clothes pile. Brother had worn those shoes and shirts and underwear. He had opened those drawers and watched himself move in that mirror. He'd sat on the end of his saggy bed and untied his shoes. He was the one wrapped an old stocking around and round the bedpost to hold the broken footboard. His fingers had wound it round and tied the knot. Ten years and the knot still holding. Some of the dust she was sweeping he had stomped off his feet or shrugged from his shoulders. He had carried Homewood into his room and carried out something from the Tates' into the streets. He'd coughed in his room. Had broken wind and cried and slobbered sweet wine on the mattress and the floor. She had to clean it all up, and then it'd be clean forever. Wouldn't be no Brother ever mess it up again. Ever track in mud or drip rain or bring the stink of the Velvet Slipper home on the seat of his pants.

Cleaning up that afternoon she had found the shopping bag full of pictures. At first she'd thought they were Carl's. They were on the paper he brought home from art school. Long pebbly sheets rolled in the bag so they looked like the wallpaper samples John French used to give them to play with. And they were Carl's in a way. On one side were sketches of naked women from the art school, but on the back side, the smooth side, were Brother's pictures. Had to be Brother's. Who else but Brother would put wings on all the people in his pictures? Little wings sprouting out the top of people's shoulders. Wings like little handles so you could pick his people up or set them down without touching anything but the curly nubs on their shoulders. A few

with wings on their feet. Like Brother is saying they're
my pictures and I can draw people any way I want to.
Wings or tails or color them all green because what's
it matter anyway they're his pictures and he can do
them the way he likes.

The other surprise was how well Brother could draw.
One more thing she never knew about him. Never saw
him with a pencil or a crayon in his hand. But Brother
could draw. When he made a person you could tell who
it was. The faces are like cloudy photographs yet she
can recognize the person right away even though they
have those wings and funny clothes Brother drew on
his people. Homewood people staring back at her when
she unrolled the sheets and spread them atop the piano
and held down the edges. Some of them she knew by
name. Others she'd passed a hundred times in the street,
not wearing the old-fashioned clothes Brother dressed
them in, or the wings he stuck on their shoulders, but
clearly the same Homewood people she'd been greeting
and speaking to all her life.

Lucy had carried the bag of pictures to the living
room, to the best light in the house, the bright gooseneck lamp on the piano, so she could study what Brother
had drawn. She began to understand why some faces
she couldn't name looked so familiar. Brother had drawn
the old people young again. The old clothes made their
faces young again. Mr. and Mrs. Tate. John French.
Freeda French. Young again. Owning Homewood again.
They smiled back at her under the heavy light. In their
long dresses and big hats and coveralls and eight-but-
toned suits and high collars like an extra set of tiny
wings around the men's necks.

She hurried and took her time. She wanted to see
them all but didn't want to pull the last rolled sheet
from the shopping bag. Brother could draw. It was like
listening to people who can really sing or play an instrument. Doesn't matter what they play or sing, they
put you in it and carry you away. Carl's mother and
father, Albert Wilkes, the Tates. All the good old people
and good old times. She could see Brother's hand, pale
as the paper, moving across each sheet. Like the magic
hands of the old-time healers. See him laying on his

white hands and see through them to the old Homewood streets, the people coming to life at his touch.

Brother's people had wings, had knobs on their shoulders so you could lift them and see through them, see under them and around them. So you could touch their shadows, so you could study the darkness while they hung in the air. They had wings so they could be two places at once. So they could move faster than anyone could follow and live whole lives in the air before you'd even notice they were gone.

Lucy had finally emptied the shopping bag of drawings. The long, rolled sheets of art school paper jostled each other atop the piano. A life of their own as they curled back to the shape they'd held for so many years stuffed in the bag. They belonged in the shopping bag. Pressed together, standing up like the samples of wallpaper John French gave them.

Lucy rocks in the empty house, trying to recall the last time she'd unfurled them, treated herself to the surprises each sheet held. Perhaps she should show them to Carl. And Doot. Perhaps they'd understand why she'd kept them to herself this long. Part of Brother's business she'd decided to mind. Part of Brother belonging to her because she was the one who had to clean up after his death.

Carl calls from the vestibule:

Hey Babe.

She closes her eyes. Sinks Carl and Doot in darkness and guides their steps through the Valley of Shadow they cannot see. The eyes go blind sooner or later. She wants to be ready. Wants her men to be ready.

Well, look what the cat drug in. Mr. Carl French, Esquire. And Mr. Doot.

Hi Lucy.

Hi back.

It's a mess out there. Wind blowing to beat the band. If I'da spread my arms and let the wind get up under my coat I believe I'd still be flying.

Must be typhoon and tornado and hurricane all at once out there get that ton of Iron City you're carrying around up in the air.

Told you she was evil, didn't I, Doot? Ain't hardly got my foot in the door and she's signifying already.

Just talking about how much of you there is to love. Especially if a gal loves belly.

Speaking of belly...

You know where the Iron City is.

Doot, you want one...course you do. And Miss Bad Mouth?

Gwan out my face, man, and get us two cool ones. I been thinking about Brother and Sam and little Junebug. They been heavy on my mind and I'm tired. Feel old and tired now thinking about all that.

Told Doot about Sam and Junebug. Ain't no happy story, that's for sure.

How long. How long. That old blues just creeped up on me. Wasn't thinking about any song in particular. Just sitting here rocking waiting for youall. Trying to empty my head and get ready for youall but don't you know it creeped up on me and before I know it I'm hearing it and then I'm humming it and then this chair is keeping time. Been keeping time all the while. Up and back. The music's got me and it's How long, how long. How's it go? I got the tune and got the *how long* but how's it go? What's the words, Carl?

Goes:

> *I can hear the whistle blowing.*
> *Can't see the train.*
> *Deep in my heart*
> *There's a crying pain and How long...how*
> *   long Tell me how long.*

That's it. That's what this chair's been rocking. Now you gwan and get that beer. What you grinning about? You know you can't sing a lick so don't stand there so pleased with yourself.

Is *How long* the name?

Only name I ever heard, *The How Long Blues*. You have to ask Carl, though. He's the one remembers all the old songs. You heard him.

Never heard him sing before.

Well, consider yourself lucky. He knows the words

and that's enough. I ain't gon talk about him cause he ain't here, but where I come from we don't hardly call what he was doing *singing*. Yeah. You heard me, didn't you Mr. Big Ears? Just get on back in here with that beer.

One for you and one for Miss Ungrateful Pup. You just ain't used to good singing. Your ears don't know what to do with it.

How long.

Good singing.

How long things got to stay the hurtin way they is? It makes me tired. Makes me feel old and tired. Like I just want to curl up in this chair and let it rock and let the world go on by.

Least Sam got a roof over her head. At least she's not freezing to death or starving to death like plenty old people still out in the street ain't even got social security. You look in the paper you read about one every day. Starved or frozen. Or burnt up in some tinderbox. Cold don't get em, fire will. It's a shame. A crying shame how they do these old people.

Who you talking about, *they?* Ain't no *they* doing nothing, Carl French, and you know it. We're the ones. We're the ones standing by letting it happen. Those old folks *our* people. *They* ain't never gave a good goddamn. *They* never have and *they* never will. You know that. So don't be blaming no *they*.

I know what you mean, but shit. What am I supposed to do? I'm just Carl French. Never had nothing. Never will. Won't be long I'll be selling pencils and rattling my tin cup. Then one day I'll get my name in *The Black Dispatch* when somebody finds my ashes. Nothing I can do about any of it. How my supposed to change what's been happening all these years? Mize well try and feed the starving babies in Africa and China as change the way things always been in Homewood.

Homewood ain't always been the way it is today. That's just why I never married you, Carl French. That's just why.

Whooo, Babe. What you talking bout?

Maybe you never had a chance. Maybe it's not your fault. But you gave up too easy. Maybe you were sup-

posed to give up easy. Maybe it's not your fault. But
even so I still couldn't marry you. I'll grow old and silly
with you. Might even be the one light the match and
send us both up in smoke, but I can't marry you. Couldn't
be faithful. That's the sticker. And I'm not talking about
body faithful. That's hard enough, but that ain't no real
problem. It's my mind. My mind would be unfaithful.
I love you more than any man, but the old Homewood
people taught me you don't have to give up. I mean
John French, your daddy. And Mrs. French and Albert
Wilkes and Strayhorn and the rest of them. The old
folks. The ones dead now. And Brother. He's one of them
now. Always was one.

Doot. Did you come to hear this song? I think somebody pushed the wrong button.

I'm gon shut up in a minute. Don't mind me, Doot.
I stopped making sense long before you were born.
Couldn't do nothing but stare all moony-eyed at you
and wonder if you'd be different. Looked for something
different in your eyes. Looked for the old folks in there.
And you just listen another minute, Carl French. Tell
me if you could ever look through your daddy and the
rest of them. Tell me if you could see through them or
if they were solid. Brother didn't even have skin, but
he stopped people's eyes. He was solid, real, like all a
them. They made Homewood. Walking around, doing
the things they had to do. Homewood wasn't bricks and
boards. Homewood was them singing and loving and
getting where they needed to get. They made these
streets. That's why Homewood was real once. Cause
they were real. And we gave it all up. Us middle people.
You and me, Carl. We got scared and gave up too easy
and now it's gone. Just sad songs left. And whimpering.
Nothing left to give the ones we supposed to be saving
Homewood for. Nothing but empty hands and sad stories.

So that's why you never married me. Hmmmmmmm.
Always thought it had something to do with the fact I
never asked you.

Believe that lie if you want to, man. Been over here
with your tongue hanging out ever since you grown

enough to know you had a tongue. And know it was
hanging.

Like the song says: *Got two minds to leave here, only
one telling me stay.*

You can whistle and waggle and try to sing if you
want to, but you know I'm speaking true.

Doot don't want to hear all this mess.

He wants to hear about Brother, don't he? Well, that's
what I'm talking about. About Brother and the rest of
them. They were special people. Real people. Took up
space and didn't change just because white folks wanted
them different. Down sometimes but they didn't get
dirty. Brother picked the way he wanted to live. And
how he wanted to die. Now how many people have you
heard of like that? Jesus maybe. And one, two others
like the Africans flying and walking cross water and
turning sticks to snakes. Believe what you need to believe, but Brother was special like that. Not some spook
or hoodoo, but a man who could be whatever he wanted
to be.

Lighten up, child. Whooa, girl. Already got the blues
three different ways.

Warned you, didn't I? Nothing but empty hands and
crazy stories. Cept I got six or seven pork chops in the
icebox and a bag of flour already salted and peppered
with a little garlic and some talking cayenne too. Waiting for the fine, eye-talian hand of my loverman and
sweetheart, Mr. Carl French, who can fry up some chops
when his lip ain't poked out. Smile now cause I got
chops and some frozen spinach we can boil and pretend
it's fresh greens. Gwan Sweetcakes and get you another
one those Irons and the grease is in a Crisco can on the
shelf under the chops. You know you love to fry meat.

The first floured chop is eased into hot grease and
makes the sound of ice cracking, the spatter and sizzle
of great ice floes colliding and breaking apart. Lucy
hears the skillet as she rocks in Mrs. Tate's ladderback
chair. The sound reminds her she is sitting, saying
nothing to her lover's nephew across the room. He's
sunk in the wingback chair. Brother's chair when he
sat still long enough to need a chair. The second Iron

City is cold, half-gone in her hand. Doot's face is shadowed. Only one light, the gooseneck lamp atop the piano,
spilling its glow so the polished wood looks wet. The
piano, spotlighted on an empty stage, waits for someone
to materialize from the dark corners of the room and
play.

Doot quiet in the chair. Like maybe he's feeling his
beer too. His face a pattern of light and darkness. More
brown in his skin than the Frenches. His mama Lizabeth married below her color. But still in the dim room
his face is mottled, the brown a kind of light against
black shadow. If her eyes were better she knows she
could pick out the places in his face which were French.
He is tall like his granddaddy and his uncle. She tries
to recall which record was playing when she got him
up to dance how many years ago in the Frenches' front
room. John French was sprawled sleeping in his over-
stuffed chair. The Victrola gleamed in its corner. Not
Sarah or Dinah or Ella or Billie singing but a man, up-
tempo, growling, belting out the tune. They had been
listening to a fight. But not for long. The Brown Bomber
had duked out his man before they even got the station
tuned in good. Static crackling like chicken in a skillet
as the announcer counted down. John French whooping
and clapping, kicking his long legs in the air. *Get em,
Joe. Whup all them crackers, Boy.* He was snoring by
the time Carl had switched from radio to phono and
played two records.

On the same gleaming RCA console combination she
had heard the news of Pearl Harbor. She thinks she
remembers snow. John French had slammed his fist
into his meaty palm and spat a long nasty string of
curses almost as bad as what she'd heard those few
times the Brown Bomber had hit the canvas. Little as
she understood world politics then, she knew the white
voice from the radio, the voice usually full of fancy
words about England and France and parliaments and
prime ministers and wars overseas, the voice which had
nothing to do with colored people, this time the voice
was speaking to Homewood. Everybody in Homewood
gathered round their radios was going to war. She knew
that and the walls of the house on Cassina started tum-

bling down. John French, hopping mad as he was about
the low blow the sneaky Japs had landed, was too old
to go overseas. Brother in his cellophane skin was too
strange. She was a girl and Doot a baby. But the walls
tumbled down, and Carl rolled out on the cobblestones.
Soft and naked and full of young blood, sooner or later
he'd have to go.

Lucy understood in an instant. Heard the rumble
and knew. The voice gone but its message hung in the
air strong as the smell of tobacco, wine and stale socks
from the corner where John French and his indignation
percolated. More bulletins then and crackling silence.
Then the *Hut-Sut Song:*

> *Now the Rawlson is a Swedish town,*
> *The rillerah is a stream...*
> *The brawla is the boy and girl*
> *The Hut Sut is their dream*

Somebody playing the song just after the news of
Pearl Harbor. Lucy hated the silly song. John French
said it ain't nothing but an old riverboat song, "Hot
Shot Dawson," he'd heard many a time in the Bucket
of Blood. Boys sing it on the waterfront when they be
loading boats. Nothing but that old nigger paddleboat
ditty the white folks got hold to and messed up like
they did everything black they got their hands on. The
silly Hut-Sut song grinning in the middle of the war
news. And the news screamed plain as day her man
had to go. Had to go fight the white folks' war and save
their silly music.

Hut Sut Rawlson on the rillerah and a brawla, brawla,
soo-it.

Played so much it got inside you. You sung it and
hummed it even though you hated it. Lucy hadn't
thought of the Hut Sut Rawlson song in thirty years
but it was still there, still lurking back there like a
sneaky belch gets up in your throat before you know
it. Across the room in the depths of the wingback chair
the young man's face is hidden. Is it his face? A French
face? Is it young?

You're awful quiet.

I'm waiting for the story you promised.

She wonders what he really wants. He raises his beer and she remembers hers, half gone, wet in her fist. She sets it down. Rubs her hands together. She can touch and smell the memory of the Frenches' front room, the room looking out on Cassina. But something is wrong. She is collapsing one time into another. The news of Pearl Harbor came in the afternoon and Doot danced his first steps after dark. Dark through the window, the image of the front room doubled, glowing on the far side of the glass. It was the same window in the story about somebody trying to shoot John French. Mrs. French punched a hole with her bare fist. The scar runs like a caterpillar across her pale hand, the light-skinned French hand like Carl's. That quiet lady punching through a window to save her man. But Lucy is confusing times. She sees John French whooping it up after a Joe Louis knockout. Kicking his feet in the air like a baby on its back. But she had been alone when she heard the war news. Alone and frightened and wanting to be close to Carl. The songs on the radio were "God Bless America" and "America the Beautiful." Then one sounded like a funeral, and she was scared. She expected any minute the drone of war planes, bombs bursting, glass shattering, sirens, machine guns. She gripped the whorled ends of the rocker's arms. Had she jumped up and turned the dial? Had she found the Hut Sut song or did they get tired of drums and trumpets and choirs and play it themselves?

Sent for you yesterday, and here you come today.

Not Dinah or Billie or Ella or Sarah. Had to be, who else could it be, Jimmy Rushing. Mr. Four by Four backed up by Count Basie. Jimmy Rushing out front. And fine as wine the Prez and Sweets and Jo Jo and Dicky, the whole shiny band, fine as fine wine and sharp as tacks, pressed clean in tuxedos and white-on-white wedges splitting the elegant black. No wonder little Doot got up and tried his wings.

No Brother stories tonight, Doot. Need to tell something happy tonight. Too much thinking on the others starting to get me down.

Whatever.

There was the time I got you up to dance. But you've heard that before.

Never from you.

Sometimes I have trouble getting it all straight. Carl going to the war and you being born and Junebug and all that other mess going on about the same time. Just a baby myself at the beginning of the war. Not even twenty years old yet. But I grew up fast. Had to. So much happening. Everybody grew up fast. Carl went in the army. Your grandmother cried for a month after he left, and Brother fussed cause they wouldn't take him too. Somewhere in there you come along and brightened up Cassina. Somewhere in there was when it got to be all right for me to visit the Frenches' house. I guess Mrs. French figured at least she'd know where we were and what we were doing if she could hear us in her front room. So it was the three of us, Carl and me and Brother, in the Frenches' or over here till Carl left. We'd listen to your granddaddy's blues records. That's where Carl learned all the words. Boy, I bet some them old records worth a fortune now. Stacks and stacks down in the bottom of the record player. You talk about blues. John French had it all. Big thick records but the kind break if you look at them cross-eyed. You know what I mean. You're old enough to remember those old seventy-eights. He used to buy them from a man come through Homewood selling Watkins products. The man got them down South somewheres. All kind of funny labels. Like Black Swan and stuff like that. Black people making their own records then. You'd go hear a group, and they hustling their records after the show. Black people making money too, till the big companies saw what was happening and started letting niggers sing for them. John French had tons of blues, and then me and Carl started buying the Big Bands. Duke and Count Basie and the rest. Wonder where all that good music went. Got to ask Carl about those records. You know what I'm talking about, don't you? You must of heard them. Know you heard them once. I was sitting right there in the room with you when that good music playing. Your Granddaddy John French's music and the sides we bought when we heard something good on the radio. We'd listen for hours. And the bands would come through here too. Play at the Masons' picnic and all of Homewood be dancing in the woods in South Park. At the clubs you could hear the bands live. The Hurricane and Ann Mulvehill's and Crawford's on the Hill and Taylors right here in Homewood on Frankstown Avenue.

Went to those places first time during the war. People had a little extra change in their pockets. War work. Hell. I was nineteen years old and had the best paying job I've ever had in my life. Wasn't Black git back, then. Was Arsenal of Democracy and overtime and time-and-a-half. If you could drive a nail or turn a wrench you had a job. Good work and good money. Women and girls making more than their men ever did. Ever would. Good jobs and good times. Thought I'd found heaven when I started hanging out in the clubs listening to that good time music. Boy, thought this child had died and woke up in heaven.

Jam sessions in the after hours joints. The Vets and the Elks. They'd go all night after everything else closed. Mrs. French wouldna never let me put my foot through her door if she'd seen me in my glory all silk-stockinged and a frilly red shimmy dress barely come down to my knees and blinking my six-inch false eye lashes at some stoned piano player just rolled in from Kansas City on the night train still going strong on Jeep's Blues at five o'clock in the morning.

Brother's always there to keep me out of trouble. I could flirt and tease and lollygag around. Have me a natural ball and know Brother'd keep me out of trouble. A young girl needs a chance to try her stuff. Just like youall. I know I must have made more than one gentleman want to wring my scrawny neck with my bodacious carrying on and then backing off from serious business. But I didn't mean no harm. A girl got a right to try her wings just like you men. Except we're supposed to get caught. I mean it's youall's game. We ain't supposed to be playing, we just out there to get caught. And once we get caught we're out. We're third prize forever once we're caught, but youall keep playing long as somebody will have you. Well, I say bunk to that. Had my chance to play. Had my chance to be a butterfly and poke my nose into a little this and a little that and I took it.

Wonder what happened to those records.

They're someplace. Got to be.

Lots of stuff in my grandmother's basement. Cartons and stuff wrapped in newspapers. No telling what's down there.

Hey, Carl. Where's all those records your daddy used to have?

Can't hear you.... these chops is talking.

Go ask him, Doot. Bet he knows.

Lucy rocks, humming to herself the old tunes. How long. How long. And if I could holler like a mountain jack. Go to the mountain top and call my Baby back. One of the brittle black discs sails toward her. She is amazed by its flight, how it glides without a wobble, like it's on an invisible turntable while it hangs graceful and weightless in thin air. But it's sailing toward her and when it lands it shudders, spinning like a top losing its balance. A swhooshing sound before settling into a hundred black fragments on the floorboards. Then another disc knifes past her, aimed at her because she had to duck to avoid its dangerous slicing edge. Rodney Jones is crouched beside the phonograph. Price tags still dangle from the record player's knobs.

All these jive-ass, old timey motherfuckers got to go.

Rodney Jones talking in his dope sleep and digging into the stack of seventy-eights and sailing them to every corner of the Tates' living room. Over prone junkies and sitting junkies and junkies on all fours and the ones who are leaving and the ones flying out the way and the ones who couldn't care less groaning in their dreams as the records smash and scatter.

Lucy thinks about crying and thinks about screaming and thinks she will kill Rodney Jones and thinks why not, why not get all the black discs up in the air at once. All spinning at once like she saw a juggler on the Sealtest Big Top get twelve plates dancing on the end of twelve sticks. They are lazy blackbirds. Crows resting their wings, laid back on currents of air. Swimming, she thinks. Like she is floating effortlessly in some medium which supports her. Stoppit you goddamn fool, she is thinking. And running as fast as she can because here comes John French through the door and he is twirling that razor strop over his head. Somebody's going to pay for breaking his records. Somebody's going to pay she knows as she flees. Big Brown Bear John French growling Who ate my porridge and who slept in my bed and who broke my Baby's chair, and she's flying down the street as she hears the pop of his strop and the squeals of the niggers he's whaling. Somebody has to pay and she is thinking *Stop*. Stop as Rodney Jones snatches another one and curls his wrist backward and sends the record careening to its death.

She wants to cry. Or kill him. Or just keep floating wherever she is. Or go for help. None of the others in the room seem to mind. Aren't bothered by the huge black snowflakes twisting around their heads. Maybe if she listens hard enough she will hear the tunes. Maybe Rodney found a new way to play John French's records. As they rotate, they magically unravel music into the air. The room crisscrossed with music, with flying songs like a net. She thinks she can hear them, the songs rushing past like the clickedy-clack steel wheels of a locomotive, all the music stored in the records exploding like a train does when it's dropped on the tracks and swallows you and then is gone. She thinks of broken pieces. Of the mess Rodney Jones is making. She knows someone will have to clean it up. Albert Wilkes sat on the wall and Albert Wilkes had a great fall. And she will have to find every piece. Dig them out of the dirt. Every splinter of shattered egg. The white pieces and black pieces and she can feel the broom in her hands and grasps it so tight it wobbles. A witch's wand. Another shaky leg to stand on. Because she needs another leg. She passes the broom over the floor like the preacher passed his hand above the open hole as the pitiful little box Brother made was lowered. She needs three or four feet to stand steady on the canvas laid round Junebug's grave. The coffin Brother sawed and nailed and sanded in Mr. Tate's basement is lowered by straps, and the apron of canvas is to keep your shoes clean and the preacher's black hand waves, scattering dust and she is the one who has to clean, who must sweep it all away, even while the gunshots boom and echo in the room.

Just told Doot what happened to those records. Don't you remember what happened to those records....hey, Babe...hey...

Look at you with that apron on. A sight, ain't he? Ain't he a sight? Chef Boy-Ar-Dee. The Cream-of-Wheat Cook. Get back on out there...finish those pork chops, man. I'm tired and hungry. I'm just weary and tired. And you go with him, Doot. Just git on out there with him. Just go on now, go on. Can't you see...

What's wrong, Babe?

Just go on and cook the greens and don't you dare burn the chops and open me a can of beer out there which I'll get to soon as I can.

I am in the kitchen of the Tates' big brick house on Tioga Street with my Uncle Carl. He turns out the fire under the skillet and puts a lid on the pot of bubbling spinach. He opens an Iron City and sits it on the table for Lucy. He says: Only the second time in life I've seen that woman's tears. He faces away from me as he says this, and after he speaks the kitchen is quiet for a long time. The burp of the spinach getting tender is a pulse measuring, accenting the silence. The pot lid rises slightly as the spinach simmers over low heat. A dribble seeps down the side of the pot into the flame which flares yellow, sputters and hisses. He turns then and says:

Shame about those records. Got destroyed just like a lot of innocent bystanders got destroyed by junk. Shame about Daddy's records and shame on us all.

Lucy joined us that evening in the kitchen, and we ate what Carl fixed and drank beer and finished the pint of Seagrams Seven Carl pulled from his coat pocket.

Then we are back in the Tates' living room and Lucy finishes the story and says, The song you danced to was "Sent for you yesterday, and here you come today." Then she turns on the FM. Not jazz and not blues and not rock and roll but it's Black music. Not fast and not slow, a little of both. The off-speed of Smokey Robinson on "Tracks of my Tears." Brother Tate appears in the doorway. He's grinning his colorless grin and pointing at the piano and Albert Wilkes starts unsnapping the duster and aiming his behind for the piano bench. I know how good it's going to sound so I start moving to the music coming from the radio. I know Albert Wilkes will blow me away so I start loosening up, getting ready. I'm on my feet and Lucy says, *Go boy* and Carl says, *Get it on, Doot*. Everybody joining in now. All the voices. I'm reaching for them and letting them go. Lucy waves. I'm on my own feet. Learning to stand, to walk, learning to dance.

About the Author

John Edgar Wideman went to school in Pittsburgh and to the universities of Pennsylvania and Iowa. He was a Rhodes scholar at Oxford, was Professor of English at the University of Wyoming, and now teaches at the University of Massachusetts at Amherst. *Sent for You Yesterday* was the winner of the prestigious PEN/Faulkner Award for Fiction. His nonfiction work, *Brothers and Keepers,* was selected as one of the ten best books of 1984 by the editors of *The New York Times Book Review.* The other two books in his Homewood Trilogy, *Hiding Place* and *Damballah,* are also available in Vintage.